Back to You

By: Angeline Larson

Published: ALH Books 2025
Cover Design: Angeline Larson 2025

ISBN: 979-8-9916346-5-6 (paperback)
979-8-9916346-7-0 (hardcover)

To all that I have judged without fully knowing your pain –

Forgive me

Note to the Reader

This is one book from a connected series. The books do not have to be read in a particular order, and the reader does not have to read the other books to understand the events in each book.

However, please understand that not every book will visit each connected scene in detail if that scene was a focal point in another book. Each book is told form a different perspective, and the scenes have different levels of impact on the characters. That is why some scenes may seem like they are being overlooked or shortened. This was done intentionally.

Please be advised that each book may contain subjects that are of an emotional nature, include foul language, have descriptions of sexual contact, discuss substance abuse, and make references to or include descriptions of harmful acts. Recommended for mature audiences.

Each character is their own person, with their own perspective, and these books act as a telling of the interconnections that these characters have throughout their lives. These are flawed characters, with issues that may or may not be resolved. These are stories about life and the people who do their best to navigate it.

This particular book is Brad's story and includes the moments that were most impactful for him. The companion novel to Brad's story is Finding You, but it is not necessary for you to read that book to enjoy Brad's story.

And now,

Back To You.

I've spent my life believing there was
nothing more for me than just being
the unwanted son. When you are told
you are not good enough, you begin to
believe it.

It was better to be ignored, attention
only brought disaster. But I could not
ignore the halo of blood surrounding
my brother. I saved him once, and
I was determined to keep saving him.

He was all I had; until I met her.

I wasn't truly alive until she came into
my life. I never knew what I was missing,
and now that I know, it is torture.

How can I live when my brother is
fighting so hard to die? He needs me,
more than she does. And I'm no good,
never have been.

What she offers is a dream, and this life
of mine has no place for dreams.
So why can't I breath unless I'm with her?

The Beginning

When does a life officially begin?

Is it when we come crashing into existence upon our conception – a mere twinkle in our mother's eyes? Or is it after birth, during our first breath of the atmospheric air? The babies' cries announce to the world that they have arrived among a mess of pain, joy, blood and tears. Such a fitting beginning for this tortured play we call life.

Not all moments in life are marked by despair and anguish, however. Many moments are pure contradictions of the promise our beginning holds. We may enter this world in such a violent manner but there are tender moments that make us forget the abruptness of life, and the agonizing defeat of death. Those are the moments we need to cling to, or we lose our sanity – the fragile hold we have on our unexplained presence in this vast universe.

My life didn't begin upon conception, or even my birth. My life didn't officially begin until many years later. I was way past the point of infancy and even childhood.

Please do not be mistaken. I did not suppress my memories of the moments before my life began; I just chose not to recall them. I found no happiness in those days despite them not being marred by physical pain. I did not want for any worldly means of survival. I had a comfortable existence but that was all I did – exist. I was simply going through the motions without actually connecting; to myself or anyone else.

My life didn't officially begin until the day – no, until the moment – I saw her. I never knew that I was a shadow of myself until she entered my life. I was a mere reflection of a man; not half, but certainly not whole. When I saw her, that was the moment I took my first breath and came to life.

It was also the moment I began to burn my whole world down to embers. The ashes consumed me, and I suffocated on them.

1

The End, Maybe

Many think that children aren't cognizant of the things they are lacking in life. Sure, everyone knows that a child will always covet what their peers have. Who hasn't bore witness to the tantrum of a young child in the toy aisle demanding they *'want it now'*?

What people don't realize is that there are children in this world that recognize early on that their lives are lacking certain comforts that other children have. Some children don't have a roof over their heads, or food in their bellies. I guarantee you those children know just exactly what their life is lacking.

I have never claimed to be one of those wayward children that didn't have the comforts of a house and food readily available for my choosing. I never wanted for any of the basic items necessary for human survival. I always had a roof over my head, food in my belly and clothes on my back. The soul, however, requires much more than the basics of human survival in order to thrive.

During my early years I didn't even know what a soul was, let alone what was required to maintain it. The concept of love was so abstract to my young self that I thought love meant physical presence. I suppose I was lucky in some respect. I did have two people in my life during my early years that bestowed love upon me. This love was displayed in embraces, focused attention, and comfort during the nights that brought me frightful visions. Perhaps it is the loss of the love I experienced early on that eventually brought about my downfall. Like a child, I threw a tantrum when the thing I desired most could not be mine.

How do I explain what child me felt when he realized that love was just as abstract as the air we breathe? We can't see it, but we know it is there. And, sometimes, we feel like we are suffocating from the lack of it. I spent so many years in a state of constant suffocation that I just became accustomed to it, not realizing that my soul was broken. That void used to be filled by my sister, a surrogate mother of sorts, and my brother, a distraction from my meager existence. My parents had never been fans of physical expression of affection. Actually, I doubt they held any affection for their children at all.

What possesses a person to desire children? I doubt I could pinpoint what motives my parents had to spawn little beings in their likeness. It certainly wasn't because they wanted to shower affection upon them or even display an interest in their future well-being. I suppose I could understand the desire to continue your genetic line but why not stop at one? Why continue and have three children when you clearly had no desire to do the parenting thing? It may seem trivial, but I can't recall a single instance when either of my parents attended a parent-teacher conference, or a sporting event. Hell, they didn't even attend my college graduation. In fact, I imagine their only presence in my life was for my conception, and perhaps my birth.

My sister, Lily, had the misfortune of arriving first. Frankly, I don't know how she survived. Our parents must have performed the basic care required to keep a baby alive, because she made it through and was present to take care of my brother and me. How unbeliev-ably lonely and barren her life must have been before my brother arrived three years later. I wasn't there to witness it, but I have been told that my three year old sister was the main care giver for my infant brother. I can picture her short, little fingers desperately clasping a bottle to ensure her young brother survived the disinterest of our parents.

As for myself, I didn't arrive until much later. There was a ten year gap between myself and my older sister. Lily and Kevin, my older brother, spent seven years together before my parents made a miscalculation and sired me. There was never any doubt during my growing years that I was the quintessential 'oops baby'. My existence was not meant to be, and I was but a burden to my already vexed parents.

Lily became my savior, the very lifeline I clung to. It was through Lily that I learned what love was, and how it was displayed. She thought she was giving me what I needed and maybe deserved. It was her I eventually blamed when that love was stripped from me. It was her name I cursed at night when the frightful visions returned, and I had no one to comfort me. She had once offered her love to me unselfishly and I resented her for it. When she left, she took all that was good about me with her and the hate set in.

Lily's absence was felt the most by my brother. Kevin simply fell apart when Lily left. At eight years old I tried desperately to fill the gap that Lily had left but it simply wasn't enough. Kevin attempted suicide for the first time when he was sixteen and I was nine. I had the privilege of finding his unconscious body sprawled across the bathroom floor amidst the red from the blood and the stark white of the tile floor. This I remember clearly.

When I first found him, I just stood there staring at the pool of blood around his wrists. I didn't comprehend what was happening. I was only nine and aside from my own minor injuries that had been the first time I saw blood, especially in that large quantity. I remember a laugh had escaped my lips. I'm not sure why I laughed because the sight before me was anything but funny. Despite that, I still clearly remember laughing. It seemed like I stood there forever before rushing to the phone to dial 911, but in actuality it was probably mere seconds. I watched my brother being loaded on a

5

stretcher and placed in an ambulance. I was not allowed to accompany him because I was a minor. Instead, I was taken to a neighbor's and waited for one of my parents to come for me.

My parents had never been great at fostering neighborhood relations, and I nervously sat on my neighbor's couch, waiting for my parents to arrive. I would wait two days before they showed up to take me home. Those two days were agony, but also heaven for me. I had no way of knowing if Kevin was alright or when I would be able to return home. The elderly couple that cared for me those two days was what I imagine grandparents were like. I had lied to the emergency services and told them my elderly neighbors often babysat me because I had heard someone mention child services and I knew from Kevin that child services were not something I wanted in my life.

The EMT had brought me to my neighbor's, and they welcomed me into their home and cooed over me for two days. This was the first time I experienced guilt, because I wished my parents, and Kevin would forget about me. It had been so long since I had experienced affection that this elderly couple began to replace my sister in my starved for attention mind and I desperately wanted to stay with them.

When my parents came to collect me two days later, I threw a tantrum and demanded I be able to stay with Mr. and Mrs. Walsh, but Mr. Walsh took me aside and explained I belonged with my parents. I didn't say it, but he was wrong. I didn't belong with them at all. I didn't belong anywhere.

Even worse than my parents leaving me at the neighbor's house for two days was their reaction to Kevin's suicide attempt. I overheard my father telling my mother that if Kevin had wanted to embarrass them he should have at least finished the job. My mother, the woman that had given birth to Kevin, comforted my father and said no one would have to know about Kevin's 'slip up'. To this day I am not sure if by 'slip up' she meant that he had tried to kill himself, or that he hadn't succeeded at it. That was the day I stopped believing in love and started to hate my parents.

As time went on, I abandoned my quest to become Kevin's champion. I couldn't bridge the gap that existed between our parents and us. No matter how hard I tried I was unable to bring joy into my brother's life, and like our older sister before him, the day came when he too left me. I was eleven when Kevin pulled out of our driveway and drove off to start his life without our parents, without me. At that age, college was an entirely foreign concept to me, and I couldn't comprehend the importance of embarking on a life that solely belonged to you, and no one else. All I knew was that when Lily left, I never heard from her again. I feared the same would ring true with Kevin. I was wrong, however, and Kevin often wrote and called me. I made sure I sounded happy during those calls because I feared if I was somehow unhappy Kevin would once again turn to that permanent solution and end his life. My life was soon marked by his phone calls because I had absolutely no relationship with our parents and few friends, which was solely my own doing. I avoided people because I did not want to overshare. I still feared the unknown child services.

Despite my desire to return to the old days, when Lily and Kevin were both in my life, time marched on. I managed to navigate my parents' lack of interest and avoid their wrath. They weren't violent but they made their desires known. I was not to make any loud noises because it would disturb them. I was not to tell jokes because it would disturb them. I was not to have friends over because it would disturb them. I was not to get bad grades because it would disturb them. I was not allowed to make my presence known because it would disturb them. I spent many years hiding in the shadows; fearful I would disturb my parents and experience their vengeance. Many times, after Kevin and Lily had left, I was locked in a closet because I had *'disturbed'* my parents. I learned quickly what was disturbing and I adjusted my behavior. I learned the dark, and the

7

silence was my friend and I pushed away those parts of me that were disturbing.

This was my world, and I never focused on how my life was lacking. I didn't notice what was missing until she entered my life. I learned what a full life could be like when I met her and like I did with my sister, I eventually resented her for showing me love.

2
Her

My parents were very driven individuals, and I spent many years mimicking that drive in a desperate attempt to impress them. My little feet would run home with my report card in hand, a grin on my face and eagerness in my heart. I was proud of my grades, and I knew my parents would be proud of them too. I would rush in the door and drop my bag, forgetting to remove my shoes before running to the kitchen to find them.

"Mom, Dad, look!" I would proudly proclaim and thrust my report card to them. Usually, Dad would be sitting, going over reports that all looked like scribbles to me and Mom would be reading. They often spent many hours in the kitchen, sitting together at the table, but never actually saying a word to one another. When they didn't immediately drop what they were doing and acknowledge me I would shift from one to the other, trying to give them my report card.

They never took it.

Mom would calmly tell me to stop hyperventilating and Dad would tell me to go to my room because I was causing a disturbance, his favorite word. Early on I would display my grades on the fridge, using a puppy magnet that Lily had gotten me one year. I stopped rushing home and displaying my accomplishments after the incident with Kevin. Suicide has a way of putting things into perspective –

even for a nine-year-old.

I accepted that I would never be able to match my parents' ambition, or impossibly high standards of accomplishment. Unlike Kevin, I just stopped trying and didn't engage with my parents. Kevin, on the other hand, desperately desired their approval and was constantly reinventing himself in a silly attempt to garner their affection. Instead, he was met with constant criticism and disdain. I knew it was only a matter of time before he too would vanish like Lily, a faraway memory from a time long forgotten. My adolescence was branded by the fear I held. Kevin became my focal point, and I knew if he left permanently then I too would be lost.

During this state of dread my parents decided their ambitions lay elsewhere and we moved out of the only home I had ever known. By this time, I had grown too big to be shoved into a closet when I disturbed my parents. I had also learned how to be absent and present at the same time. We may have lived together, but we did not co-exist. In fact, my parents were often away on business trips. That is what I was told and I never inquired further. I never once asked where they were going, and they never once provided the information. To anyone else, this would appear to be a lonely existence, and perhaps it was, but I was content to be ignored.

We left my childhood home in Pittsburgh and arrived in Wisconsin the summer before my sophomore year of high school. My parents had told me their new jobs would require even more traveling then before and while I didn't react to this outwardly, inside I was rejoicing. An increase in their travel meant an increase in the times I could be disturbing.

After Kevin had left, I needed something to fill my time and I developed two interests; running and music. The running was a parent approved hobby; the music was not. I was not allowed to listen to or play music when my parents were home. Headphones only. I knew their new schedules would provide me an opportunity to improve my guitar playing skills.

Yes, my parents got me a guitar one year for Christmas. They were always very punctual and strict about adhering to social norms. The gift giving tradition at Christmas was one they continued to practice. However, they did not get me a guitar because they noticed I had an interest in music. No, they got me the guitar because my mother had asked me one day to pick one thing they could provide me as a gift on the holiday (her exact words). I had to tell them I wanted a guitar. The gift was given to me with a disclaimer – I could not play it when they were in the house.

So, my guitar and I arrived at the new home with hope for the first time in many years. I couldn't connect with my parents but somehow my fingers were able to connect with the cords and this thing residing inside me, the thing that slightly resembled a soul, was finally beginning to wake. I may not have been able to understand people, but I understood music and it understood me. I told myself I didn't need friends because I had my music and I was content.

She changed all that.

The moment I saw her I knew I had to have her in my life. It sounds possessive, but that was not what I wanted at all. I never wanted to possess her; I simply wanted to know her. She came walking down the street I now lived on with another girl while I was unpacking the moving truck. My parents had left on a business trip the day after we had arrived at our new home, leaving the task of unloading to me. I was sifting through the boxes when I heard a laugh and looked up. There they were. Two girls that appeared to be my age walking down the street. One had dark brown hair and a deeper complexion. The other girl, the girl I just had to know, was paler with lighter features, and she was incredibly short.

Okay, maybe she was actually quite normal in size for a girl, but I was already over six feet, and I towered over my peers. I was a giant compared to her pixie size and all I wanted to do was wrap her in my arms and keep away all the bad. Besides my brother, I had never before felt such a need to protect another person from the evil of the world and it scared the shit out of me.

The girls got closer, and I realized I was staring like a complete spaz and returned to the task at hand. A few minutes later I heard a bright voice call out to me.

"Hi. Moving in?" the girl with darker features asked me as she leaned a shoulder against the moving truck, tilting her body in the process. I quickly glanced around for the pixie girl, but she wasn't there. A little disappointed, I greeted the girl before me.

"Yeah. I'm Brad," I said and extended my hand in greeting. She smiled and came off the side of the moving truck to give me her hand.

"Oh, silly me. I'm Jenny," she said as she shook my hand.

I heard a soft release of breath that clearly did not come from Jenny, the girl whose hand I was shaking. I leaned to my right and peered around the corner of the truck. Sure enough, there was the pixie. She had her back to the truck, her eyes closed, and her fists clenched. She seemed to be holding her breath in frustration. The entire scene before me was just too cute and I chuckled.

"Hello," I said and gave a half wave to the pixie.

"Hi," she replied through clenched teeth. She looked extremely uncomfortable, and I quickly sniffed the air around me to be sure my sweat drenched body wasn't emanating a foul smell, and causing her discomfort.

No rotten scent detected.

"You can come out. I don't bite," I said with a laugh again.

"Hmm, that's too bad," the other girl, Jenny, practically purred at me. Her flirting was blatantly obvious and way over the top. I was amused and I grinned.

"So, what brings you two to this neck of the woods?" I asked as I wiped some sweat from my forehead.

"Kelly lives next door. I don't live in this neighborhood, but I can always visit," Jenny said as she trailed one finger up my arm. I watched the movement but did not react. It was obvious she was trying to get a reaction from me, but I was not interested even in the most minuscule sense. My interest was solely in the pixie that wouldn't even look at me.

"You live next door?" I asked, gesturing to the house on my right.

"I only live there on holidays and some weekends," she responded hurriedly. She wasn't moving but she seemed to be out of breath.

I found her peculiarities endearing. Jenny noticed my raised eyebrows and provided an answer to my unspoken question.

"Her parents are divorced. She lives on the other side of town with her mother mostly," she said, once again positioning her body in an attempt to give me the best possible view.

I ignored her.

"It must suck being shuffled back and forth. Will one of you mind opening the front door for me?" I asked as I bent to pick up a box marked 'Living Room'.

"Sure," Jenny purred and walked to the front door and opened it.

I watched her walk away, because well, I am a man, and she clearly wanted me to watch her walk by the way she swayed her hips. I shook my head and half-grinned at the display. She was really laying it on thick and trying her damndest to draw my attention. I kind of felt sorry for her because she didn't even know that she had never stood a chance.

"Do you need anything else?" Jenny asked once I had deposited the box. I had felt the presence of the pixie, Kelly, behind me the whole time.

"No thanks. Maybe I'll see you around sometimes," I said to the pixie. She only nodded at me but said nothing else before both girls walked out my front door. Jenny gave me a sensual wave before she left. Kelly hadn't seen the wave because she had walked out first, and her back was turned. I just laughed. I found it humorous when girls gave me attention, because they knew nothing about me and for some reason it felt like a joke to me, their interest.

As soon as the door closed behind them, I went to the front windows and watched as they walked next door. Jenny continued to talk but the pixie remained silent and had her head cast downward. It was the sadness on her face that finally clinched it for me. I had to know this girl and I would do everything I could to be by her side.

The next day I gathered some courage and went to her house. My parents weren't the only ones that had developed a habit of distancing themselves from neighbors. Even though Mr. and Mrs. Walsh had been nothing but kind to me those two days I spent with them, I never again sought out their company. Life was much easier if I just stayed away from others that may ask questions. My current circumstances may not have been ideal but it was all I had known, and after losing Lily and Kevin, I knew I didn't want the only other familiarities I had left to be ripped away too. This is why my knock on Kelly's door that afternoon was so significant for me. For the first time in my life, I was putting myself out there to be vulnerable.

The door was answered by an average sized middle-aged man wearing glasses and holding a book. He smiled at me as he greeted me.

"Can I help you?" he asked kindly.

"Hello, sir. My name is Brad Klauzek and I just moved in next door and met Kelly yesterday. I was wondering if I could talk to her?" The words came out with confidence but inside I was extremely nervous. I assumed this man before me was her father and I imagined it must have been strange to see a boy you had never met standing on your porch asking about your daughter. If the situation had been reversed, I know I would have had many unwelcome thoughts running through my head.

"Welcome to the neighborhood. Come in," the man replied, still smiling at me.

I accepted his invitation and stepped through the entryway. It was quiet, much like my own home. The difference, however, was that this house was a home. It was evident the place was lived in

14

well. From the doorway you could see into the kitchen and there were two glasses and plates on the table, remnants from a shared lunch. Coats hung from a rack mounted to the entry wall. So often the only coat in my entryway was my own. I spent many days at a time in my house alone.

"Why don't we go into the living room," the man said as he gestured to the direction he wished me to go. I followed his direction and we both sat on adjacent couches. "So, Brad, I'm Paul Johnson, Kelly's father. I noticed you and your parents arrived two days ago. I also noticed you seem to be tackling all those boxes yourself. I'm not the greatest at many things but I've lifted a box or two in my day. Don't hesitate to ask for help unloading if you need it," Mr. Johnson said as he leaned back in his chair.

"Thank you, sir, but I can handle it." I wasn't sure what to say next because I was extremely nervous. This would have gone so much easier if Kelly had been the one to open the door. I glanced around the room in an attempt to hide my nervousness, but I wasn't fooling Mr. Johnson.

"It's okay, son, nothing is going to jump out at you," he chuckled. I smiled back nervously.

"I look forward to meeting your parents," Mr. Johnson changed the subject.

"Oh, they aren't really big into meeting the neighbors. They travel a lot for business," I explained, hoping I didn't offend the kind man before me. I noticed a slight tick in his jaw as he reacted from my explanation, but he did not push the issue further.

"Well, I'm not gonna keep you in suspense any longer," he said and stood. I immediately stood with him, and he smiled once again at my quick reflexive action. He gestured for me to remain where I was, and he walked to a staircase.

"Kelly, you have a visitor," he called up the stairs.

"I'll be right down," the pixie replied.

I turned so I could face the stairs and saw Mr. Johnson staring at me, still smiling. I nervously returned a quick smile before averting my eyes again. *Shit!* I really needed to get things together. I was acting like some maniac around this man. As I attempted to get my nerves under control Kelly appeared at the top of the stairs. She smiled at her father and began to almost skip down the stairs, until she saw me standing there.

Once her eyes met mine, she attempted to stop mid skip but lost her footing and stumbled on a stair. I saw her father react in case he needed to catch her, but she was able to grab a hold of the railing and right herself before the stumble became a fall. It wasn't the near fall that had me relaxing, but rather the look on her face when she saw me. She seemed to be more nervous than I was and I instantly relaxed. I didn't want my nerves to cause her any more discomfort, so I immediately swallowed my doubts and stood taller.

"Kelly, this is Brad from next door. His family just moved in a couple days ago and he came to visit you," Mr. Johnson explained to his daughter.

Kelly turned her gaze towards him and just nodded her head.

"Why don't you two talk in the living room? I'll be in the kitchen if you need anything. Brad, it was nice to meet you, and I meant what I said about helping you. Anytime you need it," Mr. Johnson repeated his offer.

"Thank you, sir, I appreciate it," I replied and turned to Kelly. She was still standing at the bottom of the stairs just staring at me in shock. Mr. Johnson excused himself and I was left alone with her. She didn't move to the couch, and I realized she was afraid to come near me.

"Do you want to sit down?" I asked, gesturing to the sofas. She just stared at me.

"I was hoping I could ask you a few questions about the school here. Tomorrow is my first day and I am a bit nervous," I said in an attempt to spark a conversation. I noticed the moment her shoulders relaxed, and she was able to breath normally again.

"Sorry," she said and began walking to the sofa her father had sat on earlier. "I guess I was just shocked to see you here." She sat and placed her hands on her knees.

I sat down too and did my best to look apologetic.

"Yeah. I didn't mean to just spring this on you. You are the only one I've met, and it would be nice to know someone at school. I thought you could give me some pointers, or something."

"What do you want to know?" She asked as she rubbed her hands up and down her upper legs. It was obvious she was still nervous. I leaned back on my sofa trying to project that I was comfortable here, hoping she would soon relax too.

"Any teachers I should avoid?" I asked and she laughed slightly.

"Oh sure. If you get in Mr. Thornton's class avoid the front row because he tends to spit. I think he has a gland problem or something because no one should create that much saliva," she said with a laugh. I laughed with her, and she relaxed further, discontinuing the movement of her hands.

"That is good to know. I would hate to get a spit shower. What is your favorite class?"

She smiled brightly at me before she answered, and I swear my heart missed a beat. That is entirely a girl thing to say but I was there, and I promise, my heart definitely miss fired in that moment.

"History. I know most people think it is boring but every time we learn about a new time period, I just can't help but wonder what it must have been like for the people alive at the time. I can't even imagine a life without electricity, but it didn't always exist and I just can't help but wonder what it was like." She now responded quicker and without a hint of hesitation. I found I really liked her answer. My brother was a history buff and the happiest memories I have of him involved him talking about some historical event and he would always end with, *'Can you believe that?'*

"What is your favorite subject?" Kelly returned the question.

"I guess English. I like to read so I don't mind all the books they assign."

"What's your favorite book?" Kelly asked and leaned forward a little.

"All Quiet on the Western Front."

"I've never read it. What's it about?"

"War and how it affects the men that fight it. The main character is a German soldier in World War I, and he doesn't feel like he belongs at home anymore because of what he has seen and done during the war," I explained.

"What happens to him?"

"He dies," I said simply.

"That's awful," she exclaimed, and I laughed at her horrified expression. She narrowed her eyes at my laughter.

"Not every ending is a happy one," I replied.

"Well, they should be. Life is hard enough without the books we read ending so horribly," she said and crossed her arms over her chest and leaned back against the couch. I just continued to smile at her.

"That's the point of the book. Life and war doesn't end happily for everyone. Sure, the fighting ends, but the war never really leaves those that did the fighting and, in the end, they didn't even really matter," I explained my take on the book, as well as life.

"Everyone matters," she replied simply.

I know she wasn't talking about me specifically but for some reason I truly believed her words were meant for me. After living for so long believing I hadn't mattered it was like her words had been presented to me at the exact moment I needed to hear them, and I knew my life would never be the same.

3

Her Friend

Kelly and I talked for a few more hours before I left that day. She told me about the rest of her classes, some of the neighbors and her parents. She seemed to be much closer to her father than her mother, but she didn't go into specifics. I told her I had parents but didn't offer much more information than that. I did mention I had two older siblings but once again didn't offer many details. Mostly I told her about my interest in music and how I spent most of my time practicing guitar and running. She made a face of disgust when I mentioned running and I laughed at her. She explained she wasn't allowed to play sports and that she was mostly okay with it because the majority of sports involved running and she avoided that as often as she could.

I laughed but did not ask her to explain why she wasn't allowed to play sports. I just assumed she did not care for them because most involved running and she clearly had a disdain for running.

I spent that night plucking at my guitar strings and thinking of Kelly. I had never really been interested in song writing but I wished I could find the words to immortalize my interaction with her that day. I could hear the cords and was able to construct the melody that described how that conversation had made me feel but after many failed attempts to match words to the music I decided to be satisfied with just the music. Song writing was not in my future.

The next day was my first day of school and I intended to find Kelly. We hadn't been able to determine if we had any classes together because I hadn't received my schedule yet. Standing there in the front office I hoped the lady creating my schedule had managed to place me in some of Kelly's classes. I had tried to look for her when I arrived, but I was not successful.

"First bell has already rung so you will be arriving late to your first class. Here is a map of the school, I've circled your classes and the cafeteria you will be eating in. First bell rings promptly at eight and your first class begins at eight o' five. Do not be tardy. I have written you a pass this time, but we take tardiness very seriously here. Here is a list of items you will need for your classes and a copy of the school song. Learn it. Do you have any questions?" The plump woman behind the desk asked me.

I shook my head, not wanting to prolong this interaction.

"Travis," she called to a boy behind her. He was a little on the skinny side and his hair desperately needed to be cut. He swung his head as he stood in an attempt to get his falling locks out of his eyes.

"Yes, Mrs. Alexopolous?" Travis said and came to stand beside the plump lady. I was impressed that he was able to pronounce the name with ease. When I saw her nameplate, I knew there was no way I was going to attempt saying that name.

"Will you take Mr. Klauzek here on a quick tour? I have excused him for being late to his first class but I would like you to point out where all his classes are, so he won't get lost."

"Sure thing Mrs. Alexopolous. I'm Travis," the boy said as he came around the desk.

"I'm Brad. Thank you," I said to Mrs. Alexopolous and followed Travis out the office door.

"So, where are you coming from?" Travis asked as we walked down the hall.

"Huh?" I asked, not understanding his question.

"Where did you move from?" Travis clarified as he once again tried to swing his hair out of his eyes.

"Oh. Philadelphia," I said looking down at the map.

"That's cool. Don't worry about that map. It's crap," Travis said and took the map from me. He crumpled it up and tossed it in a nearby trash can. I didn't appreciate the action, but I said nothing. The last thing I wanted on my first day was to get kicked out of school for punching a guy.

"Basically, you just need to know that there are two main hallways and three ways to get to the other. One entrance the way we just came. This one coming up and the last one is down there. It can get a bit crowded between classes, but you shouldn't have any trouble. The class numbers increase in this direction, and we are in Hallway A. Hallway B is that way and the three mini halls are C, D and E. Very inventive, huh?" he asked but didn't wait for me to respond.

"Your cafeteria is off to the right up here. The food isn't gag worthy but it isn't exactly the best either. Avoid the pot roast at all costs. No one knows what the meat is, but it isn't beef, that's for sure," Travis said.

As we walked he pointed out the classes that were mine and he also took me to the back of the school and showed me the various sports fields. I noticed the track and for the first time since this tour began, I perked up.

"How is the track team?" I asked.

"Eh, we aren't terrible," he said and moved his hair from his eyes. Based on his response I gathered he was on the track team.

"Why don't you just get your hair cut?" I asked. It was obvious his hair was bothering him.

"This?" he asked gesturing to the part that kept falling in his face. I nodded and he laughed. "I told my mother I didn't want her cutting my hair anymore and she freaked. She said she wasn't going to spend perfectly good money on something she could just do herself. So, we are now in a standstill. She refuses to let me have a professional cut it, and I won't let her cut it. It's a battle of wills, really. And I think I'm winning. She'll cave before the end of the week, trust me," Travis chuckled, and we went back inside.

I grinned behind his back. Despite him yanking the map out of my hands earlier he seemed to be an alright guy.

"Come by the track this afternoon and talk to coach if you're interested in joining. We just had a guy sprain his ankle and we need an alternate, so you have a good chance of getting on the team," Travis said as he dropped me off at my first class. I thanked him and said I'd definitely be there.

My first class was Biology, and I was glad I had missed the majority of it. Kelly wasn't in there and I quickly realized I probably wouldn't be very productive this first day until I was able to see her.

Unfortunately, she wasn't in my next class either. Her friend was though. The same friend I had met two days ago while I was unpacking. I didn't realize it was her at first, but she remembered me and made her presence known.

I was staring out the window to my left as the teacher prattled on and someone kept throwing little pieces of paper on my desk. I ignored it at first, thinking they just had really bad aim, until one hit me on the cheek. I turned; ready to blast a guy when I saw it was a girl with brown hair wildly waving at me two desks away.

I narrowed my eyes in confusion before she mouthed, "It's Jenny," and I recalled meeting her the other day. I gave a slight wave back and gestured to the front of the class and the teacher. She nodded, understanding that I didn't want to grab the attention of the teacher.

When the bell rang, releasing us, Jenny came quickly to my desk.

"Hey. You sure were focused on that window. I must have gone through two full sheets of paper before you noticed," she said, holding her books in front of her.

I gathered my things and put them in my bag.

"I noticed. I thought someone just had bad aim," I explained and she laughed. We walked out of the class together.

"Let me see your schedule," she said and took it from my hands.

What was with people at this school taking things out of my hand?

"Not too bad. You don't have Mr. Thornton so that is good. Unfortunately, I do have him fourth period. It looks like we have two classes together. Second and fifth period. We don't have the same lunch hour though. Oh, you have the same lunch as Kelly," she said and my ears perked up.

"Do I have any classes with her?" I asked.

"No," she said shaking her head and my hopes were dashed. Still, it was good to know I would see her at lunch.

"Hey, there she is now," Jenny said and quickened her pace. She called out to Kelly, and I saw her at a locker. She turned at the sound of her name and smiled at Jenny. It felt like I had been gut punched when I saw her smile like that. I watched Jenny and Kelly embrace in a quick hug before Jenny gestured back to me.

Kelly saw me and waved. I quickly joined them.

"Hey. I see you found Jenny," Kelly said.

"Actually, she found me," I replied.

"We have second period together and he was just so cute sitting in his chair, looking out the window clueless to his surroundings. I knew I needed to rescue him," Jenny joked. Kelly continued to smile at the two of us.

"That's nice. Where are you heading next?" She asked me.

"History, room A120," I said disappointed that I wouldn't be in the same History class as her. I would have loved to see her enjoyment.

"I'm going to Chemistry. I wonder if we have any classes together," she said.

"You don't. I already checked his schedule," Jenny said, handing the schedule back to me. I took it but continued to stare at Kelly.

"Yeah. It would have been nice to know one person in my

classes," I said.

"You do. You know Jenny," Kelly said as she closed her locker.

"Yeah, guy. You know me," Jenny joked and pinched my arm.

I really didn't like her touching me, but I didn't want Kelly to think I didn't like her friend, so I didn't say anything.

"Well, I'll see you around. Have a great first day," Kelly said.

"Thanks. You too. I mean, have a good day, not a first day. This isn't your first day," I replied quickly, nervously running my hands through my hair. Kelly smiled and said goodbye. I watched her walk down the hall until she disappeared around a corner.

Once Kelly was out of sight I turned and found Jenny staring at me in a weird way. She almost looked mad at me, but I couldn't understand why.

"I'll see you later. Enjoy lunch," she said flatly and walked away.

The whole scene was completely awkward, and I couldn't make any sense of it. Why would she be upset? I quickly rid my mind of the questions when I heard the warning bell go off, reminding me I had five minutes to get to class. I ran the rest of the way and made it to the door just as the bell rang.

Later, I stood by the cafeteria doors and waited for Kelly. I had run here too, ensuring I could arrive before her so I wouldn't miss her. She smiled at me when she saw me, and she waved. She sure did wave a lot. I walked up to her and fell in step beside her.

"Do you need to get any food from the line?" she asked me.

I shrugged. "I brought a sandwich but if you are going through, I'll go too," I said.

"I just need to get something to drink," she said, and we walked to the growing line.

"How are you liking your first day?" she asked.

"It's alright. I think I'm just trying to get used to everything and haven't really been paying attention in class. How is your day going?" I asked as I grabbed a bag of chips.

"Fine. We had a surprise quiz in Geometry, and I don't think I did that great but the rest of the day is going well. I'm glad you have some classes with Jenny," she said and smiled at me.

"Yeah," I replied quietly, not sure if I should mention my weird interaction with her friend.

"Are you okay?" Kelly asked, staring at me with concern.

"I'm fine. I guess I think Jenny is mad at me or something."

"Why do you think that?" she asked softly as she turned to grab a soda – Cherry. I took an original.

"Just a feeling." We paid for our items, and I followed her to her table. She greeted her friends and introduced me to everyone. They all said hello and quickly returned to their conversations. I sat next to Kelly and we both began eating our lunch.

"Thanks for letting me sit with you."

"Of course. I'm glad you waited to find me. I was worried I wouldn't be able to find you," she said, and I smiled this time. She wanted me to find her, and I was glad to hear it.

"I think you should give Jenny another chance. She's been going through some things lately and just hasn't been herself. Give her time. She will grow on you," Kelly explained, and I just nodded my head in agreement. She could have asked me to jump on the table and cluck like a chicken and I would have agreed to do it, maybe.

She talked to me about school, and I told her I was going to try out for the track team that afternoon. She wished me luck and by the time lunch had ended I was actually enjoying this new school. She promised to meet me in the same place tomorrow and as we parted, she waved goodbye.

Jenny came up to my desk during the next class we had together and acted like our previous encounter hadn't even happened. She was once again back to her talkative, energetic self. I found this girl to be really confusing. This time, she managed to get the kid next to me to switch seats with her and chatted at me through the whole class. I only half listened because I was pretty sure she was flirting with me, and I had absolutely no interest in that. When the class ended, she put her arm through mine and walked out into the hallway with our arms linked. I looked down at her not at all pleased with this development.

"Jenny, what are you doing?" I asked her. She looked up at me and laughed coldly.

"Relax, Brad. I'm not going to jump you. I think it's sweet you have feelings for Kelly," she said and released my arm. I narrowed my eyes at her.

"Sweet?"

"Yes. She is really nice and innocent so I can understand why you find her appealing. But she is so clueless about these things. I wouldn't waste your time," Jenny advised, inflecting caring in her tone but her eyes revealed anything but.

"Thanks for the advice but I don't know what you are talking about." I turned in the direction of my next class.

"She is only going to hurt you," Jenny called to my back, and I turned my head slightly to look back at her. "I'm just trying to help you."

"Of course you are," I replied and left her standing in the hall.

She was one strange girl.

4

Running

After school I met Travis by the track, and he introduced me to the coach. The coach explained the same thing Travis had told me earlier about one of their teammates being out due to an injury. I explained I was more of a long-distance runner but that I wasn't completely terrible at the dashes. The coach, Mr. Tennor, told me to go change and join the rest of the group. He said today was a try out and he was going to see how my times matched up with the others. I did as he asked and spent the next two hours running through drills he gave me. While I didn't beat my previous best times, I was faster than the others I ran against. At the conclusion of the practice Coach Tennor told me I had a spot and instructed Travis to get me up to speed on the schedule.

Since I had already missed my bus Travis, who was a year older than me, offered to take me home. During the drive to my house Travis filled me in on the upcoming schedule and the other competitors. He told me for the most part everyone got along but they were still highly competitive with one another and sometimes tempers had to be cooled. I wasn't worried about my own competitiveness because I didn't run to beat those next to me. I ran to beat myself. When I ran my mind just went blank and I was able to escape the nagging fear that my brother would try to end his life again. Besides, living with my parents had taught me to keep my emotions in check and I didn't have much of a temper. If anything, I was probably too detached from my emotions.

I thanked Travis for the ride when we got to my house and exited his car. Much to my surprise, and dislike, Travis got out of his car too and followed me to the front door. As I was unlocking the door, I gave him a questioning look.

"Just checking out the mansion," he said in reference to my parent's one-story house. I shrugged and let him in. If he wanted to waste his time checking out my house, I wasn't gonna stop him.

I went straight to the kitchen and dropped off my bag in a chair and took a soda out of the fridge. Travis wandered for a bit, looking at his surroundings. Then he joined me in the kitchen, grabbed a soda for himself and took a seat.

"You really have no boundaries, do you?" I asked him as I leaned against the counter and drank from my can.

Travis shrugged. "Nah. I have like a gazzilion brothers and sisters and even more cousins. You wouldn't survive in my family if you didn't just go for things. What about you?" he asked and opened his can.

"I don't have a gazziolion siblings," I replied.

Travis lifted his eyebrows at me. "I figured. The house seems pretty quiet."

"Yep."

Suddenly, Travis burst out laughing and I narrowed my eyes at him. I didn't see the humor in a quiet house, or his presence in the house.

"You are one closed off dude. Thanks for the refreshment," he said gesturing to me with the can. He stood, pushed his chair in and began walking to the front door.

"See you tomorrow, man," he called and let himself out.

I slowly made my way to the front room and watched his car pull out of my driveway and disappear down the road. People in this town sure were strange. Between Travis and Jenny, I felt like I was in an episode of *The Twilight Zone* or something. Or maybe that other show that came after that was such a knock off of *The Twilight Zone*, *The Outer Limits*.

Whatever science fiction show I had somehow landed on I knew I didn't really care for how nosy these people were. At my last school, I had been there since day one and the other students had grown accustomed to my desire for solitude. Even those I ran track with knew to keep the subject solely about the running. I never invited them over to my house and they eventually stopped inviting me out with them. It seemed I would have to go through the same process here and endure the beginning curiosity until people became bored with me.

Despite just running for two hours and working up a sweat I put my running shoes back on and took off down the block. I am not sure how far or how long I ran before I came across a business that was a landscaping business. There were trees and all kinds of plants surrounding the building. The sign said *Farley & Sons* and had a picture of a tree with snow on it. The smell appealed to me, and I slowed so I could walk the line of trees. As I was coming around a corner to walk down the next row a middle-aged woman was at the other end of the row, just waiting for me.

"Do you need help with anything?" she asked me as I approached. Her long black hair had streaks of grey in it and she held some work gloves in her hands. She wore jeans and a T-shirt that held the logo and name of the business.

"I was just running by and the smell…," I trailed off because I wasn't sure what I was trying to say. How could I explain that the smell made me stop and I just had to get closer? It seemed I didn't have to explain because the woman nodded in understanding.

"Yeah. It gets me every morning. Feel free to look around and if you change your mind about needing anything I will be over there pruning," she said pointing to a row of bushes. She didn't wait for my response and turned on her heels to leave me alone.

I wandered for a bit more before I had an idea. I needed a job and the only person I saw working here was the woman. Maybe they needed some help. So, I went to where the woman was, kneeling in the dirt and using hand shears to prune the bushes.

"Excuse me?" I said. The woman continued to prune.

"Yes?" she asked.

"I just noticed that there seems to be a lot of work to do here but you are the only one here. I was wondering if you, maybe, were hiring?"

The woman stopped pruning, looked up at me momentarily before returning to her task.

"Do you have any experience in landscape?"

"No ma'am. Not exactly. I have had multiple odd jobs the last two years. I did household repairs, worked at a gas station, cut grass and trimmed bushes but I never really did landscaping. I'm a hard worker and I learn fast," I added to make myself sound more appealing.

The woman stood, wiped her hands on her soiled jeans and dropped the shears in a nearby bucket. She picked up the bucket and gestured for me to follow her. I fell into step behind her and walked into the building with her. It seemed to be a small showroom of photos, but it was mostly an office that housed filing cabinets and two desks.

"I'm Reyann Farley. I own this place," she said and placed the bucket down beside a desk. She noticed my gaze go to the emblem on her shirt.

"The Farley that started the business was my father. He never did get over the fact that he never had any sons. He said if he couldn't have them in real life than he would have them in his business. He was an odd man, but the name is appropriate now," she said and sat down at the desk. She gestured for me to sit in the chair across from her.

I did.

"What's your name?" she asked me.

"Bradley Klauzek."

"Well, Bradley, the only people that work here now are myself and my two sons, Jeff and Tom. It just so happens I will be losing Tom when he goes off to college this year and I do need a replacement. Do you have a license?"

"Not yet ma'am. But I can get one," I said in a hurry. She nodded.

"I have two company trucks. You and Jeff will be responsible for the transport of the orders and planting. I do the designs and make the plans. Tom will teach what you need to know before he leaves after the summer. It's hard work but if you do it well you will get a raise after the first three-month trial period. The pay is $12.50 an hour. You'll receive a raise to thirteen dollars an hour if you last three months. I don't have a health insurance plan for you so you will have to figure out alternative arrangements for that," Reyann said and handed me some papers.

"Fill these out. If everything checks out you will start this Friday," she started to stand but stopped at my voice.

"I am still in school so I can only work nights and weekends. But I also run track so I might not be able to work every Saturday," I told her.

"That is fine for now. Tom is here. But I do expect you to be full-time during the summer months. Those are my busiest," she said and pointed a finger at me to place emphasis on the information.

"Yes, ma'am, I can do that," I assured her and picked up a pen to begin filling out the paperwork.

When I finished, Reyann told me she would give me a company cell phone on Friday and introduce me to her sons. I thanked her and took off running back to my house. By the time I returned home it was nearly nine p.m., and the sun had long set. I stumbled into the house; grateful my parents were still away. They wouldn't have appreciated my late entry and the stench coming off me.

After a shower and completing some assignments for school I took out my guitar and began perfecting the score I had begun the previous day. After an hour of playing and making adjustments, I decided to call it a night and put the instrument away. It was after midnight when I turned my lights off and fell into sleep.

It had been one of the best days of my life.

5

Acclimating

The days fell into another, and I developed a routine. I still pretty much kept to myself, with the exception of Kelly during lunch and Jenny during classes. While I didn't exactly encourage Jenny's attention she continued to flirt and ensure we sat next to each other every day. Sometimes she would pass me notes but I never responded to them. She assumed it was because I didn't want to get caught and she found my fear of our teachers humorous. I never corrected her. It wouldn't do any good to hurt her feelings, so I just kept my silence.

Travis continued to seek me out as well. It didn't seem to bother him at all that I never really engaged in the conversation with him. One day he told me he was determined to break through and make me laugh. He was still a strange guy, but he was growing on me. He told me he didn't understand why I wasn't having parties all the time since I had the whole house to myself days at a time. I just shrugged and he sighed at my complete ineptitude (his word). He had finally won the battle of wills against his mother and got his hair cut from a professional. The day after the cut he announced that he missed his longer hair and would let it grow out again.

Track was turning out to be a success. My times kept improving and Coach Tennor assigned me to the long-distance races. I was the alternate for the shorter events, but my strength definitely came with the endurance runs. The other teammates quickly learned that I liked to be alone, and they tended to keep their distance. Only Travis ever spoke to me about things outside of track. Mostly I just listened to his chatter but sometimes I would ask a question here and there, which always sent Travis into a momentary freeze of shock.

Every day I looked forward to my lunch hour and talking to Kelly. She told me something new about her every day and I really loved it when she smiled. Sometimes she would ask me questions and I would give what I thought would be a good enough answer. One day, however, she called me out on my lack of proper responses.

"I don't understand you," she said out of the blue.

"What do you mean?" I asked as I took the pickles off my sub sandwich. She immediately reached over and took them off my tray and ate them. I smirked at her. I wasn't exactly sure when we had become so comfortable with one another that we were taking food off of the other's trays, but I was pleased by the development. She smiled back at me and covered her mouth while she chewed.

"I like pickles," she explained after she had swallowed.

"I can tell."

"Seriously, though, why don't you ever answer my questions?" she asked, returning to the previous topic.

"I do answer your questions. See, answered," I said calmly and took a bite of my sandwich.

"Funny, and no you don't. You give half answers or somehow you manage to give an answer that isn't really an answer but a way to change the subject. It's very confusing," she said and took a sip of her drink.

"How do I do that?" I asked.

"I can't give you a specific example right now. Wait…you just did it just now! Oh! And yesterday I asked you why your parents are gone all the time, and your answer was, *'they like to travel'*." She replied and deepened her voice in a poor mockery of my own. She gave me a smug look like she had finally stumped me.

"Well, they do," I said and shrugged.

"My Dad likes to travel but he isn't gone twenty-five days out of a month like your parents," she said.

"My parents have a different kind of job than your father does. They travel for work. Do you like to travel?" I asked.

"Oh, no you don't!" she said shaking a finger at me.

"What?" I asked innocently.

"You are not going to change the subject. We are talking about you, not me," she said and leaned back, crossing her arms over her chest in frustration.

"But you are way more interesting," I smirked and winked at her. She scowled at me and narrowed her eyes.

"Stop fooling around. Why don't you like to talk about your parents?"

I put my sandwich down and sighed. It didn't appear she would be giving up this particular line of questioning any time soon. I knew that I would have to give her an actual answer if I wanted to keep talking to her.

"My parents aren't exactly the friendliest people," I began.

"Okay. But what does that have to do with you?"

"Let's just say they prefer it if I am out of their sight and out of their minds." I hoped that would be explanation enough. It wasn't.

"That is horrible. Do they even talk to you?" Kelly asked, uncrossing her arms and leaning forward out of concern. She really was the nicest person I had ever met.

"Of course they talk to me. You know, pass the salt, make sure you shovel the driveway, don't track mud into the house," I said and laughed at my joke. Kelly didn't laugh. She just continued to stare at me with sympathy in her eyes.

"I don't mind it. They stay out of my way, and I stay out of theirs," I said and picked my sandwich back up.

"Yeah, but don't you go crazy sometimes with all the quiet?"

35

Kelly asked.

"Kelly, can we please talk about something else now?"

She must have picked up on the pleading in my voice because she dropped the subject and changed it immediately.

"When is your next track meet?"

I told her the day and time and she said she would be there to cheer me on. I told her she didn't have to do that, and she told me to shut up. A smile grew as I watched her continue on with another topic. She was just so damned nice.

That weekend I began my new job and met Reyann's sons, Tom and Jeff. Jeff was older but he had opted to take a few community college courses because he intended to take over the landscaping business once his mother was ready to retire. Tom said he hated always having dirt beneath his nails and was more than happy to step aside and give Jeff the business. Jeff then promptly punched his brother on the shoulder. I watched the brothers interact and was struck with envy. This was the type of easy relationship I wish I had with my own brother, instead of the strained, twisted mess we had.

"So, Brad, how are you liking our little version of Pleasantville?" Tom asked as we loaded a truck with some small bushes and flowers.

"It's fine," I replied and went back for another load. Tom and Jeff exchanged a look between them.

"That bad, huh?" Jeff asked when I returned.

"What? No, it's alright," I replied, worried I had somehow offended them.

"No, I totally get it. I can't wait to get out of here and away from that dump they call a school," Tom said. He was currently a senior at the same school I attended.

"I thought you were in the running to be class valedictorian and a pretty decent player on the basketball team," I said not understanding his desire to get away at all.

"Well, sure it's not all bad but this town is just too small for my ambitions," Tom said, and Jeff pushed him. They laughed and began to scuffle.

"Boys! Knock it off. Finish loading that truck and get on with it. We lose daylight the more time you waste goofing off," Reyann called from the office door.

"Yes Mother," Tom said apologetically, and Reyann went back inside.

"Yes Mother," Jeff mocked his brother.

"Shut up," Tom shoved the laughing Jeff. "You're the one that has to deal with her when I'm gone," Tom pointed out and climbed into the passenger seat of the truck.

"Yeah, but I'm her favorite so she treats me like royalty," Jeff chuckled and waited for me to climb into the little seat in the back of the cab before he climbed into the driver's seat.

"You are so lucky you don't have an older brother, Brad. They are obnoxious know it all's," Tom turned to me.

"I have an older brother," I replied.

Tom blinked at me.

"Oh. Well, does he annoy the shit out of you as much as mine does?" Tom asked and received another punch on the shoulder from said obnoxious older brother.

"Something like that," I replied and averted my gaze so the conversation would end.

For the next four hours Tom showed me the basics of his job and taught me what I would need to know once he left for college. Reyann had been right. This was hard work, but it was also very rewarding. We transformed a barren yard into a welcoming garden. The lady of the house even brought us lemonade and talked to us for

37

a bit. When she disappeared back inside Tom and Jeff engaged in another taunting fest. This time Tom accused the lady of the house of having designs on Jeff and Jeff tossed the rest of his lemonade at his brother, telling him to mind his manners.

"Don't let this mild-mannered bloke fool you Brad. He has a girlfriend at every job site," Tom laughed as he gestured with his thumb to his brother.

"Fuck off," Jeff spit back.

"See. You know it's true because he gets so mad whenever I bring it up," Tom laughed.

"I get fucking pissed because you do it at the job site and one of these days our customers are gonna hear your stupid ass and you'll cost us money," Jeff scolded as he came behind his brother and smacked him upside the head.

"Hey. Come on. Watch the hair. I've got a date tonight," Tom objected and smoothed out his hair.

"Really? You gonna shower first?" Jeff asked disgusted.

"Nah. Lucy says she likes me sweaty."

"She is either lying to you or she can't smell because you reek. Take a shower," Jeff said as he loaded the last of our tools into the truck.

"Brad, tell my brother women like a man to smell musky." Tom enlisted my help.

"I don't know. There is musky and there is horse shit. You are very close to horse shit. Take a shower," I advised and threw my gloves into the bed of the truck.

"What do you two know? I'm the one with the date."

"Hooking up in the back of your truck three times a month isn't a date. She's using you, man," Jeff said and got into the driver's seat.

"Hey, if that is how Lucy chooses to spend our time together who am I to complain?" Tom said chuckling. We both climbed into our seats and Jeff started the engine.

"What about you Brad? Meet anybody *'special'* since you've

been in town?" Tom asked.

"Not really," I said. My answer was not satisfactory for Tom.

"Do you even like girls?" he asked.

I immediately turned my head towards him, my eyes wide.

"Of course I do," I said.

"Hey, no judgment here. It's cool if you're into dudes," Tom replied, holding up his hands in a mock show of peace and apology.

"I like girls," I said.

"Me thinketh he doth protesteth too much," Tom laughed.

"Knock it off Tom. Ignore him Brad, he's being stupid," Jeff glanced at me in the rear-view mirror.

"Yeah, I'm just fucking with you. What's her name?" Tom asked.

"Who?"

"The girl that has you all twisted," Tom explained.

"I don't know what you mean," I said and looked out the window again.

"Wow. He's got it bad," Jeff said, and the two brothers laughed.

I took it back. If this was how brothers were supposed to act, I didn't want it.

6

Nightmares

It had been many months since I had experienced the gut-wrenching nightmares I used to have. They always started the same. I would be returning home from school and call out for Kevin, but he wouldn't answer. I went in search of him and went from room to room until I eventually found him lying on the bathroom floor, motionless. Sometimes it would be just as I had discovered him, lying in the blood. Other times he would be awake, and his blank eyes would stare at me but his mouth would move and he would say, *'you let me die'*. Other times it wouldn't be Kevin lying there at all, but a monster that would suddenly reach out for me. I usually woke before the monster could touch me. Every time I would wake in a sweat, breathing heavily and feeling desperate for a run. If my parents were home, I would have to forgo the run because I didn't want to wake them. If they weren't home, I would put on my running shoes and blast out the front door.

My route took me to my place of work, and I would climb over the fence to walk among the trees. The scent always soothed me. The weather had turned colder, and I knew I would miss my midnight walks among the trees once the snow came. Reyann told me they sold Christmas trees leading up to the holidays and I knew I would have my midnight runs until December.

That night, as I made my way back home from my midnight run,

I saw Kelly sitting on the swing on her front porch. I glanced down at my watch and saw it was almost one in the morning. It was a weekend, but I knew it was also Kelly's turn to be with her mother, so I was surprised to see her sitting outside her father's house. I jogged up to her porch and she watched me the entire time, silent.

"Hey," I said as I stopped before her. She had her knees drawn to her chest and a blanket was covering her legs. As I took her in, I noticed she had streaks of tears running down her cheeks. I was immediately concerned and dropped to my knees before her.

"What's happened?" I asked. My hand instinctively reached out for her, but I withdrew before I touched her. I wasn't sure she wanted me to touch her. Touch was meaningful, and I lacked that in my own life. Doubt had me pulling my hand back from her.

"My mother dropped me off here today. She said that since she is going to marry Fred soon it is time for me to move in with my dad," Kelly sniffled and wiped at her nose. I knew Fred was her mother's fiancé and that she didn't really like the guy. I also kind of gathered that Kelly didn't really like her mother all that much but she was just too damned nice so she would never admit it.

"I'm sorry Kelly," I said.

Honestly, I wasn't sorry at all. If she lived with her father full time, then I would be able to see her more. I didn't like that she was hurting but deep down I couldn't muster any anger towards her mother because she had unintentionally given me something I wanted, access to Kelly.

"I just can't help but feel like something bad is about to happen. I know I sound silly, and I probably look dreadful right now but when she was saying goodbye to me, I could tell something wasn't right," Kelly closed her eyes and fresh tears began to fall. This time I didn't think about touching her, I just sat on the swing with her and pulled her into my arms. She willingly leaned into me and snuggled her cheek against my chest.

To her, this was just a hug between friends. For me, it was

41

everything. To offer my arms for her, knowing how important touch was, gave her a part of myself that I had never offered up to anyone before.

"I know this is hurting you now but maybe this will be a good thing. You'll get to see your father more. You are always telling me how you wish you could see him more. And you will see Fred less, another thing you have told me you wanted. Another bonus, you get to hang out with me more often. I know how much you miss me when I'm gone," I joked with her, and she snorted out a laugh.

"You're impossible," she whispered and snuggled closer to me. I adjusted the blanket, so she was properly covered.

"Yeah, but you like me that way," I teased. She nodded.

"What were you doing out so late?" she asked, looking up at me.

I hesitated. I didn't want to tell her the truth. That I had woken up in a panic from a nightmare in which I relived the moment I found my half-dead brother lying in his own blood. Instead, I told a half truth.

"I couldn't sleep and decided to go for a run," I lied and rested my chin on the top of her head.

"You shouldn't be running by yourself so late. Something could happen to you."

"You worried about me?" I smiled.

"Of course, I am. One friend in trouble at a time is all I can handle," she replied.

"What do you mean?" I asked, not understanding her at all.

"It's just Jenny. Her mother is a bit of a nightmare, and I think things might be getting worse. I don't know what to do about it though. Jenny won't tell anyone, and she made me promise I wouldn't tell either." Kelly immediately sat up in a panic and stared at me with wide eyes.

"Oh no. Don't tell her I told you," she said and bit her lip nervously.

"I won't," I promised and opened my arms back up so she could come back to them. She sighed and lay against me again. The touch was now more for my benefit than hers, but I didn't tell her that as she settled back in.

We sat like that for another hour before I noticed her eyes started to drift closed and her breathing evened out. Despite how much I want to just stay like that with her I gently shook her awake and told her to go to bed. She yawned, thanked me for talking to her and told me to stop running so late at night. I didn't want to make her a promise I couldn't keep so I didn't say anything. She hugged me goodbye and disappeared behind her front door. The moment she was gone I was struck by a desire to run in after her.

Jeff was right. I had it bad.

The following Monday I couldn't help but think of what Kelly told me about Jenny. I always knew her behavior was kind of strange, but I just chalked it up to her wanting attention. She was constantly flirting with me, but she flirted with every guy. Sometimes I didn't like the way she talked to Kelly but it wasn't my friendship and it never seemed to bother Kelly. I watched Jenny a bit more closely and actually listened to what she was saying to me.

There were moments when she didn't think anybody was looking, she would drop her guard, and her flirtatious demeanor would slip. I would see the pain in her expression and once she noticed someone was looking, she would instantly return to her flirtatious self. She would often compliment people but cleverly sneak an insult into the compliment. I overheard her tell this one girl that her outfit was daring because usually somebody with those hips couldn't pull it off. The girl looked hurt, but she thanked Jenny and Jenny smiled back at her like she hadn't just called the girl fat.

Another time she walked right up to a boy and told him about this new acne cream that would work wonders on his problem (the guy had like three pimples – hardly a problem), but he thanked her awkwardly and she offered to get the cream for him.

I watched and I listened. One day, when I wasn't giving her the attention she seemed to want, she told me Kelly was thinking about asking a guy in her Chem class out. I reacted to that, of course. It took me a moment to realize that was exactly what Jenny had intended. She wanted to get a reaction out of me, and she knew Kelly was the button to push. She smirked back at me, and I decided I wasn't going to play her game. I ignored her and returned to my notes. She huffed out her breath and started to write on her paper. A few minutes later she dropped her pen and when she bent to pick it up the sleeve of her shirt inched up and I saw some purple marks on her arms. She noticed me staring and she quickly pulled the sleeve back down and went back to her assignment.

It was then I knew that my nightmares were in my dreams, but Jenny's nightmares lived and breathed. No wonder Kelly was worried about her. I decided I needed to stop pushing Jenny away and try to understand why she acted the way she did. Kelly was her best friend and was always nice to her, but Jenny sometimes would lash out at her and say such awful things. She knew I liked Kelly, but she continued to flirt with me. It was clear she had some issues at home, but she refused to tell anyone about it. Something was certainly rotten in the state of Denmark, and I intended to find out.

I followed Jenny out of class and to her locker. Normally she would hang back and try to flirt with me some more, but I knew she was trying to avoid me because of what I had seen. When she stopped at her locker, I stopped beside her and just waited for her to finish putting her things away.

"What do you want?" she barked at me.

"Do you want to talk about it?" I asked, gesturing to her arm. She immediately pulled her arm behind her back.

"I don't know what you are talking about," she feigned ignorance.

"It's okay, Jenny. You can tell me," I said encouragingly.

She stared at me for a moment, and I witnessed the change I had seen so many times before. Her eyes hardened and she smirked at me.

"I can think of other things we could do besides talk," she said and moved closer to me. Her fingers brushed up the side of my arm as she caressed me. I looked down at her fingers and took a step back.

"You don't have to do that," I said without emotion.

"Why? Because you think Kelly will find out? She barely knows you exist. You should just give up on that and take what I'm offering," Jenny spewed out.

"You aren't going to get to me. When you decide you need someone to talk to, I'll be here," I said and turned to go to my class.

"She doesn't like you!" she called behind me as I walked away.

That time, and all the times after, I ignored her.

7

Disaster

It turned out Kelly had been right that night on the front porch swing. Terrible things did follow. Kelly's mother took off with her new husband and Kelly hadn't heard from her since. She was devastated by this. I knew that they didn't exactly have the greatest relationship, but Kelly loved her mother and she felt betrayed that her mother had chosen a guy over her child. I tried to comfort her but how do you provide comfort for something you don't entirely understand. I was used to having my parents absent for long periods of time, and on the rare occasions that they were home we avoided each other as much as we could.

Unfortunately, Kelly's mother leaving wasn't the worst thing to happen. Jenny just seemed to spiral further into her mean habits. I kept letting her know that I was there if she needed to talk but she never actually took me up on it. I had gotten my license and bought a used truck since starting my job and one day after school I followed Jenny home. She was shocked to find me standing on her doorstep and was not happy to see me once the shock wore off.

She wouldn't let me in, but I could see the mess from the doorway. I told her I just wanted to make sure she was alright, and she told me to mind my own business and slammed the door in my face.

Sometimes, if I didn't have a track meeting, I would follow her home and we would repeat the same scene. Other times, when I couldn't sleep, I would drive over to her house and just sit in my truck. She caught me one night and really laid into me. She accused me of stalking her and threatened to call the police. I told her to go ahead and do it, but it wouldn't stop me from making sure she was okay. That quieted her down and she went back into her house.

After that I saw her look outside her window on the nights I was there to check for my truck. She would see me, nod, and close her blinds. I would usually sit there for a few hours before going home.

I don't know why I did it. If anyone stumbled upon me lurking outside her house, I would not blame them if they thought I was her stalker. My behavior resembled one, and it did give the appearance that I was obsessed with her, but I wasn't. In fact, my actions probably had nothing to do with Jenny at all and were a product of my own deep-rooted fears. She reminded me of my brother and there were times when I looked at her I pictured her lying on that bathroom floor, surrounded by a pool of blood.

One day at school, as we continued our usual routine of me asking if she wanted to talk and her ignoring me, she asked me to follow her. I thought, maybe today she would finally tell me what was going on. I had a pretty good idea. I'd seen more bruises on her when her shirt shifted, and they came into view. She always ignored my stares and questions or lashed out in anger. So, when she asked me to follow her that time, I thought something must have happened and she was ready to tell me.

I was wrong.

She took me to an unused classroom and when I turned around, she was locking the door. Again, I thought nothing of it because I wouldn't have wanted to be interrupted either. I watched her put her things down and walk to me without saying a word. She walked up to me and leaned forward like she was trying to kiss me and that was when I reacted. I grabbed her arms and took a step back, holding her away from me.

"Jenny, that isn't what I wanted," I said and turned my head away from her. The expression on my face had to be a cross between shock and disgust.

"All guys want this," she replied and tried to kiss me again.

I tried to push her away, but I didn't want to hurt her, and she managed to break free of my hold and her lips met mine.

I just stood there. I let my arms fall to my sides and let her kiss me, but I didn't return to the kiss. I remained stoic and waited for her to finish. Once she realized that I wasn't into it she broke away from me and began to shout.

"God, what is your problem, Brad? I'm throwing myself at you and you couldn't care less! Kelly doesn't want you! She will never want you," she unloaded on me and walked up to me again. She reached out with both hands and began to rub my arms softly. "But I want you. You can have me, Brad. Right now," she said and kissed me again.

Once again, I remained still until she broke away.

"Fuck Brad! What is your problem? You think I'm ugly, don't you? You won't kiss me back because I'm ugly!"

She turned from me, took a few paces forward before bending to pick up a nearby chair. She threw that chair as hard as she could, but it didn't go very far. I watched her shoulders sag in disappointment as she watched the chair clatter to the floor. She began to cry, and she dropped onto the floor.

Slowly, I went to her and knelt down behind her. Hesitating, I put my hand on her back and tried to soothe her, then wrapped my arm around her, awkwardly. She continued to sob in her hands. I wanted to do more than just offer her some half-assed attempt at a hug but touching her seemed wrong. Something in the way she shook told me to keep a slight distance.

"You aren't ugly, Jenny," I said.

"Then why don't you want me?" she asked, sobbing.

I sighed heavily, because I was not equipped to know how to navigate my way through whatever was happening. I felt entirely at a disadvantage, but I still answered her.

"You're hurt. I can see the bruises. I see you and you don't need some boy to take more from you. Jenny, has somebody ever forced themselves on you, physically?" I asked. I dreaded the answer, but I knew I needed to ask it. Her behavior was just too bizarre to ignore. She immediately stopped crying and stiffened beside me.

"No," she said sternly.

"Are you sure?" There was doubt in the question.

She withdrew, stood, and walked over to the window. I followed her and we both looked out into the growing storm in the afternoon sky. I gave her some time, but she didn't speak so I pressed on.

"Jenny, you can tell me anything."

"My mother hits me sometimes," she said so causally, like we were talking about the weather and not how her mother hurts her.

"What about others? Has anyone else ever hurt you?" I looked at her this time. Deep down, I willed her answer to be no. I wanted it to be no.

She nodded, closed her eyes and let the tears fall. When she turned to face me, I pleaded with her.

"Let me help you."

"No one can help me," she said on a sob and shook her head.

"They can. If you let them," I replied and looked into her broken eyes. She didn't respond and I didn't want to push her any further.

We stayed in that classroom and watched the storm roll in. A harbinger of things to come.

I increased my nightly visits to her house, and she would even come outside and join me. We would go for walks, often not saying anything to each other, but I could tell she was grateful for my presence. She still would lash out at me at times and call me names or tell me Kelly would never love me, but I never responded. I knew she was only saying those things because she was hurting, and she didn't know what else to do. I had finally decided enough was enough and I was going to tell her that I was going to report her mother, but before I could do that Jenny's mother attacked her and nearly killed her.

I visited her in the hospital, and I cried as she slept. I stood over her and saw every bruise and broken bone as my own failure. All my visits and questions hadn't done a thing to help her. My failure to act had caused her to be in that place at the time her mother snapped. I hadn't gone to her house that night because I had been working on my music.

I should have been there. Instead, I was selfish and stayed at home.

When I noticed Jenny stir, I dried my eyes and sat in the chair beside her bed. She opened her eyes, stared at me, but didn't say anything. I didn't say anything either. I did reach out and link my fingers through the one hand that wasn't in a cast. Her fingers tightened around mine and we continued to just stare at each other, saying so much without actually speaking.

Of all the touches in my life, up to that point, that single touch of our fingers was the most crushing. Wrapped between our fingers was her pain and my guilt.

Her cousin came into town and took custody of her soon after. I thought maybe things would finally work out for Jenny and she could finally be happy, but as usual I was wrong. She did get better for a little while, until she got a boyfriend, and then things went straight to shit.

I met the guy, Mark Knight, one day at Kelly's house. Kelly and I had been hanging out, arguing about which flavor of soda was superior, when Jenny brought her boyfriend over. I knew who he was from school, and I had never liked him. He was such a tool, and his older brother still had a reputation, even though he was now in college.

Everyone knew who the Knights were and nothing I had heard made me feel like this guy was any different from his brother. He walked around school like he was the golden boy and the last thing Jenny needed was some pompous dick face making her feel inferior.

So, I wasn't exactly nice to him and Kelly accused me of being jealous of Mark because I wanted Jenny for myself. I was utterly shocked. How much clearer did I have to make it that the person I liked was her, not Jenny. Still, I didn't come right out and tell her. I don't know why. Maybe some part of me actually believed all those things Jenny had told me. Maybe Kelly really didn't feel the same about me and that was why she kept telling me I liked Jenny. Maybe, Kelly didn't want me to like her as anything other than a friend.

I decided that if the only thing Kelly wanted me to be was her friend then that was what I would be. I finished my first year of school pretty much just working, hanging out with Kelly, running, and improving on my guitar playing. I played for Kelly a few times and she told me she loved to listen to me play.

One day, while we were doing just that, she asked me one of her prying questions. The kinds of questions she knew I didn't like.

"Why don't we ever go over to your house?" she asked while I was writing down a cord change. I stopped writing momentarily to gather myself before answering.

"Because your house is much more cozy," I smiled at her and she narrowed her eyebrows. She always knew when I was feeding her bullshit.

"Be serious," she told me.

"Because I spend enough time there and I like it over here better. Your father and his girlfriend are much better cooks than me," I once again tried to deflect.

Kelly's father had begun dating this woman, Tasha, and I suspected a marriage was soon to follow. Tasha and her daughter had already moved in with Paul and Kelly and they had all acclimated to the new family structure with ease. Even Kelly seemed much happier since her mother had left.

"Take me over there now," Kelly said and stood up from the bed. I was sitting on the floor and quickly put my guitar down.

"I really don't want to," I objected as I stood.

"Well, too bad. We've known each other for almost a year now and I have never been over to your house. It's just weird, Brad. Are you embarrassed?" she asked as she put her shoes on.

"No," I replied and ran my fingers through my hair. I didn't have anything to be embarrassed about. My parents weren't home, so I wasn't worried about them. I had just never had a girl over to my house before. Travis came over sometimes, but we usually just watched some games and ate pizza. I imagine it would be different with a girl.

"Then let's go," she said and grabbed my hand.

She pulled me down the stairs and as we passed the living room she called out to her father and Tasha sitting in the living room.

"Brad and I are going over to his house. I'll be back soon."

"Okay. Dinner is at six," Paul called back.

I let Kelly drag me to my house and through the front door, which I had left unlocked. She took off her shoes in the entry and waited for me to do the same. I did, slowly, trying to prolong this event. She grew impatient and tapped her foot in frustration. When I was finished, she grabbed my hand again and pulled me into the living room. She looked around for a little bit then went into the kitchen. The rest of the 'tour' went exactly the same. She pulled me from room to room, looked around, and then went to the next room without a word. We eventually came to my room, and she dropped my hand to step inside.

I leaned against the door frame and let her wander around. She picked up the book on my nightstand, flipped it over and read the back cover before returning it. Then she went to my desk and her fingers floated over the sheets of music I had on there. She scrolled through the playlist I had up on my computer and hit play. The last song I had been listening to flowed through the speakers.

"Who is this?" she asked when the female began to sing.

I told her the name of the group, one I knew she had never heard of, and continued to watch her move around my room.

After she ran her fingers over the clothes in my closet she went and sat on my bed. She was the first girl to be in my room, the first girl to sit on my bed, and I didn't know what to do. I watched as she picked at a string or something off my comforter.

"Can I tell you something?" she asked me, picking at the string.

"Always," I said.

"Remember how Jenny brought her boyfriend over to my house that day?"

"Yes," I replied, still leaning against the door frame.

"Well, I kind of feel guilty because I think I'm jealous of Jenny. Does that make me a bad person?" She wouldn't look at me and I pushed off the door frame to enter the room. I didn't like where this was going at all.

"Jealous of what?" I asked and sat at my desk.

"Of her and Mark," she whispered.

"You like this Mark guy?" I asked, trying to keep the venom out of my voice.

She shrugged and said, "I don't know."

Even though I wanted to shout at her and beg her not to fall for Mark and his charms I did what I always do. I kept my emotions in check and spoke like nothing was bothering me.

"He is Jenny's boyfriend," I said flatly.

"I know. I don't know if it has anything to do with him or maybe I just wish I had the same thing, you know?"

"No," I replied, and she sighed. I was messing this up.

53

"Nevermind. I'm just being silly. Thank you for showing me your room, finally," she joked and stood. "Well, I'm gonna head back home. Do you want to join us for dinner?"

Sometimes I would eat dinner with her family since Paul and Tasha had discovered I am so often left alone. Of course, I never revealed just how often and for how long I was left home alone.

I shook my head at her invite.

"No, thanks."

After hearing her reveal she might have feelings for Mark Knight, the last thing I wanted to do was sit across from her at a joyful family dinner.

"Okay. I'll see you at school then," she said and left.

I should have spoken up that night and told her how I felt. Maybe, if I had she wouldn't have been available for Mark Knight to swoop in and take her from me. I knew he wasn't any good for Jenny and I bore witness to hurricane Mark as Jenny began to spiral out of control once again. This time she turned to drugs and alienated everyone that cared about her. When I found out Mark was pursuing Kelly, I wasn't happy about it all. The guy was so damn cocky, and he flaunted his presence at me and when I tried to talk to Kelly about it she got upset with me and once again accused me of being jealous because I liked Jenny.

"I could really use a break from all your questions. I'm just so tired of you putting me in the middle of your little soap opera with Jenny and Mark. Just tell her you like her and get it over with. Please, put me out of my misery," she huffed and threw her arms up in the air.

We were leaving school after Mark had appeared with her and he gave me one of his typical smirks that attempted to tell you he was better than you. I hated that guy, and I really hated that Kelly still thought I had feelings for Jenny.

"For the last time," I grumbled, "I do NOT have feelings for Jenny. I just don't like that guy, okay!" This was the first time I had ever shouted at Kelly. She looked at me in shock before she answered.

"Okay," she whispered.

We walked the rest of the way home in silence and when we got to our houses, we didn't even say goodbye. I don't know what she was thinking about the entire walk, but I was thinking that Jenny had been right this whole time. Kelly didn't, and never would, like me the way I liked her. And it was becoming too hard to just be her friend and watch her with Mark. It was like she couldn't see the kind of guy he really was and no matter what I said to her she simply wouldn't listen. I couldn't stand by and watch her get closer to him.

So, I resorted to my old safety net, and I withdrew from her. I stopped walking to and from school with her. I stopped eating lunch with her, and I stopped going over to her house. I figured she would eventually seek me out, but she never did.

I discovered a few weeks later why she never tried to talk to me. Jenny and Mark had broken up and Kelly was spending a lot of her time with Mark. I often saw him at her house, and it killed me every time I saw his stupid black Audi in the driveway. I wanted to slash his tires but that would require caring, and the Klauzek's didn't care about anything.

So, I just continued on existing, just like I had done before her. And I was content.

8

Old Wounds

Tom had been away at college for many months now and Jeff and I were keeping things under control. He would often try to engage me in the lighthearted banter him and his brother used to engage in but I wasn't very good at it, and Jeff let me know it. He was constantly telling me I needed to lighten up or get the stick out of my ass. I would just shrug and keep on working.

"Seriously, man, if you keep going on like this you are going to explode one day. You gotta let loose once in a while. If you were twenty-one I'd take you out drinking but you aren't so my next advice is to get laid," Jeff said as he hauled a Concolor Fir from our trailer.

"I'm not gonna go have sex just because you say so," I said as I grabbed the next sapling.

"Okay, don't do it because I say so. Do it because you need to. You are just wound so tight," Jeff said as we began to place the trees in the mapped out spots.

While I thought Jeff's advice to get laid so I could loosen up was not exactly a stroke of genius I had to admit I was interested in the act. I was a sixteen-year-old hot-blooded male after all. Of course I was interested. I hadn't been interested in anybody but Kelly since I moved here, nor had I attempted to connect with any other girls. Aside from Jenny I hadn't exactly struck up any conversations with the girls that had shown interest in me. I decided if Kelly was going to date someone else then it was time I cut my losses and went on my own path. It was time I let go of this infatuation I had with her.

The very next day, after having my epiphany, I witnessed something that brought me crashing back into Kelly's life. I was standing outside of the school talking to Travis and a couple other guys from the team when I heard shouting. I looked towards the doors and there was Kelly, yelling at Jenny. I heard her call Jenny a hypocrite and a slut. And then I heard Kelly accuse Jenny of sleeping with Mark's brother and half the school. I was stunned. This wasn't the Kelly I knew. The Kelly I knew would never have said anything to hurt Jenny. Once again, I was struck by my hatred for Mark. I couldn't prove it, but I had a feeling he was the cause of this fight.

As I was fantasizing about punching Mark in his face, I watched as Jenny did just that to Kelly. People around them scattered as Kelly went down from the impact. Jenny didn't say anything else to her, she simply turned on her heels and left Kelly there on the ground. It looked like Kelly had been knocked out, so I ran over to her. No one else around her was trying to help her and once again I was reminded how much people sucked. I picked up her bag and bent down to scoop her up.

She opened her eyes as I was placing my hands under her arms to lift her. When she realized someone was helping her, she relaxed and allowed me to lift her the rest of the way. She stumbled a bit and placed her hand on my shoulder to steady herself. She started to say thank you but stopped when she saw it was me. After a brief hesitation she smiled shyly at me, and I couldn't help myself, I smiled back and put my arm around her to offer support. We started walking towards the direction of home and I spoke to her for the first time in months.

"So, you and Mark, huh?" I asked.

"Yeah," she said and tried to touch her cheek. It was starting to bruise and she winced when she touched it.

"Hmm. Jenny sure had something to say about that," I glanced at her out of the corner of my eye and tried not to smirk, but I couldn't help it.

"You are such a jerk," she said and lightly punched me on the shoulder. If that was how she thought you were supposed to punch, then it was no wonder she hadn't stood a chance against Jenny. I laughed and pretended to rub my injured shoulder.

"They were already broken up Brad. I would never have done something like that to her," she said very seriously.

"I know. She hasn't exactly been herself lately. She's going through some things Kelly. Give her time. She'll come around," I said, not believing a word of it and realizing that Kelly had once basically said the same thing to me when I first moved there.

"And you? Do you need more time? Are you still mad at me?" She asked, her eyes cast down like she was afraid to see the answer in my eyes.

"I was never mad at you Kelly. I guess I just needed to clear some things out of my head. Sorry it took so long," I said.

"It's okay. I understand."

Even I could tell that she didn't understand at all but was too polite to question me further. We walked home in a tension filled and silence. When we got to her house, I helped her in and put ice in a bag for her. She sat at the kitchen table and once again tried to touch her cheek.

"Stop doing that," I scolded as she winced. I handed her the bag of ice, and she thanked me.

"What have you been doing lately?" she asked me as I sat across from her.

"Mostly working. Running with the team. I bought a truck," I said and used my short nail to scratch at an invisible piece of food on the table.

"I saw you driving it."

"It's no Audi," I muttered.

"What?" she asked.

"Nothing. I have to get going. Jeff is expecting me," I stood. "Try not to get punched in the face again any time soon."

"I'll do my best," she replied and walked me to the door.

I was halfway down her walkway when she called out to me. I turned.

"Don't disappear again," she said, the bag of ice pressed to her cheek. She looked so sad, and I hated that I had put that sadness there. I gave her a small smile and made the first promise to her that I would break.

"I won't," I said and walked away.

A few weeks later Jenny had taken off and no one knew where she went. Her cousin, Josh, was frantic and he filed a missing person report and even hired a private investigator to find her. He said the police weren't taking Jenny's disappearance seriously and they wouldn't give another runaway any of their attention. I helped Josh run down leads and must have gone to hundred dive bars with him trying to find anybody that knew something.

Eventually we found some people that told us Jenny had taken off with some guy named Sledge. He was a real keeper, the town drug connection. No one could tell us where they went, however, and our leads ran cold. Josh continued to employ the private investigator, but I had little faith in that panning out. I knew that Jenny didn't want to be found, and it was more than likely none of us would ever see her again. I could tell Kelly blamed herself. She thought Jenny had taken off because of her and Mark, but I knew better. Jenny had been lost long ago, and she hadn't been ready to heal. I understood her desire to run from those that knew her darkness.

My last encounter with Jenny had been purely by chance. I had been out running some errands when I saw her stumble out of some local biker hangout. She was laughing and pushing away the groping hands of some older men that looked like they had seen better days themselves.

Jenny had refused to talk to me since her fallout with Mark and I was tired of the rejection. Then, she had taken off and there she was, suddenly back in town after we had all searched for her. In my anger, I was just going to keep driving but when I saw her nearly trip I groaned and turned my truck around. I pulled into the parking lot, left the truck running and made my way over to her.

I could hear the guys trying to convince her to come back inside and she kept shaking her head. One of them reached out to grab her by the waist and I immediately took off running towards her. I put myself between her and the handsy middle aged man, pushing him away as I did.

"What the fuck?" the man grumbled as he righted himself. He seemed to be more drunk than Jenny was. His companion immediately turned to me, pissed that I had pushed his buddy.

"You must have a death wish, boy," the second man said to me and reached into his pocket, pulling out a switchblade. I listened to the click as the blade snapped out.

"And you must be dumb as hell. She's only sixteen," I said as I pushed Jenny behind me. My words must have gotten through to the guy I had pushed because his eyes widened, and he looked at his friend holding the blade.

"Fuck. What the hell is she doing here then," he said and rubbed his head.

"I just want to take my friend home. I don't want any trouble," I said as Jenny tried to get around me. I pushed her back.

"Brad, we are just having some fun. Come have fun with us," she begged, stumbling over her words and trying to break free of my hold.

"Jenny, stop," I demanded and after a brief consideration, turned my back on the guy with the blade to get Jenny under control.

"You sure seemed to want trouble the moment you pushed my

friend," the guy with the blade said and took a step closer to me. I saw him out of the corner of my eye and side-stepped, taking Jenny with me.

"I just want to get her home. Sorry I pushed you," I apologized to the other guy and pleaded with my eyes to get him to stop his advancing friend.

"Put that away. They are just kids," the guy I pushed said and put his hand on his buddy's arm. "We don't need any unwanted attention drawn to us. Put it away."

The guy brandishing the blade hesitated, but he eventually complied and put the blade away. As I was walking Jenny to my truck blade guy called out a warning to me.

"I don't ever want to see your face again. If I do, I will kill you," he said as calmly as someone reading a grocery list. I took one last glance at him and shoved Jenny into my truck. Once I was back inside, I sped out of that parking lot and finally let out the breath I had been holding.

"What the hell Jenny?" I said as we were about a mile away. She just laughed and slapped my arm.

"You almost died," she laughed and burped at the same time.

"You think that's funny? What the fuck are you doing with those guys?" I demanded as I slammed my hands on the steering wheel.

She looked at my hand and shrugged.

"Just having some fun. It isn't that big of a deal Brad. Lighten up."

I snapped. I slammed my hand on the steering wheel over and over again, saying 'fuck' with every slam. Jenny just watched me.

"This isn't a fucking joke. Do you have any idea what could have happened back there?" I shouted.

"Nobody asked you to rescue me, Brad! You should just mind your own damn business!" Jenny shouted right back.

"You're my friend Jenny. You may not care what happens to you, but I do. When will you stop acting like such a selfish brat and get your shit together?" I kept driving the entire time, but she suddenly told me to pull over. I told her not a chance and she proceeded to open her door anyway.

"Fuck, Jenny," I said and pulled over to the side of the road. She immediately jumped out and I ran after her.

"Are you crazy?" I called to her.

She stopped, turned, and pushed me against my chest, causing me to stumble back.

"Yes, I'm fucking crazy! Go away Brad!" she shouted and continued to walk away from me.

"When you decide you want to start caring about yourself again, I'll be there," I called after her.

She stopped momentarily but didn't turn back to me. She continued walking down the road and I got back in my truck and drove away. It was the second time I had failed her, and she was gone for good a few months later. She returned at some point to her cousin's house and cleared out with her belongings.

I blamed myself for not trying harder to with her.

Amidst that chaos with Jenny, my brother continued to pressure me to get back in contact with our older sister, Lily. I hadn't spoken to her since the day she walked away from us, but apparently, she had reconnected with Kevin. He seemed to be happy about having her back in his life, but I wasn't ready to go down that road again. I still hadn't forgiven her for leaving. I knew that Kevin never would have tried to kill himself if Lily hadn't just walked out on us like she did. I didn't understand how he could forgive her so easily when all of our problems started the day she so selfishly turned her back on us. She hadn't even tried to call us, or write, when she left. She just vanished and it had hurt Kevin to the point he felt ending his life was the solution. I hated her for that.

"I don't understand why you won't just talk to her," Kevin said to me one night as we talked on the phone. My parents were gone, again, and I was free to walk about the house.

"Because, I'm not ready yet," I said. I didn't want to tell him the real reason because I didn't want to upset him. He was so easily upset, and I refused to be the one that set him off the ledge.

"She's our sister. She loves us," he pleaded with me.

"Kevin, can we please change the subject? How is grad school going?" I asked.

He sighed but obliged my request.

"It's fine. My thesis is near complete," he said.

"What is it about again?" I knew if I could get him talking about his thesis, he would forget about everything else. My brother lived for the past.

"The battle between state and federal government and the shift from a fractured state structure to a centralized, overreaching whole…"

He continued on and talked about the framers of the constitution and their intentions. I was only half listening to him and before I knew it thirty minutes had passed. I told him it was all fascinating and wished him luck on completing the paper. He said he'd call again in a couple of days, and I told him I would call him tomorrow. I called him every day, he knew that.

"Yeah, yeah. Don't you have a girlfriend or someone to hang out with instead of calling me every day," he teased.

"No. No girlfriend. Besides, if I don't call who else is gonna remind you to set your alarm," I joked right back.

It took me a moment to realize that Kevin and I were engaging in the lighthearted banter I had witnessed Jeff and Tom do. This was not something Kevin and I normally did. I smiled because this was a good sign. It meant Kevin was taking his meds.

"Whatever little brother. I'm a grown man and don't need a babysitter. Oh, crap. I have to go. Talk to you soon," he said and quickly hung up. For the first time in years I laughed at my brother, and I had hope that things would be alright. Despite Jenny's absence, I thought, maybe, this time, things would be different.

9

Used

The school year ended, and a new one began. Kelly continued to date Mark, and I continued to avoid the jerk. At school, whenever he approached her, I would leave. I still didn't join her at lunch, because he was always there. Instead, I ate with my teammates. Travis knew something was up with Kelly and me, but he never brought it up. After all, we weren't that kind of friends.

The only time I ever actually hung out with Kelly was after school and at her house. Her father had married Tasha, and they had a child together, a little boy. Also, during that time Stacey had gotten knocked up by Josh, much to everyone's surprise. Stacey moved in with Josh and I think Tasha kind of used me to replace the loss of Stacey. She started bringing me casseroles or asking me over for dinner, even if Kelly wasn't there. Sometimes I would go over to their house to help Paul, Mr. Johnson, fix things. He wasn't the greatest when it came to household repairs.

Tasha was such a kindhearted person and so welcoming that I found myself opening up to her about my family. I told her why my parents were gone so much and that my sister had abandoned us. I told her about finding Kevin on the bathroom floor and how I feared he would try again someday, and she shared with me the story of her first husband, Stacey's father. Tasha's first husband had been diagnosed with stage four colorectal cancer and after months of treatment and increasing pain he couldn't take it anymore and ended his life. I don't know why I decided to open up to Tasha in the first place but after she shared her story with me, I was glad I had. She understood me in a way no one else had before. Her kindness and understanding was what drew me back every time.

One day I was helping Mr. Johnson fix the leaky kitchen sink when he broached the topic of his daughter. I was putting the finishing touches on our repair when he just blurted a question out.

"Brad, how long have you liked my daughter?"

I dropped the wrench I was holding, and it clattered against pipes. Quickly, I recovered and returned to my task.

"I'm not sure what you mean, sir," I pretended to be clueless.

"I think you know exactly what I mean. Come on out from under there," he said, and I scooted out from under the sink, reluctantly. I wiped my hands on a towel from my back pocket as I stood. Mr. Johnson suggested we sit down, and we both sat at the kitchen table.

"I'm not blind, nor am I fool," Mr. Johnson said.

"Of course you aren't Mr. Johnson," I replied.

"Paul," he said. No matter how many times he told me to call him Paul, I just couldn't do it. It felt wrong to me for some reason.

"I knew the day you knocked on my door that you had intentions toward my girl," Paul said pointing a finger at me.

"Sir, I have never done anything inappropriate towards Kelly," I denied, holding my hands up before me in defense.

"Calm down, son. I know you've been nothing but honorable towards my daughter. She would tell me if you hadn't, and you would not be allowed back into my home. But that isn't what I'm trying to say to you." Mr. Johnson let out a long breath before continuing.

"I know you know this Mark putz she's dating," he said and a laugh escaped my lips. "Yeah, I can't say I am too fond of the guy either. I know his parents too and they aren't much better. Kelly, though, she likes to see the good in everyone and she isn't seeing what is right in front of her," Mr. Johnson said looking at me pointedly.

"Sir?" I questioned.

"I spent many years in a marriage that made me and my wife miserable. And then I spent many years trying to cater to my ex-wife because I didn't want to make her or my daughter unhappy. Basically, I spent a good portion of my life trying to make others happy and forgot to be happy myself. I don't want that for my daughter, and I don't want that for you. Don't wait too long, Brad. If you do, you might look around one day to find your chance passed you by long ago."

The two of us sat there in silence for a minute before Mr. Johnson slapped his hands down on the table and stood.

"Well, that sink isn't going to fix itself," he said and picked up the wrench. He walked to the sink like he was going to finish up but when he got there he paused and looked back at me sheepishly. I laughed, stood and took the wrench from him.

I didn't take Mr. Johnson's advice. Well, not exactly. I still talked to Kelly, and I knew that she was stuck on Mark and any confession of mine would not go over very well with her. She already knew I didn't like Mark and had accused me of being jealous of him in the past. The last thing she would believe is that I was suddenly confessing long-held feelings for her now that she was dating Mark. Besides, the guy knew I had feelings for her, and he made sure she was never alone with me at school. In fact, he had even gone so far as to warn me to stay away from her. I thought the attempt to threaten me was laughable.

I towered over Mark. He wasn't as short as Kelly, but he was nowhere near my height. I must have outweighed him by twenty pounds but he still had the nerve to approach me one day at the end of school. I was in my usual spot outside the front entrance, talking to Travis about practice when Mark came up to us. He had a couple friends with him, back up I suppose.

"I need to talk to you," he barked at me.

I was sitting on the brick wall beside the sidewalk and slowly turned my head towards him. Even though I was half sitting I was still taller than him and had to cast my head down slightly to meet his gaze.

"I'm busy," I said and brushed him off. I turned back to Travis and continued our conversation.

"Stay away from Kelly," he ordered me.

After that, I stood, and I saw Mark's little friends back up a step. Pussies, just like their leader.

"You don't tell me what to do," I said and crossed my arms over my chest.

"I do when it's my girlfriend you are trying to steal."

I gave Mark some props for actually standing his ground. Even if his ground was boggy as hell.

"She's, my friend. She was my friend before you came along and she will be my friend long after you are gone," I said calmly.

Mark smirked at me.

"That's right. You're her *friend*," he placed emphasis on 'friend' and I'm sure everyone watching had picked up his meaning. He said the word like it was meant to cut me and I suppose it did in a way.

"It's time for you to walk away," I told Mark and his henchmen.

"I mean it. Stay away from her," he threatened, shaking his finger at me before walking away with his buddies.

I slowly sat back down on the wall and glared at their backs. A whistle beside me broke me from my glaring and I turned to Travis.

"Intense, man. I thought you were going to wring his neck," Travis said.

"I wanted to," I replied.

"So why didn't you?" Travis asked.

"I would have killed him," I said coldly and stood. Travis looked at me, his mouth agape.

"I'll see you tomorrow," I said and walked away, leaving the stunned Travis sitting there.

I never told Kelly what Mark had done. She still believed he walked on water, and I was tired of hearing about how amazing he was. I was also tired of waiting around for someone that clearly didn't want anything to do with me. So, I finally gave in and went to a party with Travis. He was beyond surprised when I said I wanted to go with him. This was his senior year, and he was determined to make it the best year ever (his words).

That was why I found myself on a couch, in a house of a person I did not know, making out with a girl whose name I could not remember. Beer had been involved and maybe a game of truth or dare. I couldn't really remember the events that had brought me to that moment. But I remember the girl asking me to go upstairs with her and I remember going.

She took me to a bedroom and locked the door behind us. I let her take my clothes off and I may have helped her take hers off, maybe. I remember her asking if I had a condom. I didn't. It was okay, she had one. And that was how I lost my virginity. Drunk and with a girl whose name I still don't remember.

After she was finished with me, because it was clear she had no interest in my name either, she thanked me for the good time and left me alone in the bedroom. I sat on that bed, naked, with my head in my hands. If a guy could ever feel used, I definitely felt it that night. I never had visions of perfection or anything like that regarding my first time, but I would have liked to have known the girl's name. Or at the very least remembered how I had even met her in the first place.

I looked around that room and hated everything it stood for. There wasn't anything memorable about it. No distinguishing items to identify who the room belonged to. It seemed it was just another room in just another house that I felt completely alone in, even though the house was filled with people. I sat on that bed, feeling

68

used, and useless at the same time. It was a terrible feeling.

10

Changeling

After that night at the party, I decided I was done with avoiding Mark and Kelly and I entered my senior year of high school deciding my presence would be known. Mark wanted me to stay away but I was going to do the exact opposite. I was going to flaunt my presence in his face, just like he had done to me. I was there before he had even known Kelly existed and I wasn't about to let him run me off.

Kelly thought I was finally coming around and getting to know Mark. I even started sitting with them at lunch and Kelly just said she was glad we were finally getting along. We weren't, of course, but neither of us could show that in front of Kelly. I knew my presence pissed off Mark and I reveled in it.

One of the benefits of staying near was that I was able to hear things I was pretty sure Mark didn't want me to. One day I heard him bragging to his friends that he and Kelly were going to the next level. I clenched my fists in anger and once again visions of punching him in the face popped into my head. I wanted to hit him, but he hadn't exactly said anything crude. If he had said he was going to fuck her, or pop her cherry, or something along those lines I would have beat the shit out of him. But prim and proper Mark was just talking about how he and his girlfriend were becoming more serious.

God! The guy couldn't even brag to his friends in the right way.

Besides, if I hit him Kelly would be mad at me and I would be right back where I had started, pushed aside. I decided the only way to ensure Mark's prediction didn't come true was to talk to Kelly about it. I really didn't want to, but I didn't want Mark touching her even more. So, I brought the subject up one day while I was over at Kelly's house watching a movie.

"Kel," I said getting her attention.

"Hmmm, mmmm," she kind of mumbled, still watching the movie.

"I have something I want to say but I don't want you to get mad at me or take it the wrong way," I said.

She paused the movie and turned to me.

"You really shouldn't start things off like that. I'm already half-way to panicked," she said.

"It's about Mark." I ran my fingers through my hair, nervous to speak to her about this.

"Brad, if this is a rehashing of how you don't like him, I really don't want to hear it," she said and turned away from me.

"It's not about that. I am not entirely sure how to say this, so I am just going to ask you straight up. Have you had sex with him?"

"Brad! That is none of your business!" She moved back into the couch, shocked at my question.

"Yeah, well I'm making it my business, okay?" I said, all trace of tact out of my voice. "I worry about you Kelly. Mark says he loves you and you say you love him. I get it, love all around," I said sarcastically. "But sometimes when a person says love, they can mean something else. Do you understand what I'm saying?" I ran my fingers through my hair again. I hoped she didn't slap me or kick me out.

"I think so. You are worried about me, and you want me to make sure I think before I act on anything?" she asked, unsure.

"Yeah, something like that. Just be careful and if he ever does anything out of line you let me know. Promise," I said to her.

"I promise," she said and crossed her fingers over her heart. I laughed at the childhood gesture but did the same with my own fingers and then called her a dork.

I wasn't sure if my warnings were enough to convince her, but I had to try. Despite my attempts, Kelly continued to see Mark and I waited for the day I would overhear him bragging about him and Kelly hooking up to his friends, but that day never came. The year continued on and talk soon turned to our plans for the future.

Kelly told me what her top college choices were, and I applied to the same ones. I ended up getting a sports scholarship to Kelly's top choice school and when I told her she was thrilled. She even jumped into my arms and gave me a tight hug.

"I'm so glad we will be staying together," she said as she hugged me.

"Me too," I said and hugged her back. It was only the second time she had embraced me, but it was even sweeter than the first time, because she wasn't sad this time. I was elated and I might have even sniffed her hair.

"Mark won't be going to Marion, though," she said sadly and disengaged from the hug.

Marion was the university we had both been accepted to.

"I'm sorry," I said, even though I wasn't sorry at all. She gave me a look that told me she knew I wasn't sorry.

"I just don't know why he waited so long to tell me," she said and moved away from me.

I was once again over at her house, sitting on the couch in her living room.

"I don't know." I didn't want to talk about Mark. I never wanted to talk about Mark.

"Are you going to Prom?" Kelly asked. For a brief moment I hoped she was asking because she wanted to go with me, but she dashed that hope with the next statement. "Maybe you and your date could go with Mark and me."

"Maybe," I grumbled and then told her I had to go home.

Like a masochist I ended up attending Prom with Kelly and Mark. We shared a limo and went to dinner together. My date was just some girl in one of my classes that I had randomly asked. At least I knew her name; Mandy. Part of me felt bad for using her just so I could attend but she didn't seem to mind. She was an okay girl, and she tried to get me to have fun but I wasn't the greatest date. I resorted to one-word answers most of the night and didn't dance with her much. She was a perky girl though and managed to spend most of the night dancing with her friends.

When the dance was over the limo took my date and I back to my house. After we had gotten out of the limo, I turned to help Kelly out but Mark waved me off.

"Our night isn't over yet," he said and smirked.

I turned to Kelly, concerned for her, and she smiled reassuringly at me.

"I hope you had fun tonight, Brad. It was nice meeting you Mandy," she said.

"You too. Thanks for dropping us off," Mandy waved goodbye and Mark closed the door.

The limo drove off and I just stood there staring after it. After several minutes passed, Mandy cleared her throat behind me, and I jumped. I had forgotten she was there.

"I'll take you home," I said and took my keys out. I was unlocking my truck when she came up beside me.

"You don't have to take me home yet," she said and placed her hand on my arm.

I looked at her hand, then into her eyes. I knew what she wanted from me, but I really wasn't interested. Then I looked down the street where the limo had driven off and decided my lack of interest didn't matter. I locked my truck back up and took Mandy into my house. Once again, my parents were gone, and the house was dark.

Mandy followed me as I made my way through the house, turning lights on as I went. I took her to the kitchen, dropped my keys on the table, took off my suit jacket, loosened my tie and begun unbuttoning the top buttons of my shirt.

"Do you want anything to drink?" I asked her.

"Sure," she replied. She put her purse on the table next to my keys and I took out some bottles of water. I gave her one and downed half of my mine before she even had hers open. I watched her over my bottle of water, and she looked around the kitchen nervously.

"Want to go to my room?" I asked her.

"Okay," she said and followed me when I started walking towards my room.

I turned on my bedroom lights and placed my water bottle on the small table beside my bed. Mandy walked into my room and took off her shoes. She bent down and held them in her hands, unsure where to put them. I took them from her and put them by my closet. She stared at me the entire time I moved around my room. I took out my wallet and placed it in the top drawer of my desk.

"Do you want to sit down?" I asked her and gestured towards my bed. She swallowed and nodded. While she sat down, I turned to my computer and put on a playlist that seemed appropriate for what was about to happen. She seemed to relax a little when the music came on.

I took my tie off from around my neck and placed it on the back of my desk chair. Then, I joined her on my bed. She just continued to watch my every move. I lifted my hand and caressed her shoulder nearest to me. She closed her eyes when I touched her. She really did have soft skin. I slipped my fingers beneath the skinny strap of her dress and pulled it off of her shoulder. She moaned when I dipped down and kissed her collarbone. I felt her hands on my sides and her head tilted back as I continued to kiss up her neck and her jaw until I landed on her lips. She kissed me back, moaning into my mouth the entire time.

I removed the other strap from her shoulder and reached around to unzip her dress. Once I had it unzipped enough, I pushed the top of her dress down and was pleased to see she had no bra on beneath. I dipped my head and tasted both of her breasts. Mandy continued to moan as I moved down her body, removing more of her dress as I went. She eventually lay back on the bed so I could remove the dress completely.

Once she was lying before me naked, I looked down at her and for a brief moment thought I should stop this. I had no intention of ever seeing her again and a part of me knew this girl on my bed probably thought I liked her. Just as quickly as the moment came, it left, and I returned to the task at hand.

I explored her body, touching everywhere, kissing her all over and at one point I even bit the inside of her thigh. She cried out but didn't tell me to stop. When I returned to her lips, she began to unbutton my shirt the rest of the way and it became a mad frenzy to rid me of my clothes. While she worked on my shirt, I removed my belt and freed myself from the confines of my pants. As I reached over to my nightstand for a condom, she pushed my pants and boxers down, freeing me the rest of the way. I quickly put the condom on and thrust into her.

It wasn't until she cried out in pain that I realized this was her first time. The thought that I should stop this once again entered my mind but this time it left with more haste. I was already inside her. The damage had been done, might as well finish it.

So, I did.

11

Journey

I took Mandy home after we finished and told her I would call
her, but I never did. She tried calling me a few times and even left
me some messages, but I never called her back. I saw her one last
time at graduation, but she didn't speak to me and I didn't blame her.
I probably wouldn't have spoken to me either.

Sure, she signed up for what had happened in my bedroom, but
she had actually believed I liked her. She didn't deserve to be used
like that, and I was ashamed of my behavior, but not noble enough to
apologize for it. Instead, I just stood my ground and held her gaze,
like the jerk I was, until she turned and walked away.

I spent the rest of the summer working alongside Jeff and
training the new guy. I would still work for Reyann when I returned
in the summers, but she still needed an extra pair of hands during the
off season. On my last day of work before leaving for college Jeff
said he wanted me to stick around after closing. I did as he asked,
and we sat on the bed of one of the trucks. Jeff handed me a beer and
I took it but looked at him quizzically.

"Don't tell anyone. Especially Ma, she'd kill me," he said and
opened his bottle. I shrugged and opened mine. We both sat in
silence for a few minutes, drinking our beers and enjoying the night.

"You are one tough nut to crack, Brad. But you are one damn
fine worker," Jeff finally said.

"Thanks," I said with a chuckle.

"I'm being serious. It has been an honor to work alongside you these past few years. Take care of yourself at college and don't do anything stupid," Jeff advised.

Part of me was a bit resentful that my parents hadn't taken the time to give me any advice about my college career, but another part was thankful they just continued to exist around me. Jeff had always been good to me, and I would miss his silly attempts to bond with me. The guy was relentless, and he never gave up.

"That girl going with you?"

"What girl?" I asked, taking another drink from my beer.

"The same girl you've been skulking after all these years." He rolled his at me, letting me know he saw through me.

"I don't skulk," I said offended. Jeff laughed loudly at me.

"Yeah, you do. You skulk all the time. Tom and I were never able to get a name out of you, but you always have that look," Jeff said and opened another beer.

"What look is that?"

"Like someone has grabbed a hold of your balls and won't let go."

"Gee, thanks," I said and tossed my empty bottle into a bucket.

"You only get one. Ma would kill me," Jeff repeated and we sat in silence again before he told me I could finally drive home. I left him sitting on the back of the truck, drinking beer and gazing at the sky.

When it finally came time to leave for college my parents were actually home that morning. They didn't see me off of course. They had things to do. Mother told me to drive carefully, and Father handed me some cash for the road, which was more than I expected from either of them. Kelly's family, on the other hand, were emotional wrecks.

I hadn't seen much of Kelly over the summer because she had spent the majority of her time with Mark. She was still fearful about attending a separate college than him, but I was grateful to be rid of the bastard. He didn't even come to say goodbye to his girlfriend.

As I loaded the last of Kelly's things in my truck she said goodbye to her parents. I came around to the driver's side and Mr. Johnson came up to me.

"You take care of my daughter and watch out for her," Mr. Johnson said.

"I will," I said and offered my hand. Mr. Johnson took it and when I was about to pull away, he pulled me in for a hug. I heard Tasha and Kelly laugh at my look of surprise.

"Don't wait too long," Mr. Johnson whispered to me before letting me go. I was too stunned to say anything back. Tasha and Kelly were saying their goodbyes, and I waited for them to finish.

"Oh Brad, what are we going to do without you helping Paul fix things around here," Tasha asked before she pulled me in for a hug.

"Don't worry Mrs. J. I taught him well," I said and heard Mr. Johnson laugh.

After one more final goodbye, Kelly and I got in the truck and drove away. The beginning of the ride was spent in silence. I could tell Kelly was having a hard time leaving her family. She actually loved hers. I just merely tolerated mine and had no problem driving away from them.

"How did things go with your parents this morning when you said goodbye?" Kelly asked, pulling me away from my thoughts.

I sighed. I really didn't like it when she asked me questions about my parents. To buy myself a little time I readjusted my position and placed my arm on the windowsill.

"Oh, you know. The usual. Hugs all around, tears, emotions of love and all that," I joked and grinned at her. She narrowed her eyes at me, letting me know she saw past the bullshit.

"Mom said be careful on the drive and Dad wished me luck before they both left after breakfast," I said.

"How's Kevin?" she asked.

It seemed she was determined to hash out all my family drama on this drive. I debated changing the subject, but her father's words echoed in my ear. Now that Mark wouldn't be around constantly to fuck things up, I just might actually stand a chance with her and I didn't want to start it off by avoiding her questions like I usually did.

"Kevin is Kevin. He's doing better. Working for a former college professor of his and staying on his meds. He said Lily and him go to lunch once a week and sometimes go to a show on the weekends, so he gets out a little," I said.

"Lily is your sister, right?" she asked.

"Yeah. She moved to Philly a few years back and they rekindled a connection or something like that," I paused, not sure if I wanted to reveal this next part.

"She wrote me a few times. She said she didn't think I would take her calls if she phoned. She was right. I guess Kevin had a different reaction." I said.

"Have you written her back?" she asked hesitantly.

"Nah, nothing to say," I shrugged, dismissively.

She didn't ask me any further questions about my family, and we fell into silence again. After a few minutes she asked me another question.

"So, why did you choose to go to Marion?" She asked about our college.

I certainly didn't want to tell her the truth; that I couldn't picture myself going anywhere she wasn't, so I settled for a half truth.

"The price seemed okay. It was far enough away from the folks that I could live on campus, and I had another added incentive," I said.

"Oh, what was that?" she asked.

"I heard my best friend was going there too," I said and smiled at her. I winked and she laughed.

After we arrived at our college destination I helped Kelly bring her things to her room and met her roommate. Kelly's roommate,

Serena, seemed a good contrast to Kelly's shyness. I left Kelly soon after and went in search of my own lodging. I had lucked out and was placed in a dormitory that housed mostly students that were on the sports teams. In fact, two of my roommates were on the cross-country team with me and the other was on the baseball team.

Fortunately, I had a room to myself and only had to share the common areas. This would be the first time I would be living in close quarters with other people in years. I was used to my solitude, and I wasn't sure how well I was going to adjust to having other people around.

During my last two years of high school, I had begun to venture out and attend social gatherings, but I hadn't really felt comfortable among all the people. I would usually stay for a couple hours, have a couple beers, and leave with talking to as few people as possible. It may not have made for epic memories, but it suited me just fine. I figured if my new roommates began to get on my nerves I would just retreat to my private room.

When I arrived, there was already a bustle of movement in the main common area and there were definitely more than three people here. In fact, not all the people here were of the male gender. Two girls were sitting on the sofa and laughing as they talked. I walked through the doorway, my arms loaded with bags and my guitar case when all of a sudden, a warning was called out.

"Watch out!"

I dropped my bags and fell back into the door as a Frisbee went sailing past my face, missing me by mere inches. I quickly glanced to my left, the direction the Frisbee had come from, and saw a red headed guy jogging towards me. I glanced down and saw I was still clutching my guitar case and sighed a breath of relief. The rest I could easily replace, but not this.

"Sorry about that. Noah and I were just testing out the space. Didn't think anybody would come walking in the door," the red head said as he bent to pick up the Frisbee.

"Woa, dude, you almost got creamed," another guy said, this time from my right.

"Yeah," I said and bent to pick up my things. So far, first impressions weren't the greatest.

"Are you alright?" One of the girls sitting on the couch asked me. She stood and came over to help me pick up my things. "Don't mind these two lug-heads. They aren't as destructive as they first appear. I'm Addy and this is Clark," the girl said as she handed me a bag. I took it and she put her arm around Clark, the red head. He put his arm around her and kissed the top of her head, both were very familiar with the contact.

"I'm Denise," the other girl said and joined the other guy, Noah.

"I'm Brad," I said and juggled my bags. "I'm just gonna go put my things down in my room. 2A?" I asked the group.

"To your right. Last room in the hall," Noah gestured behind him, pointing out the direction of my room.

"Thanks," I said and walked around Noah and Denise to get to my room. After I unlocked it and stepped inside, I heard a new voice yelling at Noah and Clark.

"What the hell guys! Where did you put my clothes?" The others laughed and a scuffle broke out in the common area based on the sounds I heard. I turned and closed my door to drown out the noise.

Kelly and I had attended orientation earlier in the week and had already gone through the customary introduction to our new college campus and had been given our keys to our rooms. I hadn't met any of my roommates before today. That was my doing. I had skipped the meet and greet and didn't provide any contact information when signing up for housing. That had been a battle with the housing people. I lied and told them I would be moving and didn't have any information to give out.

As I glanced around my room and continued to listen to the scuffle and laughter coming through my door, I was struck by a sudden sense of loneliness. I was usually very good about pushing these thoughts away and prepared myself to go for a run.

After changing into running clothes and shoes I exited my room, locking it behind me. The noise level in the common area had quieted and the crowd was now seated around the television, watching a movie.

"Hey, Brad, this is Terrence," one of the girls said to me. I couldn't remember which one she was, but she had her arm around the red head that had almost decapitated me with the Frisbee.

"Hey, man. Sorry about these two morons. Addy filled me in. It's nice to meet you," the guy named Terrence stood and came to me, his hand outstretched. I took it in mine and gave the customary greeting.

"You headed out for a run?" Terrence asked, gesturing to my running shoes.

"Yeah," I confirmed.

"Mind if I join you?" Terrence asked, turning to pick up a pair of shoes by the chair he had just vacated.

I honestly didn't want company. I never ran with company, unless you counted my meets, which I didn't. Unfortunately, I didn't see a way out of this without coming across as a total ass, so I just shrugged.

Once Terrence had his shoes on, we left our dorm and headed down the flight of stairs to the front entrance. Neither of us said anything until we got outside and began to stretch. As I was stretching out my hamstrings Terrence spoke.

"I'm on the cross-country team with you. I looked for you at the roommate meet and greet during orientation, but I couldn't find you. Clark is on the team with us and Noah plays baseball. How far do you want to go today?" He asked me as we continued to stretch.

I worked out my quads then loosened my neck before answering him.

"I have to be back to meet a friend for dinner by seven," I said.

Terrence checked his watch.

"That's in four hours," he said, and I nodded. He raised his eyebrows, shrugged and told me to lead the way.

For the next three and a half hours we ran. Terrence matched my stride evenly and I suspect he could have left me behind, but he stayed in step with me. I had already scoped out the trails near campus on a previous visit and knew my way around pretty well, so I wasn't worried about getting lost. I just put one foot in front of the other and ran until my mind emptied of all thoughts and all I focused on was my breathing. Neither Terrence, nor I, spoke during the run and it wasn't until we returned to the entrance of our building that words were said.

"You have great lung capacity," Terrence said as he started to loosen his tight limbs. I began my usual post run stretching routine and nodded. "Not much of a sharer?" He asked and I realized that I was being a colossal ass, and all this guy was trying to do was get to know his roommate.

"Yeah, sorry. I'm not used to being around a lot of people," I explained, and Terrence laughed.

"One is a lot?"

I looked up at him and grinned at that. He had a point. I should be able to hold a conversation with one person. This needed to be my new start. I needed to let go of the past and start fresh. Not being an asshole was probably a good place to start. I finished stretching and stood.

"Same time tomorrow?" I asked Terrence and he agreed.

After showering and changing I met up with Kelly and her roommate, Serena, for dinner. Serena dominated the conversation, but I was glad she was there. If I had to be in a group setting then I preferred others carried the conversation and Serena filled that role perfectly. I returned to my dormitory after dinner and walked into a scene that I usually avoided.

My roommates had orchestrated a party in my absence and our

common area was overrun with people. Music was playing, drinks were being passed around and people were having fun. I immediately tensed and tried to slip past the crowd unnoticed but was not successful.

"Brad, get in here," Clark called to me. He stumbled his way over to me and put his arm around my shoulders like we were the best of buds. I let him drag me to the crowd of people around the couch because I had never been one to cause a scene. I actually hated being the center of attention.

"Everybody, this is Brad, our other roommate and teammate. Brad, that is Clyde, Drake, and Justin. And these are the girls," Clark said and swept his free hand before him to point out the girls. They giggled at him, and some told him to shut up. The guys all greeted me in various ways with 'heys', head nods or simply brief glances.

"Want a beer?" the guy identified as Drake asked me.

"Sure," I said. If I was stuck socializing, then I wasn't going to do it sober.

Drake returned and gave me a can of some cheap beer I had never heard of before and I spent the next hour or so just listening to the conversation. I answered their questions but never asked any of my own. I went to the kitchen area to get another beer after I finished my third one and debated dipping out when Addy came up to me.

"You look like you want go running again," she said and reached around me to get a beer for herself out of the fridge.

"Is it that obvious?" I asked her as I stepped back and opened my own can.

"Very. But don't worry. They are too drunk to notice," she said, pointing back at my teammates gathered around the sofa.

"I'm just not the best in social gatherings," I explained and leaned back onto the small counter next to the fridge.

Addy moved positions so she could talk to me and still keep an eye on the crowd on the couch.

"I hate to break it to you, but you are probably going to have to get used to this. Clark and Noah like to party a lot. We all went to high school together and they were big into parties," she said.

"That's unfortunate," I replied, and she laughed.

"I think you are going to fit in just fine," Addy said, tilted her beer to me in a little salute and returned to the group on the couch.

The party didn't break apart until nearly two in the morning and I was beyond wasted. I recall stumbling into my bed and passing out, but nothing else.

12

Good Riddance

Everyone has heard the term beer goggles and some people have even experienced the after math of beer goggles. The following morning, after my first night at college, I had the pleasure of experiencing the aftereffects of beer goggles.

I woke, entirely hungover with a raging headache to find a girl in my bed with her arms wrapped around me. I racked my brain, trying to recall who she was. Through the haze of booze, I remember she had been one of the girls on the couch after I came back from dinner.

Her name was…Fi! Yes, everyone kept calling her Fi because her name was Fiona, and she had told me she hated it.

Now that I remembered her name I tried to determine if I had done anything other than sleep beside her last night. I lifted the blanket and saw I still had my boxers on. Fi was still clothed as well. Breathing a sigh of relief, I tapped Fi on the arm to wake her. She stirred, blinked a few times before opening her eyes and yawning.

Once she had woken, she smiled at me and I cringed inside. I didn't want her to smile at me because in about two seconds she was most likely going to hate me.

"I need to get up," I said to her so she would get out of the bed. She was on the outside of the bed and blocking my exit. She nodded and sat up, stretching as she got out of the bed.

As soon as she was clear I jumped up and went to my dresser, withdrew a shirt and put it on. I turned in a circle, trying to find my pants. I found them resting against my desk chair and quickly put them on. Once I was fully clothed, I turned back to Fi.

"Look, I'm sorry but I don't remember what happened last night," I said as I ran my fingers through my hair, a nervous habit I couldn't seem to shake.

Fi looked up at me and laughed.

"I'm not surprised. You were pretty wasted," she said and bent to pick up her shoes.

"Yeah. We didn't…I mean, did we…do anything?" I asked, gesturing to the bed. Fi followed my gesture and shook her head.

"Oh no. You weren't in any condition to do much of anything last night. We made out for a little bit, and you passed out," she explained and finished tying her shoes. She stood, looked around my room until she found her purse and picked it up.

I stood by my desk and watched as she walked up to me. She stood on her toes and placed a kiss on my cheek. I just stood there, staring at her. How could I tell her that I hadn't meant to do anything with her last night, let alone wake up next to her?

"See you around," she said and left my room.

The moment the door closed behind her I breathed a sigh of relief and waited a few minutes, ensuring she would have left my suite entirely, before I went to get some juice from the fridge.

I was pouring some orange juice into a glass when I heard a voice in the common area call out to me.

"Yeah, Brad! Scoring with the chicks already," Clark said from the couch.

"You're so crude," Addy said to Clark and slapped him on the arm. He laughed, buried his nose in her neck and made some sort of snorting noise. Addy laughed and tried to push him away.

"You like me that way," Clark said as he released Addy. She rolled her eyes and returned her attention to me.

"How are you feeling? You had a lot to drink," she said, concern in her voice.

"I'm fine. Nothing a little OJ won't fix," I assured her, tipped the glass towards them and started walking back to my room. I heard Addy giggling at something Clark said before I closed my bedroom door.

So much for my new start. Not even twenty-four hours into my college experience and I was already falling into old habits. It was time for a run.

That first week unfolded without further incidents and I often joined Kelly and Serena for lunch, when our schedules permitted. I would usually eat dinner with Kelly as well. That is, I did, until the weekend Mark came to visit. She told me he would be coming, and I knew she was telling me I wouldn't see her again until he was gone. I understood her desire to keep me separate from her boyfriend since I had never been exactly timid when it came to my opinion of the guy, but I hated being pushed aside when he was near. I knew Kelly didn't belong to me, but damnit, she was mine first!

The first night Mark came to visit her I had decided I was gonna shut myself in my room and focus on my music. As long as I kept playing the strings, or running, I wasn't overwhelmed with thoughts about what Mark was doing with, or to, Kelly.

As I recorded the notes, tweaked the chorus, I heard my room-mates once again hosting a party. After an hour of trying to ignore the increasingly louder commotion coming from the common area, I determined it was impossible and put my guitar away. As I was debating going for a run there was a knock at my door.

I opened it to find Addy, Clark's girlfriend, on the other side.

"Just wanted to see if you wanted to join us? I feel bad that we are all out there and you stay in your room all the time. Come mingle with us," she hiccupped. It was clear she was well passed mingling and had entered tipsy. I started to decline her offer when Terrence called to me from the small kitchenette area.

"Brad, come on out. We could use someone sensible to tell this football player that long distance running requires far more stamina," Terrence gestured with his hand, encouraging me to join the group.

I sighed and squared my shoulders. The first step to breaking old habits – be friendlier with the roommates. I made sure I had my key before I locked and closed my door. I didn't often know everyone my roommates invited over, and I didn't like people *accidentally* ending up in my bedroom. Addy clapped when she realized I was joining them, and she skipped back to Clark. He laughed as he caught her, and they both nearly toppled over. Clark leaned down and kissed Addy's nose and she beamed up at him.

Lucky bastard, I thought and took the beer Terrence held out to me. He clapped me on the back of my shoulder, and I walked with him to the group in the common lounge area.

"Justin here foolishly believes that football requires greater stamina than our long-distance running. Educate him," Terrence said and used his beer bottle to point out Justin. I recognized him from that first party on my first night here.

"Hey, man," Justin greeted me as I sat on an open folding chair. I nodded back in greeting.

"I'm not saying football requires more stamina. But sure as hell requires more talent. There are so many moving parts that you have to take into consideration that one small slip could mean the game. Football definitely requires more mental stamina then placing one foot in the front of the other and just going until someone tells you to stop," Justin said and leaned forward to grab a handful of chips from a bowl on the common area's cheap wooden table.

"I've seen this guy run for five hours straight and not break

89

concentration," Terrence said, clapping me on my back again. I forced myself to not cringe away from his touch and just took a drink of beer.

"But can he catch a ball while he does it," Justin asked, settling back in the couch and laying his arm over the back of it. His position clearly demonstrated that he had made his final point.

"I try to stay away from balls. Not my thing," I said.

Terrence, Addy and Clark busted out in riotous laughter. Justin just blinked at me. I thought he was being stoic, but I finally realized he hadn't understood the joke.

"I don't like balls in my face," I said and swept my hand across my face in a sweeping motion. Justin finally understood and he grinned.

"Understandable," he said and stood. "Anybody need a refill?" he asked.

"Yeah, grab me one," Clark said. I glanced around and noticed we were down one roommate. A caring person would inquire about said missing roommate, and since I was trying to not be an asshole I asked about Noah.

"He is out with some girl he met in class. I give it another hour before he brings his sorry ass back here in shame," Clark said and took the beer Justin had brought him.

"What happened to Denise?" Justin asked as he sat back down.

Right...there had been a girl with Noah that first night.

"He dumped her two days after classes started. Said he needed to be free or some shit, the jack ass," Addy answered, clearly upset with Noah's life choices.

"So, Denise is available?" Justin asked, his eyebrows raised.

"Oh, no you don't! Stay away from her Justin. The last thing Denise needs right now is you sniffing around her," Addy said and wagged her finger at Justin.

"The ladies like me. That isn't my fault," Justin chuckled.

"That may be true but that doesn't change the fact that you love em and leave em," Addy countered.

"Come on Addy, lay off my brother. He doesn't give them anything they don't want," Clark said and nuzzled into Addy's neck. She was currently sitting on his lap with Clark's arms around her.

I looked between Justin and Clark. Brothers? I didn't see the resemblance at all.

"You two are brothers?" I asked. I just couldn't wrap my mind around this.

"Step-brothers," Justin replied and picked up the remote. He began flipping through channels on the television.

That made more sense. Clark had distinctive red hair, long limbs and a scrawny physique. Justin was darker in complexion, had jet black hair and had the typical football player frame, wide shoulders and arms bigger than my face.

"Is there anybody at this school you don't know?" I turned to Addy. She laughed at my question and tipped a little bit, but Clark tightened his hold on her and righted her.

"I don't know you," she said and pointed at me.

The room fell into an awkward silence until Terrence broke it.

"You all are boring as shit. I'm heading over to Drake's," he said, stood and left our dorm room.

"I heard some music coming from your room earlier, Brad. Do you play guitar?" Addy asked me, ignoring Terrence's abrupt exit.

"Yes," I said and finished my beer.

"Will you play for us?" she asked. I saw Justin and Clark turn their gaze to me, raising their eyebrows.

"No," I said and stood to get another beer.

"Why not?" Addy asked, pretending to pout.

I shrugged in response.

"Do you suck at it?" Justin asked, back to flipping through the channels.

"I don't know," I said as I returned to my chair.

"Play then. We'll tell you if you are bad," Justin said matter of fact.

I wanted to be offended but his face was expressionless. Justin obviously didn't give two shits if I was any good at playing guitar, or bad for that matter. He was just letting me know he wouldn't placate me. I could appreciate that, but I still wasn't going to play in front of them.

"I don't play for others," I said.

"Never?" Addy asked, horrified.

"Just Kelly," I said before I processed what I was saying. I noticed the moment Addy perked up at what I had just revealed. She sat straighter on Clark's lap and leaned towards me.

"Whose Kelly?" she asked.

I groaned. I didn't want to answer her, but I didn't see any polite way of getting out of this. Once again, I found myself regretting trying to be more social.

"She's a friend. We lived next door to each other."

"Oh. Where is she now?" Addy asked, her attention squarely on me. Clark had rested his head on her shoulder, and he was staring at me but I doubted he was listening to what I was saying. Justin was focused on some sports news channel on the television.

"She's here," I said and pretended to be paying attention to the show Justin had on, hoping Addy would drop this line of questioning. No such luck.

"Well, invite her over," Addy said excitedly.

"Her boyfriend is visiting this weekend," I replied.

"So? Invite them both over," she said as if I was the dumbest person alive for not thinking the same thing.

"No," I quickly answered and cast a stern look in her direction.

Justin, who I thought was enraptured with guys talking about other guys throwing balls, suddenly turned his attention to us.

"Have you fucked her or something?" he said bluntly, and my gaze landed on him, my eyes narrowing.

"No."

"Sounds like you want to," Justin pointed out and returned to the show. Clark started laughing and Addy slapped his shoulder and told him to shut up.

"Is that true? Do you like Kelly like that?" Addy asked. I didn't respond and she started nodding her head.

"Boyfriend is in the way, huh?" she said, and I just stared at her.

"Dude, break them up. Get in there," Clark said and leaned forward to place his beer on the table before us. None of them picked up on how uncomfortable this conversation was making me, and I began to fidget in my seat.

"He can't do that. She would never forgive him," Addy said to Clark.

"Well, then what should he do?" Clark asked and shrugged his shoulders.

"You should tell her how you feel. Tell her that being her friend isn't enough. Tell her that you need her and that if you have to you will wait for her. I would love to hear that," Addy said with sigh.

"Hey! Who the hell would be telling you that?" Clark reared his head back, upset that his girlfriend was daydreaming about some other guy right in front of him.

"It's hypothetical, baby. Don't worry about it," she said and kissed his cheek.

"I couldn't do that," I told her.

"Then you don't want her bad enough," Justin said, his gaze still glued to the television.

I glared at him and decided I no longer appreciated his bluntness. In fact, I was starting to become very annoyed with this over-confident, selectively clueless football player who constantly bogarted our television when he was over.

The weekend passed, Mark returned to his college and I once again began spending more time with Kelly. I noticed something seemed to be off with her but when I would ask, she would just tell me she was fine and the subject would shift. I figured she needed some time to process whatever it was that was bothering her, which was something I understood all too well. I usually needed to retreat inside myself to process things as well. Kelly always gave me the space and time I needed so I returned the courtesy and just let her be. Serena had also picked up Kelly's shift in mood, but she didn't believe in giving Kelly the space she needed like I did.

One evening, we were hanging out in their room, watching a themed movie that Serena had chosen – this was quickly becoming one of our weekly traditions – when Serena all of a sudden turned to Kelly and demanded she fess up. I watched the scene unfold, but didn't contribute.

"Kelly, I've had enough of your doppelganger, and I want my roommate back. Whoever this depressing girl is before me needs to go. Do you hear me? Snap out of it!" Serena said as she took Kelly by the shoulders and shook her. Kelly just sat there and let Serena shake her.

"Sorry. I've just a bit preoccupied I guess," Kelly said when the shaking stopped.

"From what?" Serena asked, settling back down.

"The breakup I guess," Kelly said softly.

"What breakup?" Serena asked, turning towards Kelly. My ears perked up and I abandoned the movie completely, also focusing on Kelly.

"With Mark."

"Back up…you broke up with Mark?" Serena asked, clearly surprised.

My eyes narrowed as well because Kelly hadn't mentioned this to me at all.

"No. He broke up with me."

94

"When the hell did this happen? And why didn't you say anything?" Serena was back to her usual animated self, her hands flying in every direction as she asked her questions.

"A couple weeks after he came to visit me. I just needed some time to think or something and I didn't want to make a big deal out of it," Kelly explained. She started pulling at some fuzz or possibly a string on her pants as she spoke, her head cast down, so she didn't have to look Serena in the eyes.

My gaze remained focused on her hands trying desperately to find something to cling to. I was suddenly struck with the desire to reach out and take her hand, but I didn't.

"You could have told me. What happened?" Serena asked, her animation was now under control.

"He said it wasn't fair to me to be in a relationship with a guy that couldn't see me more often. He said it would be best for me if he let me go."

My jaw clenched and my hands fisted at Kelly's description of Mark's words. What a complete tool. He basically made the breakup sound like it was Kelly's fault and he was only doing what was best for her. It sounded to me he just used her well-being as an excuse to get out of something he didn't want to be burdened with anymore. No wonder she had been so closed off these last couple of weeks. She probably thought it had been her fault and believed the bullshit Mark had fed her.

As my thoughts ran wild with anger directed at Mark, Serena began to laugh so hard that she eventually snorted. Both Kelly and I were now looking at Serena as she clutched her stomach during the laughing fit.

"Serena?" Kelly questioned.

"I'm sorry. I don't mean to be insensitive. That Mark guy is a breakup genius. Please tell me you didn't believe the lines he fed you?" Serena asked as she wiped away the tears that had begun to form due to her laughter.

"No?" Kelly said it more like a question and I had never wanted to hit Mark more than I did in the moment her voice broke.

"He just wanted out and didn't want to come across as the bad guy. It was easier to just say he was really breaking up with you for your own good. Even when he is breaking up with someone, he is still so polite," Serena said and stood. She excused herself and disappeared in the bathroom.

Kelly and I sat there in silence for a moment. I was still wrapping my brain around the fact that Mark was out of the picture when Kelly turned to me.

"What are you thinking about?" she asked.

"Just that I'm glad you finally left that shit show," I replied.

She looked at me questioningly but didn't respond. We finished the movie, and I returned to my own room soon after.

As I sat on my bed, strumming my guitar, my thoughts went to Kelly and my own feelings for her. Addy had encouraged me to tell Kelly how I felt but I couldn't do that so soon after her boyfriend had broken up with her. She was still clearly affected by it and if I just swooped in and suddenly declared I wanted to date her she would probably reject me. The timing just wasn't right, and I decided I needed to give Kelly her space so she could move on from that asshole.

Later, I would come to regret my decision. A decision that I made out of fear that she would reject me. I had once told Jenny that if I had to choose between not being in Kelly's life or just being her friend, I would choose to be her friend. I used to think just having her in my life would be enough but there is only so much a man can take before he breaks.

13
This is What I Get

After reading the email from Kevin I left my desk, went to the kitchenette, pulled a glass out of the cabinet, filled it with water, took a sip, held the glass before me and promptly chucked it into the sink. As the glass made impact with the sink it shattered, shards flying up and water splashing out. I clenched my fists and held my breath.

Fuck that email.

Fuck my parents.

And fuck Kevin.

As soon as the thought was complete, I immediately wanted to take it back. It wasn't Kevin's fault our parents were unfeeling pod people that didn't give a shit about Kevin's accomplishments. He was just doing what normal children do with their parents all the time. He just wanted them to visit him and celebrate the completion of his thesis and acceptance into the P.h.D. program. It wasn't his fault that they had rejected him, once again.

But it was his fault that he had foolishly believed they would accept his invite. And it was his fault that he allowed their rejection to affect him so. His email had been full of hints that he wasn't taking the rejection well. It was only a matter of time before he relapsed, and I was thousands of miles away. I couldn't do shit about it and Kevin knew it. Sometimes I wondered if he did this deliberately in an attempt to guilt me into action.

"Dude, I wouldn't move if I was you. Glass is all over the floor now," Clark said.

I quickly turned my head in the direction of his voice and saw him sitting on the sofa, the television on mute before him. I hadn't noticed he was there when I came out.

I wasn't embarrassed by my outburst, but I did regret having an audience. I didn't like others to see me like this. The Klauzek's didn't display outward emotional demonstrations. No, we kept everything inside because emotions were complicated. We all did this, except Kevin. He wore his emotions on his sleeve and displayed them often.

"You're not wearing any shoes," Clark pointed out and gestured to my feet. I looked down and saw shards of broken glass surrounding my bare feet. I shrugged and took a couple steps back. Shards pierced my skin, but I didn't care. This pain was temporary and not worth my attention.

I bent and started picking up the glass.

"Your feet are bleeding," Clark said as he walked to me.

Once again, I just shrugged.

"You are one strange dude." Clark grabbed a broom and began to sweep up the smaller pieces of glass. "What set you off?" he asked.

My hand paused as I reached for a glass shard. How did these roommates not understand that I was not a sharer? Why did they continue to insist on asking me personal questions? I was just going to ignore him when I remembered that I was trying to be friendlier with others. Damage control was probably warranted since Clark had witnessed my outburst.

"My brother," I said and deposited the glass shards in the trash can. I moved on to the sink and counter next.

"Yeah. They can be annoying sometimes. Justin and I may not be related by blood, but he can be a dick," Clark said and emptied the dustpan into the trash.

"If you ever need to…you know…talk or whatever…I can listen, or something," Clark said to me hesitantly.

I could tell he was uncomfortable with the offer, as was I, but the significance of the offer was not lost on me. I nodded my head, acknowledging the offer without actually talking about it. Clark nodded back and returned to the show he had been watching.

When I returned to my room, I read the email again and made a decision. I may not be close enough to Kevin to make a difference, but I knew of someone that was. All this time I had been avoiding her out of pride, and even a sense of revenge, but in order to save my brother I would reach out to her. My sister, Lily, had been in contact with Kevin for years now and I knew she lived fairly close to him. She needed to know about this development so she could do something.

I pulled out the latest letter she had written me and found the phone number she always included on the bottom. I hadn't written her back and I wasn't entirely sure why I continued to read the letters she sent, but I did. Keeping them seemed a bit sentimental but I was glad I had kept them so I could call her now. I dialed her number and waited for the call to connect.

"Hello," her voice rang out as she answered. I hadn't heard her voice since the day she had left and something about it reached a part of me that I had long repressed. I was frozen by that voice because it had long been the only voice of love I had heard and here it was, sounding in my ears once again.

"Hello? Is anybody there?" Lily asked.

I shook my head and snapped out of my trance.

"It's Brad," I said and once again silence stretched out.

"Brad?" her voice cracked when she said my name and I swear I thought I heard tears in that voice.

"Yeah. I need to talk to you about Kevin. He just sent me an email. He said he asked our parents to come visit him in November and celebrate the completion of his thesis and stuff, but they turned him down. They said they were far too busy to entertain his recent fad career goals or some shit like that. He's taking it pretty hard, and he won't answer my calls. Can you go check on him?" And again, I was greeted with silence. I waited for a minute or so before my frustration set in.

"Look, if you don't want to do it, I can figure something else out," I said.

"No! I can go check on him. We usually meet up every couple of days but if he really is in such a bad way then I can go there now. I'll look after him Brad, I promise," Lily said.

"Okay, thank you. Let me know how it goes," I replied and started to hang up before Lily's voice called out to me again.

"Wait! How are you doing? I've written you. Have you gotten my letters?" she asked in a rush before I could hang up.

I sighed and ran my fingers through my hair. This was why I had avoided contacting her. I knew she would want more, and I just wasn't ready for that.

"Yeah, I got them. Look in on Kevin and tell me how he is. I have to go," I said.

"Okay. I would like for us to talk some time, Brad."

"I'm really busy. Just take care of Kevin," I said and hung up before she could call say anything else. My eyes closed and I rested my forehead against my closet door as I composed myself. Hearing Lily's voice affected me more than I thought it would. It was both amazing and painful to hear her again after all these years. The pain of losing her all those years ago resurfaced and in typical fashion I pushed those feelings back down. Turning, I grabbed my running shoes and prepared to do what I do best – run.

The next few months passed by with regular updates on Kevin from Lily. Most of the updates came in the form of emails since I had given her my contact information. She always began the messages with a status update on Kevin and ended the emails with questions about me. I never answered them. The only comments I made were in reference to Kevin and I never asked her any questions about her. I didn't want to give her any false hope that we would somehow have a relationship of our own. I was grateful she was near Kevin and he had someone that loved him to watch over him but I was not Kevin. I still hadn't been able to let go of the anger I had towards her for abandoning Kevin and I when we needed her most. His suicide attempt was still so fresh on my mind and her absence during that time was stamped clearly on my heart.

Kevin spent the Thanksgiving holiday with Lily and her friends, and I decided that I would go to Philly to be with him during Christmas because Lily had to go out of town for work. I did not want Kevin to be alone during the very time of the year where family is the focus. I hadn't told Kelly yet that I wouldn't be going to her house this year, like I normally did.

Kelly seemed to be in a better place since the break-up with Mark. Serena convinced her to get a part time job, and her mood had improved significantly since she started working at the campus bookstore. I still ate lunch with her most days but hadn't been hanging out with her as often at night. I'd been distracted by Kevin's continued depression and my track season just recently ended. Between my courses, the team, Kevin, and my music I hadn't really had much free time. I had even distanced myself from the parties my roommates continue to have and have stopped drinking alcohol. When Kevin got in his depressive state, I tended to become hyper focused on him and shut all other distractions out.

A few days before we were set to leave for the holiday break Serena, Kelly, and I were watching a movie, a ritual I had been absent from for some time. Kelly suddenly declared she wanted to go to a party. I turned to her, surprised. She hadn't attended a single party since we had gotten to college. Her shyness usually turned her away from such scenes.

"Not my scene. But if you two want to venture out I won't mind. I have plenty of reading to catch up on," Serena said as she stretched out her legs.

"I guess I don't mind going out. I know my roommates are throwing a party. I came here to get away but if you want to check it out, I will go with you," I said to Kelly. I wasn't about to let her wander out to some party with strange people all by herself. If we went to my room, I would know some of the people there.

"Yes, let's go!" she said, jumped up and knocked over the bowl of popcorn we had been snacking on. Serena and I both laughed.

"I'll clean it up. Go have fun," Serena shook her head while she laughed.

I took Kelly to my room. She had been over a few times before but only briefly so we could collect something. Sometimes I would bring my guitar to her room and play for her, but I never played for her in my room because my roommates were nosy bastards. After I had revealed to them Kelly was the only one I played for, they continued to rip on me about her and I had avoided bringing her around. I hoped my roommates didn't mention anything to Kelly.

I could hear the music in the hallway as we approached my room. I hesitated before I opened the door.

"You just let me know when you want to leave. And don't leave without coming to get me," I advised her. She nodded, looking nervous as usual. I smiled at her and opened the door. It was crowded in our suite. This was the most people I had seen attend my roommates' parties.

"Hey, Brad, where have you been all day?" Clark called to me as we stepped in the room. I closed the door behind us and took the hand Clark offered to me in greeting.

"Oh, just hanging with Kelly. This is Clark," I introduced Kelly and she smiled at him.

"Yep, roomies. Want a beer?" Clark asked us.

Kelly nodded and I narrowed my eyes in concern. I didn't think she had ever had alcohol a day in her life. She laughed at my concerned look.

"Don't worry Brad. Everything is going to be fine. I'll take a beer," Kelly said to Clark, and he went to a cooler on the floor and took out two cans.

"Have a good time. Don't do anything I wouldn't do," Clark called to us and moved on through the crowd.

I watched Kelly open her can and take her first sip. The face she made was priceless and I chuckled. She gave me a stern look and took a longer drink this time.

"Slow down, Kelly. You don't have to guzzle it down," I said in warning. She smiled at me and asked me to show her around.

We walked through the crowd, and I introduced her to the people I knew. We ended up in Terrence's room where an impromptu poker game had been set up. He invited Kelly and I to play, filling seats of people that had already bowed out. I knew Kelly wasn't the greatest poker player, but she said it seemed like fun. So, we joined in. I put the buy in for both of us and we played cards for the next hour.

I was ahead by fifty bucks when Kelly announced she was finished playing. I started to cash out and go with her, but she put her hand on my arm, stopping me.

"Stay. Finish the game. I'm just gonna go into the common area," she said and stood.

"Don't leave without me. And if anyone gives you a hard time you come and get me," I instructed. I really didn't like her wandering off by herself but it was clear she didn't want me to be her watcher.

"I promise. It was nice to meet you Terrence," Kelly said and left the room.

"So that was the girl, huh?" Terrence said to me when Kelly had left. I tore my gaze away from the door she had just exited and looked at Terrence.

"What?" I asked.

He shuffled the cards and laughed at me.

"The one that you are hung up on. That's her," he said and gestured towards the door with the cards.

"She's my friend," I replied and put my chips in the pot.

"Yeah, but you want more," Clark said from behind me.

I turned in my seat and glared at him.

"Where's Addy," I asked.

"She left for home early since she finished her finals already," he said without pause.

The game continued and they let the subject of Kelly drop. After another hand we were joined by Justin, and I cringed when I saw him. I hadn't seen him since he told me I didn't want Kelly bad enough and I wasn't thrilled to interact with him again.

"Hey, who is the blond girl wearing the black and white flower dress in the kitchen?" he asked as he approached the table. He picked up Terrence's drink and took a swig.

"Hey! Get your own!" Terrence said and took his drink back from Justin.

"What is that?" Justin shuddered.

"Hennessey on the rocks," Terrence replied and pushed his drink further away from Justin.

"Tastes like shit," Justin said and sat down next to me in the chair Kelly had vacated.

"So, whose the girl?" he asked again.

I clenched my jaw because I knew exactly who he was asking about. It was Kelly and I didn't want him to know that.

"It's Kelly. Brad's friend," Clark revealed from behind me. I turned my head slightly and glared at him as he spoke.

Fucking idiot.

"Really? She's hot. No wonder you want to tap that," Justin said

104

and once again reached for Terrence's drink. Terrence saw and picked it up, protecting it from scavenger.

"Come on. Get your own," Terrence repeated.

Justin chuckled and leaned back in his seat.

"I don't want to *'tap that'*," I said between clenched teeth.

"No? Alright. If you aren't interested then I'm gonna go for it," Justin said and put his hands behind his head.

"She has a boyfriend," Terrence said as he passed out the cards.

"Nah. They broke up," Clark announced

. I threw him a sinister look and this time he noticed, stepping back a bit from my glare.

"Addy told me," Clark said to me as if this was a defense.

"Yeah? So, she's available," Justin said and sat up.

"She's not," I said angrily to Justin.

"Why? Are you two dating now?"

He looked at me, waiting for my response but I provided none.

"Man, if you aren't gonna go for it then someone else will," Justin said, stood and left the room.

I continued to glare at the doorway until Terrence told me it was my turn. I finished that hand, and the next, before frustration got the better of me and I bowed out.

I left the room in search of Kelly and eventually found her on the couch. It wasn't until I got closer that I realized she was sitting next to Justin. At first, I was annoyed to find him there but as I approached and saw the way Kelly was staring at him I became angry. She was looking at Justin like he was the greatest thing in the world, and I wanted to grab her, throw her over my shoulder and take her out of there.

"There you are," I said when I got to the couch.

She smiled at me and reached out, grabbing my hand and pulling me towards her.

"Brad, this is Justin. He likes my smile," she giggled.

I immediately determined that she was drunk, and that Justin was a complete jack ass. He was sitting next to Kelly and grinning at me. He knew that I knew he was playing some fucked-up game with me and I wasn't enjoying it.

"Hey," Justin said, and I narrowed my eyes.

"How much have you had to drink Kelly?" I asked, returning my attention to her. She let go of my hand, which really sucked, and she tried to count on her fingers. She was having a difficult time and eventually just gave up and held up both hands with her fingers spread out.

"Ten? You've had ten beers?" I asked.

"She's only had two sitting here," Justin said, and I glared at him. I didn't want to talk to him. I didn't even want him here.

As I was looking at Justin, Kelly had leaned forward to grab her beer from the table but lost her balance. She fell to the side and landed in Justin's lap. The fucker laughed and put his arms around her. She laughed and looked up at him in the same way she had been looking at him before and I just snapped. I didn't like Justin's hands on her.

"Come on. You need water," I said and pulled her off of Justin's lap. Justin was the one glaring at me this time. I didn't care. He could go fuck himself.

"I have to get going. I'll see you around Kelly," Justin said to Kelly. He turned to me as I was trying to steer Kelly towards the bathroom.

"Hey, give this to her when she sobers up," Justin said and handed me a piece of paper. Kelly was watching us, so I took the damn paper, staring daggers at Justin the entire time. The fucker actually had the nerve to wink at me before he left. I crumbled the paper and shoved it in my pocket.

"What was that?" Kelly asked me.

"Nothing," I said and tried to turn her again.

"Liar," she said, refusing to move.

I sighed. "It's his phone number," I said and guided her to the hallway and into the bathroom.

I gently guided her down to the toilet and had her sit on the closed lid. I closed the door and locked it behind us then went to the sink and wet a cloth. After I had rinsed it, I returned to Kelly and began dabbing her face. She seemed to be burning up and her face was flushed from the beer.

"He liked me," she said smiling as I knelt down and wet her face.

"He liked drunk you. You really shouldn't have had so many Kelly. You are gonna regret it tomorrow," I warned and stood.

"Nope. I made a friend. Beer is good for friends," she slurred.

I saw her tilt to the right and leaped forward to catch her before she fell.

"Thanks," she said quietly.

"No problem," I said.

"Brad?"

"Yeah?"

"I think I'm going to be sick," she said and a second later she vomited on my shoes. I groaned as I examined the mess. She wiped her mouth and sat back against the toilet.

"I'm sorry," she whispered, and I watched her pass out.

After ensuring she wouldn't be falling, I set about cleaning up the mess. I removed my shoes and put them in the shower and rinsed them off. Then I cleaned up the vomit with a towel that I threw in the trash. Luckily, she had managed to avoid getting any vomit on her. Once the mess was clean, I picked her up and carried her to my room. The party had died down and only a few stragglers remained.

Once I got her to my room, I placed her on my bed and took off her shoes. I debated removing her dress and putting one of my shirts on her, but I didn't want her to freak out about it. So, I left her in her dress and put her under the covers. I changed into a T-shirt and some running shorts before going to get a glass of water from the kitchen. I knew she would wake up eventually and be thirsty. I placed the water and a bottle of aspirin on my nightstand and grabbed an extra blanket I had for myself. After I set up my makeshift bed on the floor, I looked at her. She was sleeping peacefully and looked so damn beautiful with her hair surrounding her.

I gently placed my fingers on her cheek and brushed away some strands of hair. She stirred, moaned, and rolled to her side. Sighing, I left her, turned out the light and lay down on the floor. As I stared up at my ceiling, I knew that I couldn't just be her friend anymore. I wanted more.

I woke a few hours later to the sounds of someone in my room. As soon as I realized it was Kelly I stood and went to her side. She was holding a hand to her head and groaning in pain.

"Take these and drink this," I said and handed her two aspirin and the glass of water. She took them from me.

"I'm sorry about your shoes," she said, and I laughed. She swallowed the pills and drank half the glass of water before handing it back to me.

"It's okay. They needed to be replaced. How are you feeling?" I asked.

"Like I've been run over by a truck," she said and scooted back on the bed so she could sit up better.

"Yeah. The first time is always the worst. You will probably feel like shit all day tomorrow," I said and she groaned, putting her head in her hands. I laughed again because she was just so darn cute. When I started to get back down on the floor she reached out and took hold of my hand. I looked down at our clasped hands.

"I can sleep on the floor. You should have your bed," she said and started to remove the blankets from her.

"Oh, no, the floor would only make you feel worse tomorrow," I said, stopping her and pulling the covers back up.

"Okay. We can share the bed," she said, let go of my hand and moved over. The look I had must have concerned her because she mistook it and said, "I'm not going to barf on you again, I promise."

That wasn't at all what I was concerned about. I had never shared a bed with her and the thought of doing so made me nervous.

"Okay," I finally said and joined her.

"Thanks for everything Brad."

I laid down on my back and looked up at the ceiling again.

"What was tonight about Kelly? This isn't like you?" I asked as I turned to look at her.

"I don't know. I guess I just wanted to be a new me or something," she said.

I immediately turned on my side so I could see her clearly.

"I like the old you just fine," I said and stared directly at her.

She smiled and patted my hand.

"Thanks. I know I've been a bit weird lately. You're a good friend, Brad."

I cringed at the word friend. Here I was thinking how I wanted more, and she still only viewed me as nothing but a friend. It hurt to hear her say that.

"Yeah, better than your new *friend* Justin?" I asked with a sneer.

Kelly laughed and covered her face with her hands. At first, I thought she was making fun of me, but her response told me she wasn't.

"God, I was such a mess. I can't believe he actually stayed and talked with me. Wait..didn't he give you his number?" she asked, taking her hands away from her face.

"No. He gave me his number to give to you," I clarified, clearly annoyed.

Kelly reached out and playfully slapped my arm. I laughed at her pitiful attempt.

"I don't think I will be having beer anytime soon," she said and turned to me.

"Well, there is always wine and hard liquor," I joked.

She smiled at me and settled down into the mattress. I wanted to reach out for her. "Night, Kelly," I said and leaned forward. I kissed her forehead, and I felt her stiffen beneath me when I did it. If a simple kiss on her forehead had her stiffening up, I could only imagine what her reaction would be if I told her I loved her.

Defeated, I pulled away from her and rolled to my other side. My back was now facing her as I closed my eyes and prayed sleep would come quickly.

The next morning Kelly woke up with the typical day after headache and I once again supplied water and aspirin. I laughed at her when she attempted to hide underneath the covers to block out the sun and she threw her pillow at me. I dodged it.

"Thank you for last night. You are the best friend ever," she said as she came out from underneath the covers.

I scowled at her. There was that damn word again. I was tired of having that thrown back in my face. I got it. We were friends and nothing more.

"Think you're gonna call that Justin guy?"

"Don't know," she shrugged, "I can't imagine he wants to see me after my display last night. I wasn't exactly at my best." She attempted to sit up.

"Somehow I don't think he noticed," I said and handed her the water once she managed to sit up.

"How do you know exactly what I need?" she asked as she took the glass.

For some reason her question pissed me off and I responded with a snide comment.

"Well, I don't just sit in my room and read all the time. I live with a bunch of partiers. Sometimes I join them, play a little cards, drink some beers," I said and turned from her.

"Oh," she said softly, and I immediately regretted my shitty response. Having her here right now was not bringing the best out of me. I needed some distance so I could rid myself of the anger I was feeling.

"Well, short-cake, I think it's time to venture back out into the world. Don't worry. I know it seems like the sun is poisonous right now but that is only temporary. Drink lots of fluids, go light on the food and minimize the sudden movements. Don't forget to pack your things. We will be leaving by seven tomorrow morning," I said, making sure I left any trace of anger or resentment out of my tone.

"I hate that nickname and I think I hate beer," Kelly moaned and stumbled out of my bed. She put her shoes on, and I walked her to the main door. She cringed at the sunlight in the common area and gave me a half wave in parting.

I laughed, called her drunkie to keep the mood light and closed the door behind her.

As soon as she was gone, I returned to my room and leaned against the closed door. I had wanted nothing more last night than to take her in my arms and tell her how I felt but every time I decided to do it, she would bring up our friendship. It was like she knew I wanted more but she kept reminding me that she was just my friend. I was glad I wouldn't be spending the holidays with her and her family. The last thing I wanted was to sit across from her on Christmas day and once again be reminded of the one thing I wanted that I couldn't have. This break away was serving two purposes: get me to Philly to keep an eye on Kevin and get me away from Kelly so I could figure some shit out.

14

Brothers

Even though I spent fifteen years in Philadelphia and had once called it home it felt strange to return to the place that I long ago left behind. Kevin had picked me up from the airport and he hadn't stopped talking since I had arrived two days ago. Unlike Kevin I did not find long stretches of silence uncomfortable and I gathered he felt he needed to fill the long stretches. I would contribute every now and then to the conversation with a well-placed question or obscure comment, such as 'really, tell me more.'

Even though I had grown up in the same city he had he showed me around places like Independence and Congress Hall as if I was some fresh-faced tourist learning the history for the first time. I humored him and let him tell me about the liberty bell and the history of the cracks and when he asked if I 'could believe that' I told him I couldn't.

Being back in Philly was strange but walking alongside my brother listening to him prattle on about the history of the city, something he was extremely passionate about, was perhaps even stranger. I was struck with the notion that his mannerisms reminded me of a child. The way he flitted about from one conversation to the next was exhausting. For some reason I felt like the older brother even though he was seven years my senior. I had to tell him it was time to go home when I noticed how tired he was and whined about it at one point, asking if he really had to go home. I told him I was tired and needed to rest. He conceded and we returned to his apartment.

Even though his mannerisms reminded me of a child, his apartment did not. He had books strewn all over and his decorating style screamed college professor. I knew that was his ultimate career goal. He had hopes to work for one of his college professors while he pursued his P.h.D. candidacy. I was encouraged by his willingness to share details with me regarding his future plans. His hopes for his future gave me hope that he passed his dark times.

On my first night at his apartment I had gone through his medicine cabinet and drawers, checking to see he had the medications he needed to control his depressive moods. I saw the prescriptions and relaxed when I saw him taking the medication regularly. He caught me watching one day and laughed.

"Want some?" he joked and offered me the bottle. I shook my head, and he put the cap back on.

"It only works if you're crazy anyway," he said and put the bottle away.

"You aren't crazy," I told him. I was sitting on the couch, a book in my lap. He laughed again.

"Oh, little brother, I'm a fruit cake. But these pills keep it at bay," he said and walked to the kitchen.

His apartment was a studio so I could see his every movement as he gathered supplies to cook some dinner. I pursed my lips at his fruit cake comment but wasn't sure how to respond.

He had problems, sure. But he wasn't certifiable. His emotions just overwhelmed him sometimes and he didn't know how to handle it. The medication helped him remain in control. I didn't like how easily he dismissed his condition and made fun of himself. I didn't like it at all.

Later, as we ate the meal he had prepared, he brought up our sister. He noticed me shift my position in discomfort and he sighed.

113

We hadn't spoken about Lily since my arrival, and he did not know that Lily and I had been communicating by email. Neither of us wanted him to know that we were keeping tabs on him.

"You really should give her another chance. There are things you don't know about that she can clear up. She isn't the person you think she is," Kevin told me.

I put a bite of steak in my mouth, buying myself some time before I responded.

"I just don't think it would do any good to bring all that back into my life," I said and received an exasperated sigh from Kevin in return.

"What does that even mean? Bring all what back? Your sister? She loves you."

"Look, I'll think about it. Ok?" I conceded only because I knew my brother and he would just keep going until I agreed with him anyway.

"Fine. What do you want to do tomorrow?"

Tomorrow wad Christmas. It would be the first Christmas since I moved next door to Kelly that I wouldn't be spending it with her and her family. I saw them before I left, and Tasha had been thrilled to hear I would be spending time with Kevin. She knew all about his history and my strained relationship with Lily. Tasha, like Kevin, was encouraging me to reconnect with Lily but I just wasn't ready, and I didn't like to be rushed into things. I had a process when it came to making decisions and rushing recklessly into things was just not my style.

It took me a moment to realize that Kevin was staring at me, waiting for my response. I had been so lost in my thoughts that I hadn't given him an answer.

"Staying here is fine. Didn't you want to show me your research?" I asked, bringing the topic back to his obsession. It worked wonderfully and for the next hour he filled me in on his latest project. My brother got lost in history better than anyone I had

114

ever known. He talked about the past like it was a living, breathing creature and his eyes lit up every time. It was the only time I ever really believed my brother could be happy.

I called Kelly on Christmas to wish her and her family a happy holiday. Her father answered the phone and spoke to me for a bit about my visit with Kevin. I could tell he wanted to say more, and I waited. Mr. Johnson, like me, took his time before he spoke his mind.

"How are you doing, Brad?" he asked.

"I'm fine, Mr. Johnson," I said.

"Are you?" he asked. His tone told me he knew very well that I wasn't fine, but how could I tell him that I was torn up over his daughter. Kevin also had me worried. Sure, he was fine now but I knew from history that he could deteriorate back to his old ways in a flash.

"Paul, who's on the phone?" I heard Tasha ask in the background. Her presence allowed me to keep from answering Mr. Johnson's question.

"It's Brad," he said, and I heard Tasha squeal.

"Give me the phone," she said, and I heard a scuffle and then Mr. Johnson laughed.

"Should I be worried, wife? Have I lost your love to the neighbor boy?"

"Don't be silly, Paul. You couldn't get rid of me even if you tried. Now give me the phone," Tasha said.

"Come see us when you return and take care of yourself," Mr. Johnson said to me before he gave the phone to Tasha.

"Brad? How is Kevin?" Tasha asked once she had the phone.

"He's doing well. He's taking his meds and is excited about applying to an assistant position with a former professor of is."

"That's great. I'm happy to hear he is improving. How is the rest of your visit going?"

I spent the next ten minutes filling Tasha in on the places Kevin had taken me, and she told me about the shenanigans happening back home.

Home.

When had I started thinking about Wisconsin as home? And when had I associated the Johnson's with home? The thought frightened me. I was used to being unattached to places and people. It was easier to get through the disappointment that way. I didn't want to be attached to anyone enough that their presence equated to the feeling home evoked. Feelings like that only caused disappointment and I had enough of that in my life.

Once Tasha had finished talking with me, she called Kelly over and gave her the phone. She greeted me with happiness and her voice made me wish, once again, that I was home.

"It's a shame you aren't here. We lost Pictionary," she said, and I laughed. Every year the teams were Tasha, Paul and I against Stacey, Josh and Kelly. Tasha and Paul were freakish creatures and had a connected mind and knew instantly what the other person was drawing. They were unstoppable, until I came along. I was a terrible artist, and they could never guess my pictures. Kelly and Stacey said I was the great equalizer. Which was really just their way of telling me I sucked at drawing.

"Sorry to hear that. You will have redemption next year," I said and smiled at her answering laughter.

"Promise?"

"Promise." The second promise I gave her that I would break.

"When do you come home? We miss you," she said and the familiar pang returned. She didn't say *she* missed me. She included her family, and I was reminded of her constant need to call me her

116

friend. Just once I wanted her to miss me and to ask me on behalf of herself.

"In a few more days. Lily will be back, and I need to get some work in before break is over."

I still worked for Reyann and Jeff every time I returned home. I knew they really didn't need me, and I was grateful they still let me work there and paid me. I didn't have a steady job when I was in school and relied on various odd jobs I had acquired for spending money. I had a full scholarship, but I still had minor expenses that needed to be covered. My savings covered most of them, but I didn't like to replete my savings and tried to bring money in as often as I could.

"I'm glad you called. It feels strange being back home. I think I'm ready to return to school," Kelly said.

"I know what you mean. Even though my roommates are a bunch of jackasses most of the time I think I might miss their ugly mugs," I agreed.

We engaged a bit more small talk before she said she had to go. Their dinner was ready. I hung up the phone and found myself wishing I was there with them. Instead, I was miles away in a city I no longer felt connected to, with a brother I struggled to connect to. I wrestled with my warring desires the rest of my time with Kevin.

He wanted me to stay and wait for Lily to get back, but I knew I could only handle one needy sibling at a time. I had deliberately booked my return flight for before her arrival flight. I was boarding my plane as hers was landing. After dropping me off, Kevin waited for Lily's flight to arrive. He hugged me goodbye at security, and I patted his back during the embrace. It felt strained to me, but Kevin didn't notice. He held on to me and told me he loved me. He said he would miss me. My response?

"Thank you."

15

The Start of Disaster

It didn't take Kelly long to go out with Justin as soon as we returned to school. A matter of days was all it took for her to contact him and the next thing I knew she was seeing him regularly. She told me their first date hadn't gone well, and I thought that would have been the end of it. I was wrong. I tried to convince her that she was wasting her time with the conniving jock, but she brushed aside my concerns and did something much worse.

"I don't understand why you would go back out with him after you said he wasn't what you expected," I said to her as we ate lunch together one afternoon.

"It's complicated," she replied.

"What's so complicated? He bores you. You have nothing in common and there is no future there," I said, dumbfounded by her response. It wasn't complicated at all. She should just move on and not waste any of her time.

"I can't talk to you about this," she said and took a drink from her soda can.

"What does that mean? You talk to me about everything. You puked on my shoes, remember? I have seen you at your worst. What couldn't you tell me?" I asked.

For years she had confided in me about everything, from the pain she felt when her mother left to her feelings for Mark. She had never before held back on telling me things and I was a bit pissed that she felt she couldn't talk to me now. After all, in her own words, I was the best of friends.

"It's about sex. I can't talk to you about that. You're practically my brother," she said, moving her fork through her food and not looking me in the eye.

I just froze.

Literally froze.

The fry I had been bringing to my mouth was stuck in mid-air and my gaze was fixed in the distance. I wasn't really focusing on anything because I was blindsided by her comment.

Friend – got it.

But brother? I was far from being her brother and her suggestion that I was *'practically her brother'* set me off.

"Brad?" she asked quietly.

"I am *not* your brother Kelly!" I threw my fry down on my plate.

"I know that. I just meant talking to you about me having sex with another guy would be extremely awkward. I can't do that," she said and tried to reach out for my hand. I pulled it away as if her touch was a burning fire. I saw her eyes register hurt but in that moment, I didn't care. All I cared about was how I would never be anything more to her than her trusty sidekick.

"Look, I get you don't want to talk about that with me but don't ever call me your brother again. And I really wish you would think about this Justin guy some more before you jump in the sack with him. He isn't good for you, Kelly. You're better than some cheap roll between the sheets with Justin fucking Long," I said, seething.

"You make it sound so gross. You've had sex with girls, Brad. Why is the thought of me having sex with someone making you act so mean?" She cast her eyes down and folded her hands together on the table.

Now I really felt like a complete asshole for hurting her. She might have hurt me first, but she didn't do it on purpose. I, on the

119

other hand, had reacted out of spite and wanted to hurt her. I needed to pull myself together and push the emotions back down. Nothing good ever came from letting your emotions out. I took the lesson my parents had taught me and barricaded my emotions away.

Reaching out I took hold of her hand.

"I'm sorry. I'm not doing it on purpose. You're my friend and I don't want to see you hurt again and I think this Justin guy is gonna hurt you," I said, all anger removed from my voice.

"Well, don't worry about that," she said and squeezed my hand, letting me know I was forgiven, before she removed it and returned to her lunch.

"Fat chance of that," I muttered, and the last few tense moments were forgotten.

And forget I did. Amidst Kelly's sexual awakening (that is what I assumed was going on based on conversations I heard in hushed tones between her and Serena), I was experiencing a different kind of awakening.

My brother continued to see-saw back and forth between functioning and despair. His emails were erratic at best. It was no longer enough to just rely on emails between Lily and I. Not only did I speak to Kevin daily on the phone, sometimes it would take an hour of calling before he would answer, but I also spoke regularly to Lily. She managed to enlist the help of Kevin's next-door neighbor. Whenever we couldn't reach Kevin directly Lily would ask the neighbor, a retired Army Veteran, to go check on him. Our system seemed to be working. Kevin was still unpredictable but between the three of us we managed to keep him on solid ground.

I increased the times I went running and even Terrence warned me to take it easy. He still joined me for our regular run but said life was about more than running and never once joined me on my impromptu runs.

For some reason I hadn't picked up my guitar in months and it remained collecting dust in the corner of my room. Every time I went to reach for it, I was struck with thoughts of Kevin and blood, and I would rush to the phone to call him, to reassure myself that he was still alive. I was existing in a state of panic and detachment. When I felt the control starting to slip, I would do one of two things – run or get drunk.

Access to alcohol was never the problem. My roommates kept me amply supplied with both booze and women. In my quest to forget the shittyness that was my life I used women as a temporary outlet for my frustration. If I couldn't be with the one I wanted than I would be with the ones that were available. I buried my dick deep inside them, and for those brief moments, everything else just slipped away and all I cared about was chasing release.

Of course, when it was over, the thoughts would only return, and I would be plagued with such crushing guilt that I would lash out at the girl in my bed. I never let them stay and I never let them touch me when it was finished. I was quickly becoming the worst kind of person but instead of changing my behavior I blamed those around me. I wouldn't be this way if it wasn't for my parents being so distant and cold. If Lily hadn't left, I wouldn't have commitment issues. If Kelly wasn't such a colossal airhead, she would see I wanted more than friendship. And Kevin…if he wasn't such a selfish, needy bastard I wouldn't have to schedule my whole life around his breakdowns. Even the girls that willingly followed me into my bed were to blame because they knew I made no promises and offered them nothing but a few minutes of pleasure. I didn't want, or need, their sympathy or kind words. I only needed them for one thing, and it wasn't my fault if they allowed themselves to get hurt by the truth.

This is what I told myself as the latest girl sat crying in my bed, naked. I had just been balls deep inside her and she didn't under-stand why I was being cruel to her. When I had finished, I rolled off of her, put my pants back on and told her it was time for her to go. She had asked me what the hurry was and tried to pull me back to

121

the bed. I slapped her hand off of me.

"Don't fucking touch me," I sneered and pulled my shirt on over my head. The girl stared at me as if she didn't recognize me. This made me laugh. The only thing she probably knew about me was my first name. We had only met two hours ago and hadn't done much talking. Two hours a commitment did not make. She accepted this the moment she had walked through my door.

"What is wrong with you?" she asked.

"Nothing. I just don't want you to touch me. Get dressed and go," I said pointing at the door, dismissing her. Her mouth fell open at my command.

"Are you fucking kidding me! You can't just fuck me and then kick me out!" she shouted and sat up on her knees. Her hands were fisted at her sides, and she was pissed. But I didn't care.

"Yes, I can. We're done here." I bent, picked up her clothes and threw them at her. She swatted them away and glared at me.

"You are such a damn asshole! You can't treat people like this."

"Like what? The slut that you are?" I smirked.

I actually fucking smirked at her when I said that. The truth was I was no better than what I was accusing her of. I couldn't even recall the names of the girls that had been in my bed, but I threw those words at her knowing they would hurt. And now she was sitting in my bed, crying. A part of me wanted to take it back but I quashed that quickly and returned to my bitter, angry persona.

"You need to go," I said and picked up her clothes from the bed. I thrust them at her. "Now."

She took her clothes, tears streaming down her face. Quietly, she got dressed, collected her things and walked out of my room. There were still people gathered in the common area, and they saw her leave my room in tears. She quickly left through the main door, and I was greeted with many pairs of eyes on me. Among them were my roommates, Addy, and...shit...Justin.

Stubbornly, I walked into the common area and grabbed a beer from the fridge. Defiantly, I twisted off the cap and maintained eye contact with them as I tipped the beer back.

"Who are you?" Addy asked.

I sneered at her but didn't reply. As I began to walk back to my room the conversation resumed, and I heard someone say something to Justin.

"So, how is your latest fucktart?"

I froze before my door and turned around.

Fucktart?

Justin chuckled.

"Knock it off Steve. Kelly's one of the good ones," he replied.

Fucktart? Kelly? What the fuck?

I walked back out into the common area and glared at Justin's back. The guy across from him, I'm assuming that was Steve, saw me and pointed me out to Justin. Justin turned and grinned at me. The fucker grinned at me like he hadn't just been talking about Kelly like she was some cheap piece of ass.

"Do you need something, Brad?" Justin smirked.

"Stay away from Kelly," I said.

"Hmm, well, I don't think that is up to you. See, Kelly and I are together, a lot," he laughed and stood, facing me. "She pretty much likes to be together with me practically every night of the week, and sometimes even at lunch. She likes it so much that she sometimes begs for it. On her knees. Right in front of me." Justin smiled at me and lifted his bottle to his lips.

I snickered, nodded my head, placed my beer down on the table beside me and charged at Justin. Our bodies collided and we barreled backwards into Steve. Steve was slammed up against the wall and shouted at me to back off. Justin had dropped his beer in the process of me tackling him and he slammed his fist into my back. I used one shoulder to keep him pinned and my free fist punched him over and over again in his side. The crowd around us has backed off, some cheered, while others tried to pry us apart.

"Brad, knock it off," I heard Terrence yell.

I think it was him and Clark tried to pull me off Justin. They weren't having much success. I felt a fist connect with my cheek but I just stayed focused. A third person joined Clark and Terrence and they finally managed to pull me away from Justin. He didn't come after me as I was being restrained. He actually checked to see if his friend was okay first, which made me laugh.

"Brad, you're fucking toasted. Go sleep it off," Noah, my baseball playing roommate, said to me. He must have been the third guy pulling me off of Justin.

"Stay away from her!" I shouted at Justin, trying to pull free of my roommates' hands.

"You are cracked, man. You had plenty of chances with her and you blew them all. You don't fucking own her. Walk away. She doesn't want you," Justin said as he held his side.

The sight of him hurting brought me comfort. I did that. And I wanted to hurt him more.

"You don't even know her," I retorted, still trying to break free.

"No? Well I'm the one inside her every night. It's my name she moans. I think I know her better than you."

His words broke me from my rage and slammed into me like a ton of bricks. The shithead was right. He was the one that got to hold her, kiss her, wrap his body around her at night.

I was just her *fucking brother!*

"I'm fine. Let me go. Let me go!" I shouted to my roommates. They released their hold but stepped in front of me to block my path to Justin.

"Just leave Brad," Clark said. I glared at them all before turning on my heels and stalking back to my room.

I slammed the door behind me and paced, running my fingers through my hair. I felt like my insides were about to implode. I felt like the walls were squeezing me. I felt like a complete and total failure. I felt like a monster.

Through my rambling thoughts a soft knock rasped against my door.

"Go away!" I shouted.

"Brad? It's Addy. I just wanted to make sure you were okay," Addy whispered through my door.

"Go away Addy," I said. There was a pause, then silence, before she responded.

"I can see you're hurting Brad. You have to let someone help you or it's only going to get worse. Let me help you," she said.

I was suddenly thrust back to a classroom and a broken girl standing before me. I had once begged Jenny to let me help her and she refused. What followed was chaos and violence. Parts of me wanted to go to that door, open it and let Addy in, but a stronger part of me rebelled. I didn't need any help. I just needed people to leave me alone.

I opened the door, stared Addy in the eyes and promptly told her to fuck off. Then I slammed it and put on my running shoes. I bolted out the door while the group that had witnessed my rage avoided me.

The next day I confronted Kelly about Justin. I barged right into her room and accused her of fucking Justin Long. I wanted a fight. I wanted her to be just as mad as I was but that wasn't what happened.

"Hello to you too," she said and just looked up at me like I had lost my shit.

"Don't be cute with me, Kelly. I heard some guys talking about Long's latest *'fucktart'*. That's what they are calling you by the way, his fucktart," I told her, my arms crossed before my chest.

"So what? People talk all the time," she said dismissing me.

"Not about you they don't Kelly. What are you thinking? This guy is no good for you," I raised my voice and started to pace in her tiny room.

"It isn't that big of a deal Brad. Why do you even care?"

I stopped pacing and stared her right in the eyes, boring into her soul, and all I got in return was blankness. Justin was absolutely right. She didn't want me, and I was slowly starting to realize that I wasn't entirely sure I wanted her either.

"You really are completely clueless, aren't you?"

"What does that mean?" she asked.

"Nothing. Forget it. Enjoy your little fuck fest with Justin. Don't come crying to me when he screws you over," I pointed an accusatory finger at her and left the room.

I was done with her. I was done with any residual feelings I may have had for her. It was time to live my life without her. I didn't need her. Didn't want her anymore. She was just Justin's sloppy fucktart and I didn't want her anymore.

I didn't.

16

Disaster

Walking away from something you have glorified for so long is much easier said than done. I didn't sever ties with Kelly. Despite my animosity towards her not returning my feelings, I still cared deeply for her and knew I didn't want to just disappear, like her mother had. I also decided I needed to distance myself from the party atmosphere my roommates had cultivated. I didn't like the person I was becoming, and I stopped attending their nightly gatherings. I also knew I needed to regulate the time I spent with Kelly because I couldn't listen to her and Serena talk about Justin, or any other guy for that matter. I eventually started hanging around a guy from my Musical Theory class. He had approached me two weeks into the class to ask for my help. He was struggling with the course work and desperately needed a tutor. I had been helping him now for a few weeks and our acquaintance had graduated from studying to hanging out. He was a decent guy and wasn't into the party scene. He was a couple years ahead of me in school and the complete opposite of any of my roommates.

"Want to share a pitcher?" Matt asked me. We were at some local hangout grabbing a bite to eat after a long study session.

"No," I declined and set my menu aside.

"Right. Underage," he said and called the server over. He ordered his burger and a pint. I ordered my burger and a soda –

127

regular.

"How are you feeling about this next exam?" I asked Matt when our server brought our drinks.

"Oh, not very confident. Numbers I get. Music is beyond me," Matt replied, tapping his fingers off beat to the music playing on the speakers.

"Why did you enroll in this class?" I asked, grinning at his tapping fingers.

"Well, I needed an arts elective, and it had the word theory in the title. I like theories. You know, coding, probability and quantum. Those are theories I understand. I thought this would have something to do with the equation of music or something," he said and ate some of the peanuts in a bowl before us.

"Did you even read the course description?"

"Oh, hell no. I just checked the box and showed up to class," he said, and we both chuckled. "Thanks for helping me out though. I would be failing this class if it wasn't for you."

"Don't mention it," I said and shrugged.

"No, really. You're a good guy."

"No, I'm not," I replied harshly. I saw Matt kind of sit back in surprise by my reaction. "Sorry," I apologized.

"Sounds like you have a pretty harsh opinion of yourself," he said.

"I'm just not some saint, is all."

"I didn't say you were. You can still be a good guy but, you know, do bad things sometimes. Why do you think you are such a bad dude?"

I glanced at Matt and then looked down at my drink, using it as an excuse to avert my gaze.

"It's cool. I won't judge you. I'm not that great either. I used to get so jealous of the attention my little sister got from our parents that I would sneak into her room at night and cut all the hair on her dolls. I denied it of course when my parents questioned me. And

128

when they punished me, it only made me more upset with my sister. I would spread rumors around school about her. You know, she ate bugs and still wet the bed, stuff like that. Adolescent games but it hurt her pretty bad. I don't think she has ever really forgiven me for the torment I caused her," Matt said.

Our burgers arrived and we started to eat in silence.

I don't know what it was about this guy before me, but I found I wanted to confess something myself. Maybe it was because he was just such an easy guy to get along with. Or, maybe it was because he hadn't kept trying to convince me to reveal anything. Either way, I soon found myself talking to him.

"Sometimes I wish my brother had succeeded in killing himself."

There was a brief hesitation in Matt's movement before he recovered from what I had just revealed. He took a bite of his burger, a swallow of his beer and wiped his hands on his napkin before responding.

"Why?"

"Because maybe if he wasn't here, I wouldn't have to alter my entire life around his mood swings. Maybe I could actually be with the girl I want; have the life I want. Maybe I wouldn't feel like my chest is being constantly squeezed and I could finally be free of the guilt." I spill it all out. All the things I had been too afraid to say aloud before.

"You can still have all those things," Matt said.

I gave him a look that said, *who are you kidding?*

"No, I can't. Every time I even come close, Kevin has another relapse and everything just stops. I swear he has it timed perfectly. The moment I start to go after what I want, he is telling me he just can't do it anymore and wants to give up. If only I was closer to him, things wouldn't be so bad he says. If only our parents loved him then everything would be alright. If only *someone* loved him, he wouldn't feel so hopeless." I slam my burger back down onto my plate. I couldn't take my frustration out on Kevin, so I was going to take it out on the slab of ground beef sandwiched between bread.

"Sounds like your brother is a bit of an emotional manipulator. That isn't fair to you. Have you told him how it makes you feel when he says those things to you?"

"Are you kidding? I couldn't tell him that. He would use it as an excuse to pick up a razor and slash his wrists again. No. I can't tell him that. God, I want a drink," I said and rubbed my jaw.

"Why?"

"Why what?"

"Why do you want a drink?" Matt asked.

"Because this conversation is annoying me," I said impatiently.

"And alcohol will fix that?"

"What? No. I just…" I couldn't finish that thought. I couldn't reveal that I reached for a drink every time things got to be too much for me to handle. I used to use running for that purpose but when running stopped working I turned to alcohol. Of course, that didn't chase away the guilt either. So, I just kept running more, drinking more.

"It's good that you recognize the answer isn't at the bottom of a bottle," Matt said.

"Who are you? A counselor or something?" This was one strange dude.

"Ha, no. But my father is. He runs a rehab center. I used to volunteer there all the time, and I guess I just paid attention. So, tell me about the girl you want but can't have."

I spent the next two hours telling Matt all about Kelly. I told him how I had been a complete jerk to her lately and how I regretted my actions. He asked why I didn't just go apologize and tell her how I felt. I explained to him that she didn't have the same feelings for me, and he suggested we bring her along one night so he could see it for himself.

That was how I found myself hanging around Kelly and her roommate once again. Matt accompanied me and what was supposed to be an easy night of friends hanging out turned into a nightmare. Serena pretty much had a breakdown, and we all learned that she had been molested by her father when the cologne Matt had worn sent her into a flashback state or something. I was pissed when she told us. What kind of monster does that to his own daughter? Kelly sent Matt and me out of the room, of course.

I decided after that night though that I couldn't be around Kelly anymore. What Serena had revealed made me realize that I didn't want Kelly to ever witness my monster. She had glimpsed it so far during the moments I had approached her out of anger, and I never wanted her to think of me the way Serena thought of her father. It was best to just pull away.

So, I broke the first promise I had ever made to Kelly, and I disappeared again. I dodged her, made excuses to not hang out with her, and did everything I could to slowly extricate myself from her daily life. I made sure we were no longer faux brother and sister, or friends. By the time the year was over, we were distant acquaintances at best.

My first year of college was at an end and I had been informed by my roommates that they did not want me to be their roommate next year. My behavior over the course of the year had basically turned them off of me. Terrence was the only one that actually felt bad about it. He said he would still continue to practice with me but that it would be best if I got a single room next year and stayed away from the whole roommate situation. I told him there weren't any hard feelings. I even apologized to Clark and Noah for my behavior. They accepted the apology, but I wasn't convinced they believed me.

Surprisingly, the person that was the most upset about my

departure was Addy, Clark's girlfriend. She actually cried when she hugged me goodbye. I thought she was being a bit emotional. After all, we weren't exactly close.

"Take care of yourself. And please be happy," she said when she hugged me. I glanced over at Clark, who was watching the scene, and he just shrugged at my questioning look.

"Are you alright Addy?" I asked her when she pulled back.

"I'm fine. I'm just worried about you," she said and wiped at her tears.

"Don't be. I'm fine," I said and bent to pick up my things.

"You aren't fine. You're a mess," she said and shook her head.

I laughed and said she was over exaggerating. I said my final goodbye to them and went to meet Kelly. Even though we hadn't been hanging around each other I still offered to drive her back home. We did live next to each other after all.

The ride back home was extremely awkward, and we only talked about bullshit things. Mostly, she talked to me about Serena and Matt, who had started dating. I wasn't sure how I was going to get through the summer living next door to her. At college it was easier to avoid her because we had classes, work and other obligations. Plus, I didn't live right next door to her.

I ended up working extra hours with Jeff, so I didn't have to be home as much as possible. My parents were traveling a lot, and I spent most of my time with Jeff, or alone.

It was always late at night when my fingers itched for my guitar. Sometimes I would spend hours sitting on my bed in the moonlight, staring at the case propped up against the wall. My fingers would twitch from the need to create music, but I only ever made it a couple of steps toward the case before I found myself tearing down the stairs and running out the door. Needless to say, I wasn't exactly sleeping very well.

"You look like shit that's been run over one too many times," Jeff said to me one day as we loaded a truck with bags of soil.

"Wow. Thanks," I replied and moved to get another bag.

"Seriously. You not sleeping or something?" Jeff stopped working, put a hand on the truck and stared me down.

"Guess not if I look like rolled over shit," I tried to deflect. His expression remained the same. I shrugged and he rolled his eyes.

"I don't get you, man. Why do you mistreat your body like this?"

"What?" I asked, confused by his statement.

"All you do is work and run. That isn't a life, man. Broaden your horizons," Jeff said and returned to loading the truck.

After a moment's hesitation I went back to work alongside him. As long as I was working, I didn't have to think.

Lily had reported that Kevin was improving and had even gone on some dates. Lily was optimistic, but I was waiting for the anvil to drop on me. I couldn't help but feel like we had been down this path before, and it was only a matter of time before my phone would ring and I would get *the* call. I existed on a razor's edge, and it was my brother who held the razor, poised to strike at any moment.

It was those very thoughts that had me running the neighborhood streets at one in the morning. It was those thoughts that I was trying to ignore when I found Kelly sitting on the porch swing at her house, just as I had found her once before, long ago. That time, her mother was about to take off and Kelly had felt something bad was about to happen. She had been right then, and I wondered if similar thoughts had brought her to the porch at this late hour.

Other than giving her a ride home when school had ended, I hadn't seen her since. I had every intention of just running past her house and going into my own. It seemed she had other plans, however, because she stood when she saw me.

I slowed my approach, and she walked down her driveway to meet me. Once she got to me, I bent forward and took a few deep breaths. I was covered in sweat from my run and the night wasn't exactly cool. It had been a hot summer so far. I wiped away some sweat and waited for her to speak. It was obvious she had been waiting for me and I wasn't about to be the one to speak first.

"I saw you leave earlier," she said and gestured to my house with her thumb.

"Okay," I replied.

"Where are your parents this time?"

I shrugged.

I really didn't know or care where they were. They continued to leave me cash when they were gone and that was all I cared about. I was able to keep myself fed and the bills paid. I didn't need anything else from them.

"How've you been?" Kelly asked. She seemed nervous. It reminded me of that first day I had met her and, reflexively, I smiled. She saw me smile and it seemed to relax her because she smiled back.

"I don't know," I answered.

She looked at me quizzically.

"You don't know how you've been?"

"Honestly? No. I think I've been messing up a lot," I confessed.

"Like what?"

"Just stuff at school." I hadn't exactly lied but I didn't exactly tell the whole truth either. I wanted to tell her that I was sorry for disappearing again, for messing up stuff with us, but I didn't.

"You know I'm here for you, right?" She reached out and touched my arm.

I looked down at her hand on my arm and found her touch saddened me. This was the touch of someone that intended to comfort but it had limitations. Her very presence only reminded me that I would never be anything to her but a friend. Once, I had longed for her touch me. Now, I wanted nothing more than to avoid it. I gently pulled my arm away from her and pretended to stretch it out.

"I know," I nodded.

"Do you want to come sit with me?" She asked and tilted her

head back to the porch swing.

I saw a blanket resting on the swing and I chuckled. It wasn't even the slightest bit chilly, but she had a blanket. She always did get cold easily. Before I knew what I was doing, I followed her back to that porch swing. We sat side by side and she put the blanket over our legs. I was still sweating from my run, but she didn't seem to notice and I really didn't want to ruin this moment.

At first, we just sat in silence and gazed out into the night sky. Soon, she leaned forward and squinted her eyes up at the sky. I leaned forward as well and tried to find what she was looking at.

"What is it?" I asked her.

"Is that a plane or a star?" she asked.

"Where?" I asked.

"In the sky," she replied seriously, and I just turned and looked at her.

"Really?" I asked.

She turned towards me, not sure what I was asking. As soon as she realized what I meant she started laughing.

"Not very helpful, huh?"

"No. Not really," I shook my head. She just smiled and leaned back.

All of a sudden, she put her head on my shoulder and nestled up against me. I was stunned at first and it took me a minute to adjust my body to accommodate hers. Hesitantly, I put my arm around her shoulders and held her tight against me. It was hotter than balls under the blanket and with her against me, but I wasn't going to complain. Inside me, there was a battle of wills trying to decide if I should walk away from her.

"I've missed you," she said and closed her eyes. She made the decision for me, and I stayed.

Once her breathing had evened out and I knew she was asleep I responded back.

"I missed you, too."

I woke the next morning with Kelly still in my arms. The blanket had fallen to the ground during the night and Kelly must have snuggled closer to me because she was practically in my lap. I smiled at her still sleeping form. I could definitely get used to waking up with her in my arms. I had that day off work and decided I would spend it with her. It was time I just told her how I felt.

As I was brushing some hair off her cheek, I felt my phone vibrate in the pocket of my running shorts. Being careful not to disturb Kelly I pulled the phone from my pocket. The smile I still had on my face fell as soon as I saw who it was.

"What happened?" I asked Lily as soon as I answered.

"He's in the hospital. He tried again," Lily said, and I heard the tears from the cracking of her voice.

This was when Kelly woke up. She saw the expression on my face and immediately asked me what was wrong. I glanced down at her, the phone still pressed against my cheek.

"I have to go to Philadelphia," I said.

With those words, I cast aside the very decision I had come to moments earlier. I disengaged from Kelly's embrace and once again walked away from what I wanted so I could go rescue my brother from his demons.

17

Siblings

Standing beside Kevin's hospital bed, staring down at his sleeping form, was not an event I had ever wanted to experience again. When I was nine, I was completely terrified. It was eleven years later, and instead of terror, I felt nothing but resentment. The doctors said it was an accident, but I knew better. Kevin wasn't a careless driver. Like everything he did he set out to be the best and driving was no exception. Even as a teenager he had been extremely cautious about obeying the traffic laws. I didn't believe for a second that he had lost control of the car and crashed into that tree on accident. It didn't matter that it had been raining, and the roads were slippery. I knew my brother. He had intentionally hit that tree, believing he would not wake up.

In a twist of irony, something I doubt my brother would appreciate, it turned out the slippery roads saved my brother's life. His original trajectory was straight on towards the tree but at the last minute the tires had hit the perfect spot and sent the wheels slightly to the left, causing the passenger side of the car to receive the majority of the impact. As far as suicide attempts go it was probably the worst on record. Kevin hadn't even remembered to remove his seat belt.

Of course, the doctors took this as evidence that the act wasn't intentional. After all, if he was truly suicidal, he wouldn't have had his seat belt on. The seat belt and air bag saved his life. I'm sure the experts would cite this case in favor of the life-saving capabilities of the seat belt and modern air bag system – standard in all vehicles.

Unlike the medical professionals, Lily and I weren't fooled. I imagined my brother was probably returning from his latest research trip and came across a tree that looked like the perfect tree. He probably hadn't finished his research and was upset with himself for failing and saw the perfect tree before him, offering him an escape from his perceived failure. He probably convinced himself he was doing the right thing. It wasn't like anybody would miss him. No one cared for him anyway and this would just be easier on everyone. He didn't remove his seatbelt because he hadn't planned to do it, and it never occurred to him that the seatbelt would prevent him from succeeding at this plan too. I imagined when he woke, he would probably be upset with himself for failing yet again.

Lily came back into the room while I was speculating on what Kevin had been thinking before he steered into the tree. She had met me at the airport. I told her she didn't have to, but she insisted. The initial meeting wasn't like the other reunions of other airport patrons. Airport greetings usually fit into two categories – happy reunions or business. My reunion with the sister that had raised me until I was eight did not consist of hugs, tears or declarations of happy thoughts. Our meeting couldn't even fit into the business category. We didn't shake hands or discuss schedules. We didn't even say hello to one another. After I got off the plane, I went to meet her near the exit she had told me to go to.

"Got everything?" she asked when I stopped before her.

"Yes," I said and held up the bag I had taken on the plane with me.

Lily nodded, turned on her heels and walked out the doors. I followed silently behind her and when she stopped by a four-door sedan and got in I did the same. We didn't say anything else as she drove straight to the hospital Kevin had been admitted to.

While I was perfectly fine with the lack of discussion, I did glance at her out of the corner of my eye. I hadn't seen her in over ten years, and I was curious about the changes in her face. She still had her sharp features, pointed nose and deep blue eyes. She was nearly thirty, but she looked the exact same as she had the day she walked out our front door. Her hair was longer, however. She currently had it tied back, and it stopped just above the middle of her back. I wondered why she kept it long now when she had always cut it short before.

"The doctors say he should be cleared for release in the next couple of days. They just want to make sure there isn't any internal bleeding before they release him," Lily said as she set a small bag down beside a chair. She had gone to Kevin's apartment to get him some clothes and other items he would need when he was released.

She sat in the empty chair and folded her hands in her lap. I just continued to stare down at Kevin, lost in my thoughts. I wanted to shake him awake and yell at him. I wanted to tell him he was ruining my life with his selfishness. I wanted to scream at him that he did have people that cared for him, but he was too selfish to see it. I wanted to tell him that I was done with all of this and that he was on his own.

I did none of that, however. No matter how mad I was at him he was still the same brother I remembered from my childhood. The same brother that used to tie my shoes for me. The same brother that patted my head and told me I did a good job when I brought home my report card.

"You're welcome to stay at my place while we wait for him to be released. I'm not sure how long you are planning on staying but I have a spare bedroom," Lily said behind me.

Still, I said nothing.

"Brad, I'm trying here. Please talk to me," Lily pleaded.

I sighed, closed my eyes and clenched my fists.

"There's nothing to say," I replied.

"There has to be something?" Her voice was pained, and I winced from it.

"What do you want from me, Lily? You left. That's it."

"No, that isn't it. Brad, I wrote to you both when our parents forbade me to call you. You had to have known they changed the house number. They did that so I couldn't call you guys. I wrote you, I swear. I wrote you for years, but I never got a response. I didn't even know you had moved out of Philly until Kevin told me. And I had to hire a private investigator to track down Kevin. That is the only way I found him. Brad, I swear to you I never meant to hurt you." Lily stood and came to stand behind me. She tried to reach out for my arm, but I jerked away from her.

"None of this matters now," I said and walked away from her.

"Of course it matters. I'm already fighting to keep one brother. Please don't make me fight for you too," she said.

"Fight? And just how hard did you fight for us? All I have is your word that you wrote letters. How convenient for you that no one can corroborate that for you. Look, I'm not here to play sibling reunion. I'm here only for Kevin. Once he is out of here and back home, I'm gone."

"And then what? You pretend like I don't exist again? We go back to only talking about Kevin and wait for another one of his breakdowns before we see each other?"

"If it ain't broke," I shrugged.

"But it is broken!" she exclaimed and took a few steps towards me.

It was then Kevin woke up.

"Lily, is that you?" Kevin croaked. His right arm was in a cast and his face had many scratches on it from the shattered glass. His right leg was also bandaged up due to some deeper cuts. None of his major arteries had been nicked; otherwise, he most likely wouldn't be alive right now.

Poor Kevin. Couldn't catch a break.

"I'm here Kevin. So is Brad," Lily said and rushed to the bedside. She grasped Kevin's un-casted hand and caressed his cheek, careful not to touch his cuts. Kevin smiled at her.

"I'm so glad you're here," he said to her and coughed.

Lily reached to the tray-table and picked up the cup of water that was waiting for Kevin. She held the straw for him while he took some sips.

I remained in the background, observing them. It was evident they were comfortable with one another and that Kevin truly was glad Lily was there. This wasn't jealousy I was experiencing, but perhaps betrayal. I knew Kevin and Lily were close again but part of me wanted him to be upset with her, just as I was.

"I'm going to get the doctor. Brad is right here, Kevin. I'll be right back," Lily said and left the room.

"Brad?" Kevin asked, searching the room. He smiled at me when he found me in the corner.

I didn't smile back. This wasn't a happy reunion.

"Why?" I asked him and his smile fell.

"I don't know what you are asking," he said and turned away, telling me he knew exactly what I was asking.

"Why do you keep doing this? Do you want to hurt us?"

"It was an accident, Brad. I lost control of the wheel is all. Even the doctors have said that," he said, dismissing my questions.

"They're wrong. It wasn't an accident. We both know that."

"I don't know what you want me to say," Kevin turned his head, avoiding my gaze.

"I want you to say you're sorry. That you won't do it again."

"Well, I won't do it again because it was an accident," Kevin said, this time meeting my stare with his own equally stubborn glare. I was mad at him for doing this again, for only thinking of himself, and I was even more upset that he had the nerve to lie to me about it.

"Just promise me that next time you do something this incredibly stupid and selfish you make sure to follow through with it," I crossed my arms across my chest and matched his angry stare. I saw the moment my words hurt him. I saw the defeat in his eyes and watched his glare go from angry to acceptance. I instantly regretted what I had said.

"Kevin, I didn't mean,"-

"See, he's awake," Lily said as she entered with Kevin's doctor.

While the doctor went through his check and asked Kevin questions, I turned my back and looked out the window.

I was becoming versed in the art of slashing the hearts of those I loved and then turning my back on them.

18

Reunion

I left Philly, Kevin, Lily and all thoughts of mending relationships behind two days after Kevin was released from the hospital. Lily and I agreed to return to our usual email contact regarding our brother but neither of us mentioned pursuing a deeper connection. I was able to work a few more days with Jeff before classes resumed and I was due back at college. When Kelly called to ask how I was and if it was okay if she rode back with me, I told her everything was fine. The drive back to school was very strained and she once again asked how my brother was doing. I told her he was getting better but offered no further details.

Classes resumed and I buried myself in the routine of practice, class, and running. I avoided Kelly and her roommate, Serena. I still maintained contact with Matt. In fact, he was the only person at school I spoke to regularly. I wasn't counting the girls I picked up randomly when I went out to bars. It was easy for me to get into bars, even though I wasn't twenty-one yet, because I was tall and had always looked older than my actual age. I rarely got carded and there were plenty of bars within walking distance of my college. When the running wasn't enough to drown out the nightmares of blood and stark white tiles I would go to the bars and get lost in booze and women.

After a few months of this routine, I had an unexpected visitor. Someone I thought I would never see again. It was late morning, and my next class wasn't until later in the afternoon. I was reading when there was a knock at my door. The only person that ever visited me was Matt, so I assumed it would be him, and I was simply going to open the door and walk back to my desk but the person that stood on the other side of my door was not Matt.

It was Jenny, the girl I had tried to save but had failed.

She didn't look like the broken girl I had known. In fact, she didn't even look like a girl. She was a grown woman, exuding confidence and health. She looked like she had finally conquered her demons, while I was still battling mine.

"What do you want Jenny?" I asked, my eyes narrowing. It had been years since I last saw her. The night where she had almost gotten me killed at that biker bar was the last time I had seen her, and here she was outside my door looking like nothing had ever happened.

"To talk," she said, and I shook my head in disbelief.

I didn't want to invite her in, so I stepped into the hallway and closed my door behind me.

"Well?" I said.

She looked around nervously at the other residents walking in the hallway and I laughed inside. She didn't want an audience.

"Can we go for a walk?" she asked.

I didn't respond. I simply started walking down the hallway, not waiting to see if she followed. I walked out of the building and kept going until I came to a clear grassy path and immediately stopped. She caught up to me.

"I owe you an apology," she said.

"Yeah you do," I agreed and put my hands in my pockets. I started walking again. She followed behind me, speaking the entire time.

"I was horrible to you and all you ever tried to do was help

144

me. I'm sorry Brad. For everything," she said, and I stopped again. She bumped into my back, but I didn't turn around.

"That's it? You're sorry?"

"Yes. I'm sorry."

This time, I did turn around and met her gaze.

"You disappeared for years, Jenny. Years! You treated all of us like shit and you're sorry!" I shouted.

She nodded.

"Oh, well, great. Now we can all just keep living our lives because Jenny is sorry. Hey, guys, Jenny said she's sorry!" I shouted to the people that were walking passed us. She didn't want an audience, but I wasn't about to make this easy for her.

"We looked for you Jenny. Josh hired so many investigators it is ridiculous. Kelly cried over you for so long. She blamed herself for not stopping you the day you took off. Paul beat himself up because he didn't take you into his home. Stacey thought she was the reason you took off. And I,"- I couldn't finish the thought.

"You?" she encouraged me to continue.

"I fucking hated you, Jenny!" I shouted and ran my hands through my hair in frustration. She just stood there, staring at me. "Fuck! I tried so hard to get you to let me help you and you just crapped all over me. Over all of us. We loved you, Jenny! We loved you," my voice trailed off.

"I loved all of you too," she whispered.

"Then why did you leave?" I asked, just as softly. It seemed my abandonment issues had seeped into my thoughts on Jenny's departure. I couldn't decide if I was angry, relieved, or devastated at seeing her again. I decided it was best to not focus on how I should feel and just be. I willed myself to calm down.

"Because I was no good for any of you. I was beyond lost, Brad, and I didn't know how to love then."

I nodded, put my hands back in my pockets and gestured with my head to a coffee kiosk not far away.

145

"Want to get some coffee?"

She smiled and followed me to the kiosk. I bought our selections, and we walked to a nearby bench and sat down. We took a few silent sips of coffee before I spoke again.

"Why are you back now?" I asked.

"To make amends," she laughed but I just scowled at her. "I have a daughter," she said softly.

I quickly glanced at her, surprised.

"I went to California after running and didn't exactly live a chaste life. I changed when I became pregnant because I knew I had to. She saved my life. She brought me to my husband. I'm finally in a place where I feel worthy of love and I knew I had to come home and repair what I broke," she told me.

"What's her name," I asked.

"Who?"

I rolled my eyes at her. "Your daughter."

"Oh. Hope," she smiled when she said it. She pulled out her phone and showed me the photo that was the screensaver. A cute, curly-haired child smiled up at me.

"Fitting name," I said, and she smiled wider at me.

"I really am sorry, Brad. Truly."

"I know. I'm glad you're doing well. Your husband, he treats you right?" I really looked at her for the first time because I needed to know the answer to this question. I needed to know she was being treated with kindness.

"Yes. Evan is a wonderful man. He reminds me a lot of you," she said.

"Yeah. Bullheaded and clueless?" I laughed.

"No. Loyal and honorable," she said and placed her hand on my arm.

"You must be thinking of a different Brad," I said and attempted to laugh again, extricating my arm from her touch.

"I have the right one. You are an amazing man, Brad. You saved me from myself so many times. I would have ended my life long ago if it hadn't been for you," she said.

I had no idea she had ever thought of things like that.

"I would have helped you forever, Jenny," I said and squeezed my eyes shut.

"I know," she said and patted my leg.

I dreaded asking the next question, but I knew I had to.

"Have you seen Kelly," I asked.

"No. I needed to see you first," she replied.

"Why? You two were like attached at the hip."

"I saw Josh and Stacey. They told me Kelly was dating other guys, and you still haven't tried anything."

I shrugged.

"She's on this path of self-discovery or some shit. Doesn't leave much time for anything else," I said.

"That's bullshit and you know it, Brad."

"It's like you used to say, she doesn't want me," I said and looked away.

"Oh, Brad. Those things I said were meant to be hurtful, but they weren't true. I swear the two of you are the most clueless people I have ever met. Kelly would be into you if you would just tell her how you feel," she said.

"I've tried to tell her Jenny, but she only sees me as a brother," I said and leaned back against the bench and stretched my legs out. I placed a hand in my pocket and watched as people walked by us.

"I have a feeling you haven't actually told her, Brad. I know you. Always willing to be the sacrificial hero playing second fiddle to Kelly's whims," Jenny said.

"What?" I turned to her, clearly confused by her statement.

"You are so afraid that she won't like you back, so you just hide behind the veil of friendship. It's cowardly. And Kelly isn't any better. Unless someone is beating the two of you over the head with the truth you just don't see it," she shook her head at me.

"Take it from someone who has had a lot of experience with regret. Don't wait too long Brad. Before you know it, it will be too late and you will look back wishing you had the balls to say what you wanted," she finished.

"Geez, Jenny, you leave us and return all wise and shit. Married life and motherhood looks good on you," I laughed, but she narrowed her eyes at me.

"Alright. I promise I won't wait too long," I said.

"Good. Now, Superman, tell me how you've been?"

I spent the next hour lying to Jenny about how great I was. My classes were great. The team was great. My family – great. I could tell she didn't buy it for one minute and she told me if I ever needed her, she would be there. I tried to play it off as a joke and told her there was only room for one superhero, but she told me even heroes needed help every now and then.

We parted ways, promising to stay in touch. I was happy for Jenny and hoped her life would only bring her more happiness from now on. She had seen enough of the darkness and deserved the light.

I was still processing my visit from Jenny when another, different, reunion occurred a couple weeks later. I was coming out of an Econ class when Kelly suddenly appeared at my side, two coffee cups in her hands.

"Hey, stranger," she said and nudged my shoulder. I was trying to put some papers away into a binder and hadn't noticed her there until she was right on top of me.

"What are you doing here?" I asked. I was having difficulty getting the damn papers in the binder and was beyond frustrated. I had to be at work in thirty minutes and I had no time to spare if I wanted to be on time.

Kelly's smile vanished once I asked my question and once again, I felt like a total dick.

"Waiting for you. I brought coffee," she said and held out a cup towards me. I looked at it, then her before slowly reaching out for the cup.

"Thanks," I said and started to walk out of the building. She followed me, her short legs trying to match my long strides.

"Where you headed?" she asked.

"To my room. Gotta change for work."

"Right, of course," she said and kept walking with me.

I could tell she wanted to say something, but she was holding back. She would open her mouth to speak but then nothing would come out and she would close it again. She repeated this three times before I lost my patience.

"What do you want Kelly?"

"I want to know why you are being such a colossal ass!" She huffed out, her face turning red from the anger. I couldn't help it. I laughed. She looked so damn cute. Then she made a smart-ass comment and gave me a look that could kill.

"I'm not telling jokes," she said and glared at me. I really was running late and didn't have time for her to push her issues on me. I don't know why I became upset with her, but I did, and I released some of my own word vomit.

"Yeah, you are. Not everything is about you Kelly," I said and started to walk towards my dorm.

"Don't walk away from me," she said and grabbed my arm.

I let her spin me around. Had I resisted I probably would have knocked her down and the last thing I ever wanted to do was harm her.

"Kelly, I don't have time for this. I have to get to work," I said, exhausted from everything: school, my brother, my sister, my parents, Jenny's visit, Kelly's appearance.

"Well, make time mister. I want to know what happened to my friend. You just disappeared," she said, and I could see her eyes start to water.

I shuffled my feet and twitched. I had this nervous habit of running my fingers through my hair when I became uncomfortable. I was uncomfortable, but I couldn't do anything about it because I had my books in one hand and the stupid coffee cup in the other. I really just wanted to escape from this conversation. I was deliberately avoiding her because I was no good for her, but she just kept coming around, poking at me.

"Jenny came back," she said, breaking the silence.

"I know," I replied, looking down the path, avoiding her gaze.

"Oh. Did she call you?" she asked.

"No." She narrowed her eyes at my vague response, and I sighed. "She came to see me."

"She came to see me too. She looks great. And she's a mom. I can't believe how much she's changed," Kelly said.

"Yeah. She's doing really great. Kelly, I really do have to go," I said.

"Ok. Will you call me this week?" she asked, hope in her voice. I hated to do it, but I lied to her.

"Yeah, sure," I said and walked away.

Despite what Jenny had said to me, I knew it was best for both of us if I just stayed away from her. It was exactly like Jenny had described her own state before she ran away. I didn't know how to love, and Kelly deserved better than what I could give.

19

Careful What You Wish For

"He's really making improvements, Brad. He has gone to every one of his appointments with the psychiatrist and is taking his medications. I think this last stint in the hospital really got through to him," Lily said.

I desperately wanted to believe her that Kevin was finally getting better. I wanted to share in her delight that, maybe, just maybe, Kevin wouldn't try to kill himself again. But I knew I couldn't believe it. It was the believing that crushed me every time. So, I just listened to Lily go on about how well Kevin was doing and how he was making plans for the future again. He had applied for some new research position and was excited about the opportunities it would provide him. Lily seemed to be more excited, but I remained skeptical.

Kevin wasn't the only one making changes in his life. Kelly was dating some new guy. I had seen her hanging around him many times. Matt told me that the guy, William, was a constant fixture in their weekend hangout plans. Serena was smitten with him. Of course I had done some digging and found out who the guy was. He was pre-law, a son of a current lawyer and socialite wife – the country club type. He belonged to some fraternity on campus that a few of my fellow teammates belonged to. He was basically the typical frat guy, came from money and had the golden boy good

151

looks that came with privilege. So, naturally, I disliked him instantly.

The fact that she was doing exactly what I wanted her to do did not escape me. I had deliberately stayed away so she could move on and not have me holding her back. Honestly, I knew I needed to distance myself from her because I simply couldn't handle it when she sought out the company of other men. My past record hadn't exactly been the greatest when it came to handling Kelly's boyfriends. I acted more like a jealous ex instead of the best friend and I was tired of playing that role.

Still, I hadn't broken old habits. I had seen Kelly eating lunch with William one day before Christmas break and I had just flipped. I walked up to their table and told her that I would pick her up the next morning to drive back home as if I hadn't been avoiding her for the last few months. She looked at me like I was bat-shit crazy and said her sister and brother-in-law would be picking her up to take her home. When I questioned her on it, she made a comment about how we used to be friends, and I shut down. I know I'd been a shitty friend, but it never actually occurred to me that she would view us in the past tense, and I just walked away from her, again.

Now, I was sitting in my parent's home, at the kitchen table, listening to Lily go on and on about how well Kevin was doing and all I really wanted to do was run to the house next door and beg Kelly to forgive me. I knew I couldn't, though. The things I had done to her were unforgivable. I had promised her I wouldn't disappear, and I did it anyway. I swore I would never hurt her and all I seemed to do was hurt her. I was just no good for her.

"Brad, did you hear me?" Lily asked in my ear.

"Sorry, no. What did you say?"

"I said Kevin and I are going to spend the holiday with some colleagues of mine from work. I know you were still undecided on if you could make it here. If you want to come along you are welcome to. Kevin will be taking my spare bedroom, but the couch is pretty comfortable." I heard the desperation in her voice. She wanted me to come.

I glanced out the kitchen window and into Kelly's living room. She was sitting on the couch with her little brother, and they were laughing at something. Tasha came into the room carrying a bowl and set it on the coffee table before joining in the laughter. I smiled at the three of them and their sheer joy. Paul and Tasha had extended an invitation to me to spend the holiday with them again, like I used to do before I began spending it with Kevin. Watching them, together like a family should be, made me realize that I wanted the same thing. I wanted to sit on a couch with my family and just enjoy their presence. The only time I had ever felt that was when I had been inside the house next to mine, sitting beside the girl next door.

"I'm sorry, Lily, I can't. I'm going to a friend's house this year," I said without even realizing I had made that decision.

"Oh. Well, I understand. I hope you have a good time," she said, disappointment in every word.

I knew Lily still had hope that we would once again be the brother and sister we used to be but there was still too much hurt there. We hung up soon after and I went out for a run.

The next few days were spent working with Jeff and doing some last-minute shopping for Christmas gifts. Since I had only recently decided to spend Christmas day with my favorite family I hadn't prepared. Jenny had also called to tell me that she and her family would be coming in for a few days as well. I added them to my shopping list. My parents had already left for their annual winter vacation before I had even returned from school. I hadn't seen them since the end of summer, when I had returned to college. We no longer went through the formalities of gift giving for any occasion. My guitar had been the last gift my parents had actually given me. Since then, they had left envelopes of cash whenever they went away for business or on vacation. I used it to supplement my expenses when work was slow.

On the morning of Christmas, I received a call from a panicked

Matt. He was going to ask Serena to marry him, and he wasn't sure it would go so well. He said she was acting suspicious, and I told him he needed to get off the phone with me before she became even more suspicious.

Four hours later I got another call from Matt and he told me Serena had finally accepted his proposal, after some dramatics that included a bathroom door being locked and her grandmother threatening to knock the door down. I was happy for my friend and maybe it was the hope in his voice that had me thinking hopeful thoughts for the first time in a long time. Serena had experienced the ultimate betrayal when she had been so young, yet she had found happiness in another. Matt was the best guy, and they were really happy together. Jenny had pulled herself up and found her own heaven with her husband and daughter. Maybe the darkness didn't always follow us. If they could make it out, then maybe I could too. Maybe I didn't have to stay away from Kelly to protect her from the darkness that followed me. Maybe, together, we could chase it away.

I went to the house next door with gifts in my hands and hope in my heart. I wasn't going to allow my own fears to keep me from Kelly anymore. It didn't matter that she had a boyfriend again. I wasn't going to let that stop me this time. Today, I would tell her how I felt and lay it all out there. If she didn't feel the same, then I would move on knowing that I hadn't simply given up.

After knocking, and not receiving an answer, I walked into the house and called out to them. Paul and Josh, Stacey's husband, came running to help me with the gifts in my hands. They were all greeting me, but I kept searching for Kelly. She wasn't in the kitchen with Stacey, Jenny and the kids. I saw her in the living room with a man I didn't know setting up the various games we always played at gatherings.

While I was watching her Jenny called out to me. I turned and looked at her. The last time I saw her was when she visited me at school. She smiled at me as she stood, and, for some reason, I

154

opened my arms for her. She rushed to me and put her arms around me as well. We both laughed and rocked each other. I hadn't been very welcoming to her during our last encounter, and I was glad that it didn't matter now. I hugged her tighter and was once again struck with the same feeling I had the night I was talking to Lily when I saw Kelly, Tasha and Gregory laughing in the living room.

This was what mattered. This feeling. These people.

As I was hugging Jenny the man from the living room came up behind her and put his hand on her back. She came out of our hug, but kept one arm around my waist as she turned to the man, tears in her eyes.

"This is Brad," she said and the next thing I knew I was being pulled into another hug. This time it was by the man I didn't know.

"I owe you many thanks for saving her life as often as you did," the man said when he stepped back from me. I put the pieces together and realized this was Evan, Jenny's husband.

"Nah, I didn't do anything special," I said and shrugged.

"Still, many times, thank you," Evan said and put his hand on my shoulder. I nodded at him, understanding his appreciation.

After the moment had passed the rest of Kelly's family came forward and gave me more hugs and greetings. A little girl came up to me and wrapped her arms around my legs and I looked down at the little angel.

"Well, hello there," I said and waved. The girl giggled and looked up at me.

"She's a flirt," Jenny said and scooped up the little girl. I recognized her from the photo Jenny had shown me when we talked about her daughter, Hope.

"I don't mind when pretty girls flirt with me," I said and tickled Hope's cheek, making her giggle again. I heard a snort of laughter and glanced over to find Kelly in the entryway of the kitchen.

"Hi Kelly," I said, looking at her like it was the first time I had ever seen her. In fact, it was like the first time I had seen her. She looked so damn beautiful standing there with the Christmas tree and lights in the background.

"Hey," she said. It was evident she was uncomfortable, but I just kept staring at her.

Jenny finally interrupted the moment by asking if I could help the kids finish decorating the cookies so they could finish preparing dinner. I agreed and spent the next hour making a mess with frosting and sprinkles.

I tried several times to get Kelly alone to talk with her but every time I had a free moment I was roped into another task. Paul and Josh had me help fix some lights outside, Tasha asked me to get dishware down from the top shelves, Stacey asked me to clean up her son when he found the mashed potatoes she was making and got some in his hair and at one point Jenny and Evan found me. I didn't mind Jenny and Evan approaching me though. It was nice to get to know the man that Jenny loved. He looked at her like she was his world, and she looked at him like she would never let him go. I wanted Kelly to look at me that way. When Evan excused himself so he could help set the table for dinner, Jenny asked me about Kelly.

"You can't keep your eyes off of her. What is going on?" she asked, glancing at Kelly in the kitchen.

"Nothing," I said and looked at Kelly once again.

"Brad, we've known each other a long time and I know when you are lying. I swear to you that all those things I said when we were younger was complete bullshit. If you love her then go get her," Jenny said and nudged me with her shoulder.

"I plan to," I said as I still watched Kelly help Tasha with the meal preparation.

"Really?" Jenny asked, skeptical.

"Really," I said and looked Jenny square in the eyes.

"Well, it's about damn time," she said and patted my knee before joining the others in the kitchen.

Dinner was a joyous, loud occasion filled with laughter. I still couldn't keep my eyes off of Kelly and was appreciative that she had introduced me to her family. I loved these people like they were my own family. They had accepted me into their house and never once made me feel unwelcome. Paul and Tasha had extended a helping hand to me many times and I often looked to them as examples to follow. I wanted nothing more than to spend more time with these people. After dinner, we all went into the living room to do the present portion. The children were eager to tear into the paper.

Stacey insisted that Kelly and I sit together on the smaller sofa because she wanted parents and children to be together for the purposes of taking pictures. I didn't mind but Kelly seemed to stiffen when I sat beside her. I watched as Paul silently crept out of the room and up the stairs so he could put on the Santa suit he rented this year. Once he was up the stairs I spoke to Kelly.

"I heard from Matt today. He bought a ring and proposed to Serena," I said hoping that if I started on neutral ground, she wouldn't shut me down.

"Oh. She hasn't called me. What did she say?" she asked.

"She said yes, eventually." Kelly turned to me, confusion on her face from my comment. "You know how she hates surprises. He was down on one knee with the ring held out in his hands when she turned around. She took one look at him, told him she hated him and locked herself in the bathroom. He tried to get her to come out, but she refused. Her Gran had to tell her to get her cowardly butt out of the bathroom and give the nice boy an answer before she broke the door down. Matt said Serena cracked the door, called him a stupid head then threw open the door, knocked him over because she jumped into him and kept saying yes over and over again."

"Sounds just like her," Kelly said.

"Yeah." I looked at her watching the kids ripping into the presents and I swear I stopped breathing. I wanted to reach out and pull her into my side and just sit with her like I did on the front porch swing.

As I was reaching out for her I was interrupted by a jovial 'ho ho ho' coming from the stairs. Kelly and I both looked back and saw Santa coming down the stairs.

"Merry Christmas," Santa said. His beard was a bit askew, and Tasha gestured to her chin and cleared her throat. Paul immediately fixed the beard.

Kelly covered her mouth with her hands to keep from laughing and I elbowed her in the side to let her know if she lost it, so would I. We were grinning at each other and the moment was damn perfect. I was having the moment I longed to have just days before when I looked into the window of this room.

The shrill ring of my cell phone interrupted the moment. I took it out and saw it was Lily calling. I excused myself and went into the kitchen so I wouldn't interrupt anyone.

"Hello," I said with a smile on my face, instead of my customary 'what happened'.

"Brad, he's gone," she said and for the second time that night I stopped breathing.

"What?" I said. I stumbled as I reached out for the counter.

"He was supposed to meet me at my apartment an hour ago, but he didn't show and he wasn't answering his phone. I came over to his place and had to let myself in because it was locked. He didn't answer when I called for him. I found him in his bedroom. He shot himself, Brad. He was dead before I got there."

She was crying and stumbling over the words, but I couldn't process what she was saying. Gone? Kevin was gone? Dead? But he was getting better. She said he was getting better and now he was… gone?

"Brad? Are you there?"

"I'm here. I'll take the next flight," I said emotionless.

"Okay. I've tried to call our parents, but I can't reach them," she said sniffling.

"They are in Barbados I think. Call their office and leave a message. Someone there will know how to reach them."

"Okay. I will. Brad, be careful. Let me know the flight details and I'll pick you up."

"Okay," I said and hung up the phone.

I stared blankly down at the square object in my hand. I dropped it on the counter like it had stung me and stepped back. The sounds from the other room suddenly returned to me and I heard laughter.

The contrast between this moment and the moment I had just experienced had me laughing as well. Only, my laughter wasn't from joy, but pained panic. I desperately wanted to leave this moment and go back to the other one; the one where I was surrounded by a loving family and sitting next to the woman I loved while we laughed at Santa.

I slowly walked back to the living room in a daze. I was staring at the joyous family memories unfolding before me, but my eyes weren't seeing any of it. Kelly was by my side almost immediately. She grabbed my hand and asked what was wrong.

"He's gone," I whispered, and tears started to fall.

"What? Who's gone?" she asked.

"K-Kevin," I stammered.

Suddenly, Tasha was next to us, and she shuffled us into the kitchen. I could tell there was more movement going on, but I couldn't focus on any of it. Tasha guided me to a chair, told me to sit and asked Kelly what was happening.

"Something happened to Kevin," Kelly said.

Tasha knelt in front of me and covered my hands with hers. She had gone through this with her first husband. Except, her husband had decided to end his life when his body had betrayed him, and he was in constant physical pain. Kevin hadn't been ill. He just decided he didn't want to live anymore and shot himself.

"Bradley, tell me what happened," Tasha said.

"Lily just called me. She said she found Kevin in his bedroom. There was a gun. How did he get a gun?" I asked Tasha but she didn't have an answer for me. For years I had been searching for answers and had yet to find any.

"I don't know honey. What else did Lily say?"

"He…Kevin…was already dead by the time she got there. He was supposed to spend the day with her but when he never showed she went to his apartment. She said she spoke to him yesterday and he promised he would be there. He promised her," I cried out and Tasha pulled me into her arms. I let her hold me and just sobbed into her shoulder. There was more movement happening around me, but I shut it all out. The pain was too much.

"Bradley, I spoke to Lily. I'm booking you the next flight to Philadelphia. Lily is expecting you," Paul said.

I broke free of Tasha's embrace and wiped my eyes. I needed to stop acting this way. Nothing was getting accomplished if I turned into a blubbering fool. I stood and squared my shoulders.

"There's no need for that Paul. I can buy my own ticket," I said proudly.

"This isn't up for negotiation. While I take care of this, you need to gather your things for the trip," Paul said firmly.

"I'm going with him," Kelly suddenly said.

"No, Kelly. It's fine," I said as I glanced her way. I couldn't have her go with me. I was barely holding myself together as it was.

"No!" she shouted, stunning all of us. "I'm going," she said to her father.

Paul nodded and handed me my phone. I watched as Santa left the kitchen. His beard bouncing around his neck, leaving his face exposed. The kids would be traumatized when they saw him.

"Okay, both of you need to go pack right now. Be back in thirty minutes. Kelly, you will take my car and drive to the airport. Here's my credit card for whatever you may need. You will call us as soon as you land and check in regularly," Tasha said before she turned to me. "If you need anything, anything at all, you call us."

I thanked her but said nothing else as I turned to leave. I avoided the others in the living room and walked back to my house in silence. My gaze fell upon my guitar as I was packing. I had pulled it out of its case earlier in the day and had even played a bit after I had spoken to Matt. It had been months since I had played it and today, of all days, I had finally picked it back up.

With a scream I reached for the instrument, swung it up over my head and smashed it down on the floor. I repeated the movement over and over again until the guitar was a splintered mess on my bedroom floor.

After I had gotten my breathing and emotions back under control I finished packing and waited for Kelly at the end of her driveway. I didn't want to go back in that house. That house had lied to me. There was no hope. The darkness couldn't be chased away, and I couldn't ever be a part of the life that house promised.

In mere moments Kelly came out of the offending house and unlocked the doors to Tasha's car.

"You don't have to do this, Kelly," I said to her.

"Don't even start that shit with me right now Brad. I'm going with you and that is that. Now get in the car," she said and pointed to the passenger seat.

I put my bag in the back seat beside hers and got silently in the car. I didn't speak to her again until we landed in Philadelphia. I know she must have been uncomfortable the whole time, but she never once attempted to break me from my thoughts. I still hadn't fully processed what had happened and I didn't want to talk about it.

Still, I needed to stop treating her like shit.

"Thank you for coming with me," I said as I looked out the window, avoiding her gaze. She didn't say anything back, but as the plane touched down, she reached out and took my hand in hers.

20

Point of No Return

Lily picked us up from the airport and the drive to her apartment was also spent in silence. None of us knew what to say. Was there a right thing to say in these circumstances? When we got to her apartment, she showed us the spare bedroom and I told Kelly to take it but she refused. I was exhausted and didn't put up much of a fight. I left Lily and Kelly in the living room while I shut myself off in the bedroom.

It didn't take me long, however, to realize that the isolation in the room meant that my thoughts could wander back to Kevin and why he did this. These were thoughts I had been trying to avoid since Lily had called me. I didn't want to think of Kevin. When I thought of him, I only saw red – the blood against stark white tiles.

Quickly, I exited the room and went towards the living room at the front of the apartment. I heard Lily and Kelly talking. Not wanting to interrupt, I started to return to the room but stopped when I heard what Lily was saying.

"Brad would probably tell you that I am just like them. As soon as I reached eighteen, I packed my bags, took off and never looked back. That isn't completely accurate, of course. Yes, I packed up and left but I looked back often. I tried to call to talk to them, but my parents wouldn't let me speak with them. I suppose they thought I had turned my back on them as well and they felt justified in denying me access to my brothers. I used to write them letters, Kevin and Brad, but I had no way of knowing if they ever received them because they never wrote me back. Still, I continued to write. When it came time for Kevin to go to college, I hired an investigator to find him. Once I located the school he went to, I wrote to him. He wrote back and it was then I learned just how bad off he was.

"Brad blamed Kevin's condition on my disappearance. No matter how many times I tried to explain to him that I never meant to hurt them Brad just didn't want to believe me. I just couldn't stay in that house anymore. Maybe some would say I should have been grateful. I had a roof over my head, food in my belly and clothes on my back, but I also grew up in a house where I was not wanted. I never understood why our parents had children. They clearly did not want us but instead of stopping with me they had Kevin and Brad. Kevin was the best of us. He was always trying to make us happy. If only I had noticed sooner just how much he was hurting behind all those smiles." Lily finished.

"It's not your fault," I said and stepped out from behind the wall. Lily smiled at me, but I saw the pain in her expression. She was really hurting from this.

"I should have been paying more attention. I should have come back for you two," she said.

"No. You lived with them long enough. You were right to leave, and I was wrong to push you away," I said and walked up to the couch she was sitting on.

"You were so young. You only knew that I was there one day and gone the next. You couldn't have possibly understood what was going on. I'm so sorry you thought I abandoned you. I never wanted to do that, but that place was killing me," she said and sobbed.

It was then I noticed that Kelly had left the room. I sat in the spot she had vacated and decided it was time to have the discussion Lily had been trying to have with me ever since I started talking to her again.

"I blamed you for so long for Kevin's condition. I thought if you had stayed he wouldn't have been so sad. I know now it wouldn't have mattered. He just got sad so easily. I'm sorry I've been a dick to you," I said and leaned forward, my hands clasped between my knees.

"I don't blame you for being angry with me, Brad. I just wish I could have been there for you all these years. You've had to carry this burden for so long. Know that I am here for you if you ever need me. Please don't shut me out again. You're all I have left," she said as the tears began to flow freely.

I reached out, then pulled my hand, only to try again and I took her hand in mine. It was the first time I had touched her since the day she left.

"I'm not going anywhere. But I'm not the greatest at opening up and sharing. Kevin was much better at that than I am. I tend to upset people most of the time. I can't promise you that everything will be fine, but I can promise that I'll do better," I said.

"I'll take it," she said and squeezed my hand.

Right on schedule, I became uncomfortable with the closeness and withdrew my hand as I stood.

"I'm beat. I'm gonna go to bed," I said and gestured towards the spare room.

"Let me know if you two need anything," Lily said and went to her own room.

I went to the spare room and intended to just get my things and sleep on the couch but when I saw Kelly sleeping in the bed, I wanted nothing more than to be next to her. I changed into a T-shirt and boxers and crawled into the bed with her. I simply watched her sleep for a little while before I fell into sleep.

I was woken up the next morning by slight movement. I saw Kelly trying to slide out from under my arm that was draped across her breasts. She had her lower body dangling off the edge of the bed and her upper body was trapped by my arm. She saw me staring at her and I smiled at the funny look she had on her face.

"What are you doing?" I asked her, my voice croaky from slumber.

"Trying not to wake you up," she replied, and I laughed.

Quickly, I realized what I was doing. My brother killed himself yesterday and there I was laughing it up. I removed my arm from her body, threw the covers off of me and left the room.

I found Lily in the kitchen making breakfast.

"Morning. Want some eggs?" she asked me.

"No, thanks," I said and walked to the coffee pot. She already had mugs out for us, and I poured myself a cup of black coffee.

"I want to see him," I said.

Her back stiffened but she continued to plate her eggs.

"He is at the morgue. They have to do an autopsy. I don't think they will let us see him until that is finished," she said.

"I don't care. I need to see him, today." I wasn't going to relent. This was something I had to do. Until I saw him, I refused to accept this.

"I'll see what I can do," Lily said and took her plate to the living room.

I went back to the bedroom to change. Kelly was sitting on the bed staring at the wall when I entered.

"Lily and I are gonna go to the morgue to view the body," I said as I gathered some clothes from my bag.

"Ok. I'll be ready in ten minutes," Kelly said and stood.

"It's fine. You don't have to go," I said, and she stopped gathering her things to look at me.

"Don't be silly. Of course I'm gonna go," she said and left with her clothes.

Two hours later I stood before the plexi-glass window waiting for some stranger to wheel the body of my dead brother before me. The man asked me through a speaker system if I was ready and I nodded stoically. My arms were crossed in front of my chest, and I glared at the sheet covering the still form of my brother on the cold metal table. I'm not sure what I expected when the man removed the sheet but whatever I had expected seemed to disappear when I was looking down at Kevin's dead body.

He looked like he was sleeping, except the tiny hole in his head where the bullet had penetrated betrayed his current state. I stared at the offending hole for a little bit before I gestured to the man that I was finished.

The sheet was placed over Kevin and the man silently wheeled my brother back into whatever place they had come from. I just stood there and stared at the empty space. Wherever Kevin had gone after he decided to leave this world, I hoped he was feeling like shit for what he was putting me and Lily through. It didn't seem fair that we were stuck back here dealing with the shit Kevin left behind if he was able to go to some place where pain and regret never touched him again. He had no right to just disappear from our lives without thinking about how this would hurt us. Once again, he did the selfish thing without a second thought for who he hurt.

"Brad?" Lily asked as she stepped towards me and reached out to put a hand on my shoulder.

I didn't want her to touch me. I didn't want anyone to touch me. I just wanted my fucking brother back.

I started to punch the plexi-glass over and over again. I didn't say anything or scream in frustration. I just kept punching that damn fake glass wall trying to break it. If I could just break this fucking wall it wouldn't hurt so bad. I could hear Kelly screaming at me to stop but I didn't listen. I didn't even notice the blood on the wall until Lily came forward and grabbed my fist mid swing. As I stared at my blood, she unfurled my fingers and looked into my eyes. It was her gaze that made my tears fall.

"It's okay to be angry." She caressed my cheek, and I broke. I fell to my knees and wrapped my arms around Lily's legs and just held on.

"You're okay," she said and placed her hand on my head.

I didn't believe her, but it was nice to hear. I spent so much of my own time lying, that I knew her words were a lie meant to comfort me. They didn't, but it was still nice that she tried.

The next few days were spent making arrangements for Kevin's burial and cleaning out his apartment. Kelly wanted to come with us when we went to Kevin's apartment, but I told her we needed privacy. She accepted that and stayed at Lily's place. I knew I wasn't being very nice to her, but I couldn't stand seeing the compassion in her eyes any more. She looked so damn sad every time she looked at me and I couldn't handle her sadness, nor did I want her sympathy. I slept on the couch the nights after our first night there.

Today, I was going through Kevin's books, trying to decide what to do with them. He had so many. They were mostly historical in nature but every now and then I would come across a sci-fi novel and it reminded me just how little I knew of my brother.

"Mr. Watson, the building super, says if we pack up everything in boxes, he will make sure the movers get everything," Lily said walking back into the apartment. She had been talking to the neighbor that we had asked to help keep an eye on Kevin.

I had wondered how none of his neighbors had heard the gun shot when he killed himself, but Mr. Forrester had brought insight to that query. He had told us that most of the residents went out of town during the holidays. Even Mr. Forrester had been gone on Christmas day. Kevin had chosen the perfect day to end his life. On fucking Christmas, a day of celebration. The irony was not lost on me at all.

"Okay," I said to Lily because I really didn't know what else to say. I glanced at the book in my hand and decided the only thing to do with the books was throw them in a box and not think of them again. I threw the book down and just swept my arms across the books on the desk before me. They tumbled into the box on the floor, and I turned to the bookcases. He had four bookcases that nearly reached the ceiling.

"When did he have time read all of these?" I asked no one.

"He never threw a book away. He's read these throughout the years," Lily answered me anyway.

"Maybe he should have spent more time in therapy and less time reading," I said under my breath.

"He was in a lot of pain," Lily said as she abandoned her task of clearing the kitchen to come to me.

"Aren't we all," I pointed out, dismissing her comment. She pursed her lips and looked around at the books.

"I was going to wait to give you this but maybe you need to see it," Lily said and took an envelope out of her purse.

"What is this?" I asked when I took it from her.

"He wrote you a letter," she replied.

I looked at her like she had betrayed me because she never once told me he had written suicide notes. She had been keeping this from me?

"I was afraid it would only hurt you and I didn't want you to hurt more," she said in response to my accusing glare.

"Too bad Kevin didn't think like that," I said and walked away from her.

I went into the bathroom because I could lock her out in there. After doing just that, I sat on the toilet and stared at the offending envelope with my name written on it. Kevin always had been a decent writer. I couldn't write a song to save my life but he could put

168

together words like it was nothing.

I tapped the envelope against my leg, wondering what clever words my brother left for me to read. Deciding there was no point prolonging it any further, I ripped open the envelope and took out the single sheet of paper, the last thing my brother left me.

Brad,

I know I've disappointed you and for that I am sorry. I never meant to hurt you. I wish I could say that I tried to rid myself of the dark thoughts that have plagued me for years, but the truth is I've been lying to you and Lily. I haven't been going to therapy or taking the meds the doctor prescribed me. Also, there is no research position.

You were right. I did crash that car into the tree deliberately. I was driving along, saw the tree, and knew I had to do it. I can't explain why I have these dark thoughts. I just do. I've had them for many years and there isn't anything that can be done to stop them. I simply was not meant for this world. I knew this a long time ago and tried to end things then, but you found me.

I've never been the greatest at planning things and I'm always late. I know you are probably really mad at me right now, but I just couldn't pretend anymore. I hurt all the time and doing the simplest task pained me. I tried so hard to be a good brother and son but I'm just not enough. I only bring those I love pain, and I don't want to be a burden anymore.

I would ask for your forgiveness but I know you won't offer it. I know you still blame Lily for everything, but it isn't her fault. Please don't blame her for this. She tried so hard to get me to stay but I have no more fight left in me.

Live your life Brad and forget about me and all these wasted years. Find your happiness. I never could find it, so you find it for me. I love you little brother and know that this is truly for the best.

Kevin

169

I put the letter back in the envelope, stood and went to the sink. As I was rinsing my hands, trying to wash away the remnants of that damn letter I saw my reflection in the medicine cabinet. I stared at myself for a brief moment before I punched the mirror and shards of glass shattered into the sink. The cabinet opened from the impact and blood began to drip from my knuckles into the sink. It mixed with the glass and water, making a strange pattern.

I looked into the cabinet and saw rows of tiny orange bottles. I picked one up and read the label; oxycodone. The next one was codeine. There was Zoloft, Prozac and Paxil. Lithium, Clozapine and the list went on. I stared at the bottles and Kevin's words ran through my head.

For someone who had been so eloquent with words his suicide letter to me was pretty shitty. He wanted me to be happy but also wanted me to forget about him. Did it ever occur to him that part of my happiness involved him staying alive? He was sorry for disappointing me but not sorry for taking his life? He was in pain? What about me? I was in pain.

Pain.

I was holding pain killers. I turned the orange bottle in my hand and stared at the label again. I caught a glimpse of myself in a shard of glass in the sink and saw blood on it.

It is in that moment that I made a decision that caused the darkness to take hold of me and consume my very being. I twisted open that orange bottle and spilled two pills out into my palm. Without a second of hesitation, I put those pills in my mouth and swallowed them down.

Later, I returned to the bathroom and placed all the bottles into a bag. I told Lilly I was going to dispose of them, but I didn't. I kept them and hid them in my luggage. I took two more pills before I went to bed and set about doing exactly what Kevin asked me to do in his letter – forget about him by drowning out the pain.

21

Still Running

There weren't many people at Kevin's funeral. He had never been good at making friends and the lack of people at his funeral demonstrated that. Lily decided there wouldn't be a point to having a wake or gathering after the service because it would just consist of the three of us: me, Lily and Kelly.

Kelly remained the entire time and still refused to leave. I hadn't decided yet if I was grateful or annoyed by her presence. Since reading Kevin's letter I hadn't been able to feel much of anything. Lily knew something was bothering me, but I refused to tell her what was in the letter. She regretted giving it to me, but it was too late. I had read it and the rest be damned.

It wasn't until we were leaving the cemetery, and I saw my parents approaching that I even thought of them. I had never expected them to actually come and the fact that they had showed up after being absent our whole lives had me fuming with anger. They didn't get to pop in and out whenever they wanted. Kevin had done nothing but try to be the son they wanted, and they never once gave him anything he needed to believe he was good enough. They shouldn't be there.

"What are you doing here?" I demanded.

"Bradley!" My Mother replied, horrified with my disrespect.

"We came to give our respect," Father answered with distaste

171

dripping off his words.

"Respect?" I scoffed.

"Brad," Lily warned but I ignored her.

"You didn't give a damn about Kevin when he was alive, and you come here now to show your respect!" I shouted.

"You will adjust your tone when you are speaking to me, *son*." My *father* said the word son like he couldn't stomach it and I laughed.

"This is just so typical of you two. Always gone when it matters. Did you just come here so you could make sure he's dead this time?"

I didn't even flinch when my mother slapped me. I hated this woman and this man, my so-called parents. The things they had said when Kevin had tried to kill himself the first time came flooding back to me and all I wanted was for them to be dead and not Kevin.

"How dare you say such a thing? We have done everything for you kids and yet you continue to be ungrateful little bastards!" My mother shouted at me.

"The only thing you have done is gave us life and fed us, like we were nothing but your pets. You never loved any of us. Kevin deserved better than the two of you," I seethed, the sting of my mother's slap warming my face.

"Don't expect to return to our home after today," my father said to me.

"Brad, let's go," Lily said as she placed her hand on my shoulder, trying to calm me down.

"I am sure this is due to your influence, Lily. You always were the most difficult child," our mother said to Lily.

Lily just stared back at her, in shock by the attack.

"Don't. You don't get to talk to her like that. She was more of a mother to us than you ever were. I understand why he did it, now. He didn't want to spend another moment on this earth with the two of you."

"Brad!" Kelly said, surprised by my words. I had forgotten she was standing next to us, watching this whole scene, and I was embarrassed that she had to witness this.

"Let's go," I said to Lily and Kelly. The three of us began to walk away.

"You're dead to us," my father called after me.

"We were never really alive to you, anyway," I said to him and the three of us got into Lily's car. After a few moments of silence Lily spoke to me.

"You know what you've done?" she asked.

"Yes," I said.

"Where will you go?"

"It doesn't matter," I said and turned to look out the window.

I watched as our parents turned away from the cemetery and walked towards the car waiting for them. They never even went to Kevin's burial site. How quickly they forgot about the respect they had come to show.

"I have to go into my office for a little bit," Lily said when she dropped Kelly and me at her apartment.

I nodded, not bothering to check on her. I knew what a dodge was, and my sister needed to be alone. I exited her car and walked into the building and went up to the apartment. I let myself in and started to walk toward the back bedroom but stopped. This wasn't my place. As of then I technically didn't have a home to go back to. I knew my parents meant what they said. I would have to move out as soon as I returned, and I didn't have anywhere to go. Kelly found me standing in the apartment entrance just staring into space.

"Brad?" she asked me as she stepped towards me cautiously.

"I don't know what to do next," I confessed.

173

She came up to me, reached out and placed both hands on my cheeks and turned my head so I was looking down at her.

"We're going to change your bandage," she said.

I looked down and saw the hand I had been using to punch mirrors and fake glass walls had been cut open and my bandage was covered in blood. I let Kelly take me to the bathroom and push me down onto the seat of the toilet.

I watched as she gathered the supplies she needed. While she removed the old bandage and began to clean the cuts I stared at her face. Her beauty and kindness never seemed to stop amazing me and I loved her for always being there for me. Her gentle touch was making me want to confess everything to her right there.

After she had cleansed the cuts, she brought my hand to her lips and gently kissed my knuckles. The gesture was meant to be comforting but it only pained me. I didn't want her to show me kindness after the way I had been treating her. When she was finished placing a fresh bandage on my hand, I asked a simple question that was haunting me.

"Why, Kelly?"

I wanted to know why she kept coming back to me even though I hurt her over and over again. I wanted to know why Kevin did what he did. I wanted to know why I couldn't just be happy with her.

"Because you're hurting," she answered.

Her response didn't answer any of my questions, not really. I stood and brought my hand up to tuck some of her hair behind her ear. She closed her eyes when I touched her, and she sighed this long, withering sigh. I wanted nothing more than to wrap her in my arms, put my lips against her and declare my need for her.

She opened her eyes and stared back at me. It wasn't until she bit her lip that my walls came crashing down. I lunged forward and took what I wanted. I kissed her like I would never get to do it again. It was hard and needy, just like me. She responded to my kiss and wrapped her arms around my neck. My tongue plunged into her

174

mouth, and I twisted us, so she was backed up against the bathroom counter.

When she hit the counter my pelvis bumped into her and I immediately hardened. I groaned from the impact and lifted her onto the counter, kissing her the entire time. As I took her mouth I began to unbutton her shirt. Once the final button was undone, I pushed it off of her and took in the scene before me. She had a sheer bra on, and I could see her nipples through it.

Silently, I pleaded with her to make me stop. But she didn't. She reached out for me cheek and I dipped my head to avoid her touch. I sucked on her nipples through the thin material of her undergarment. She gasped and I felt her hand in my hair gripping me.

While I sucked on her nipples I reached under skirt and pulled her matching underwear off. I stepped away from her briefly to remove my pants and boxers. I quickly shoved them down and stepped between her legs. I pulled her body to mine and plunged into her. She wrapped her legs around my waist and her arms came around my neck. She nuzzled her face into my neck, and I withdrew slightly and then pushed further into her. She made a noise. I couldn't tell if it was from passion or pain, and I glanced up. I caught my reflection in the mirror and was struck by how wrong this was.

She didn't deserve to be used like this.

Despite my disgust with myself I didn't stop what was happening. Instead, I drove into her over and over again until I forgot about how wrong it was and just chased the feeling I knew would come.

Like I had done with so many before her I used her to forget my pain. Once I had my release, I stayed inside her for a moment while I glared at my own reflection, hating what I had turned her into. Hating myself for doing it to her. She was not some girl I could just use like this. She was so much more, and I had tainted her.

I withdrew from inside her and bent to pick up her shirt. I put it back on her shoulders and covered her with it. I couldn't look at her.

"I'm sorry," I said and walked out of that bathroom and away from her, away from my shame.

I got my bag, left the apartment and immediately went to the airport. I called Lily before I boarded my plane and told her I had to get back for work. She didn't believe me, but I didn't tell her that I was actually running away from Kelly and what I had done to her. Nothing I had ever done or said to Kelly before compared to what I had done in that bathroom. I had treated her like nothing more than the very girls I had used for so many years.

How could I look her in the eyes when I couldn't even stomach seeing my own reflection?

I returned home, packed up my things and called Jeff. He let me crash at his place for a couple days before I returned to school. Thankfully, Jeff let me keep the rest of my belongings at his place. He tried to get me to tell him what was going on, but I told him it was just family drama and not that big of a deal. He told me I was full of shit, but he left it at that.

I spent the next days thinking of how I was going to fix what I had done and the only conclusion I came to was that I needed to beg Kelly to let us go back to the way things used to be. Things hadn't gotten so messed up until I had started thinking I had a shot with her. We just needed to be friends again and everything would be alright.

After I returned to school, I went to her room every day but Serena told me she hadn't come back yet. I basically stayed in the hallway outside her room for two days waiting for her to come back.

On the third day she returned.

I had fallen asleep while I sat in the hallway and woke when she jostled me. I was startled at first by the movement but when I noticed it was her I relaxed.

"Hey," I said looking up at her. She didn't reply and I started to get nervous. Serena opened their door and stepped over me.

"It's about time you showed up. He's been camped out here for the past two days," Serena said.

Kelly looked at me and I shrugged. It was true, I had been there every day since school started back up.

"I'm going to Matt's. Try not to kill him," Serena said as she walked down the hall.

Kelly continued to glare down at me, her arms crossed over her chest. We remained the hall for what felt like forever, her standing, me on the floor.

"Can I come in?" I asked as I ran my fingers through my hair.

Kelly turned, opened the door to her room and left it open behind her. I quickly got up from the floor and followed her inside. I closed the door behind me and waited while she was putting her things away.

Once she was finished, she walked to her desk, leaned against it and crossed her arms over her chest again, waiting for me. I wasn't sure how to begin so I hesitated and avoided her gaze.

"Well?" she asked.

"I don't know what to say," I said.

"Oh. Okay. Well, I have plenty to say," she said and uncrossed her arms. She pushed off the desk and started to pace back and forth in the tiny dorm room. "You're an asshole. I can't believe you just left me there. You didn't even leave a note. You were just gone, and I didn't know what had happened to you. You could have gotten hit by a car or something for all I knew. You wouldn't answer my calls and your sister had to explain things to me. It should have been you, but the moment things start to get too emotional for you, you just take off! I just wanted to be there for you, and you treated me like shit," she said as she began to cry.

"You're right," I said. Her tears were killing me. I was the cause

177

of those tears, and I didn't deserve to have her in my life.

"What?" she said, surprised I had agreed with her so easily.

"Everything you said. You are absolutely right. I'm an asshole. The worst kind. You came because you cared, and I took advantage of you. I shouldn't have done that, and I shouldn't have taken off like I did. I should have told you then it was a mistake, and I feel terrible for using you like that. You're my best friend Kelly and I never wanted to hurt you," I said standing back near the door. I was afraid if I got closer to her, I wouldn't be able to stop myself from reaching out for her.

"Mistake?" she whispered.

"Yes. I care about you Kelly and I would never want anyone to hurt you. It kills me that I'm that someone who hurt you. If I could take it back, I would. Can we just forget it ever happened and go back to the way things were?" I pleaded with her.

"You weren't even talking to me," she replied, shaking her head.

"That was because I was dealing with family stuff and I needed to figure things out," I explained.

"I just can't be your sometimes friend, Brad. Whenever I reach out to you, you push me further away. It hurts and I won't do it anymore," she said and stepped further away from me.

It was the step she took away from me that had me accepting the fact Kelly would not be in my life anymore. I nodded my head and left her room without another word. I went back to my own room and reached for the pills in the orange bottles I had taken from my dead brother's medicine cabinet. I had someone else I needed to forget about now, so I doubled the pills I usually took and chased them down with a beer.

22

Spiral

It had been so long since I woke up in the morning and actually liked the person I was. In all honesty I am not sure if I ever really did like who I was. As a kid I didn't understand the concepts of loathing and self-hate. My world had been so narrowly focused on my sister and my brother that I didn't know I was developing my own identity, or just how much that identity was tied to my siblings. When Lily left, I clung to Kevin in desperation and as I grew my whole existence centered on his. I could not be Brad without Kevin and while I wasn't sure who Brad really was, I knew that discovering my identity was pointless without my brother.

After my colossal failure with Kelly, I collapsed into myself and allowed the darkness to consume me. I not only swallowed all the pills I had found in Kevin's medicine cabinet, I started faking injuries so I could get more pain pills. It was currently the off season for track, but I would tell the doctors that I still practiced and injured myself on runs. That was partially true; I did still go running often but I never actually injured myself to the point where I needed pain relief. The relief I was seeking wasn't for a physical injury, but an invisible one I couldn't chase away fast enough. The running didn't help. The alcohol only kept it at bay for a little while. The pills worked better, but the best result came from a combination of alcohol, pills and running. I would swallow pills with alcohol and go

179

running when they started to kick in.

Sometimes I would make it back to my room and pass out from sheer exhaustion and I would get a couple hours of peace before being woken by the nightmares. Other times I would pass out while running and wake up in some area on campus. There were some mornings when I would be woken by some student on their way to class, asking if I was alright. They always made the assumption that I was passed out drunk and not because I ran myself to the point of utter exhaustion and my body just gave out.

Deep down I knew that I was slowly killing myself, but I didn't care. I was doing what my brother wanted me to do – I was forgetting him. This was the only way I knew how to give Kevin his final request. I couldn't save his life, but I could make sure the last thing he asked of me was accomplished. I failed at a lot of things, but I wasn't going to fail at this.

Lily called me often to check on me and I would answer just enough so I could convince her that I was fine. She begged me to talk to her, but I couldn't. There was nothing left to say to her. Kevin had said it all in his letters to us. I didn't know what hers said but if it was anything like mine it was complete shit. I hadn't heard from my parents since the day of Kevin's funeral. In all fairness I hadn't exactly attempted to reach out to them either.

Jenny checked in on me regularly as well. She had been at the Christmas celebration when I had been told Kevin had finally succeeded in ending his life. I hadn't seen her since that day, but I had spoken to her many times. She too tried to get me to open up, but I told her everything was fine. I told her I was just really busy with classes and practice. She told me she didn't believe me.

"I'm worried about you, Brad. I know when you are lying to me, and you are lying. Let me help you, please," she begged one evening over the phone.

I had my elbows propped up on my desk, one hand holding the phone, the other on my forehead to help keep my head from falling forward. The bottle of scotch I had nearly finished was beside me and I looked at it when I answered her.

"I'm fine, Jenny. I have a friend here with me, so I have to go." I chuckled and winked at my *friend*. It stared back at me and waited for me to pick it up.

"You're lying. Brad, tell me what I can do to help you," she pleaded.

"Nothing, Jenny. There's nothing you can do because I don't need any help. I have to go, goodbye," I said and hung up on her.

The scotch really needed me to pay attention to it. I dropped my phone on the desk, stood and grabbed the bottle. I walked to the single window my room held and looked out at the courtyard below me as I leaned against the wall. I wasn't exactly steady on my feet after a few hours with my new friend.

As I was bringing the bottle to my lips I saw a familiar figure walking across the courtyard towards the library. I recognized her right away and my body twitched, ready to chase after her. It had been months since I went to her room and begged her to be my friend again. Months since she had turned away from me.

In my hazy state I started to blame her for all that was going wrong. If I hadn't been so distracted by her, I could have given Kevin the attention he deserved. Kevin would still be alive if Kelly hadn't been around to pull my thoughts away from him. If she hadn't lived next door to me, I never would have seen her family that day before Christmas and I would have gone to Philadelphia to be with Kevin. He wouldn't have had the opportunity to kill himself if it hadn't been for Kelly. I wouldn't have been given that fucking shitty letter and I wouldn't be swallowing pills and alcohol trying to forget the brother I couldn't live without.

Immediately, I threw my new friend down to the ground and ran out of my room so I could chase down the person that was the cause of all of this. If I was hurting, then she needed to hurt too. It wasn't right that she got to go on with her life as if nothing had happened.

She had no right to be happy and dating some guy when my brother was dead because of her. She was probably on her way to go meet him right now. I wondered if he knew that she had cheated on him with me. While she was supposed to be in a relationship with this William guy, she had wrapped her legs around me and let me fuck her on a bathroom counter. All these years she had me so fooled. She wasn't kind at all. She was just a manipulator that took and took until there was nothing left behind.

I stalked into the library and searched the stacks until I found her in the Criminology section. She was sitting at one of the study tables in the back, quietly reading a book and taking notes. I wasn't fooled by the picture of innocence before me. I knew who she really was now, and I wasn't about to let her play these games again.

"What are you thinking?" I demanded when I reached her side.

"I was thinking that the crime statistics from three years ago are really concerning," she replied coolly, as if my presence was nothing more than a temporary nuisance. She picked up her pen and annotated something in her notebook.

Her easy dismissal of me upset me further.

"You're dating William Wright? The guy is such a snob. Even his name screams snob," I said in an attempt to bait her.

"You don't know anything about him," she said, still looking at her damn book.

"You already had one guy like him cast you aside. Why would you get involved with another?" I waited for my words to penetrate her cool exterior.

"Maybe I enjoy his company," she remained completely at ease.

"Look at me when I'm talking to you," I shouted.

"Maybe, if you were talking to me instead of attempting to lecture me like I was a small child I would look at you. You have interrupted my studying, and this is not a conversation worthy of my time," she said and jotted some notes down.

This was not the girl I remembered. The girl I remembered

would have already started crying and apologized to me. She would have put her arms around me and tried to console me. This new girl was nothing like the girl I remembered.

"What happened to you?" I asked this stranger before me. I blinked from the light on her desk when she shifted in her seat. While it wasn't exactly bright, my eyes were not enjoying any of the light in the library.

"Maybe I finally realized that I need to start living my life for me. Maybe I recently had someone I cared about a lot tell me that I was a mistake. Maybe I came to the library to study, and I was interrupted by someone that has made it very clear they want nothing to do with me," she said, staring me in the eyes and not breaking my gaze. She delivered the words without any emotion and with complete confidence.

I was momentarily taken back with surprise by this new confidence she was displaying that I didn't notice when William had come up behind me until he spoke near my shoulder.

"Excuse me," he said and managed to sneak around me in my attempt to recover. "How's it going?" he asked me as he began to remove items from his bag.

I squinted my eyes. It probably looked like I was scowling but I was really just trying to block out some of the lights that were hurting my eyes.

"We need to talk," I said to Kelly and ignored William.

"No, we don't. I said all I need to say last time. Here are the notes you asked for," Kelly said to William, dismissing me.

When she reached across the table to hand William the pages of notes my hand shot out and I grabbed hold of her arm. In my drunk and high state, I didn't notice how both Kelly and William stiffened at my actions.

"Let her go," William said, his voice lowering with the threat he intended behind them.

"This doesn't concern you," I said quickly and turned away from

183

him, back to Kelly.

"The moment you put your hands on her it concerned me," William said and began to rise from his chair.

"William, I'm fine," Kelly said.

"See. She's fine," I confirmed. The guy needed to chill out.

"Kelly, nothing about this is fine. I'm going to tell you one more time. Let. Her. Go."

William was now standing right next to me. He was slightly shorter than me, but he was no slouch in the fitness department. I looked him over and nearly smirked, completely prepared to do whatever it took to get him out of here. Kelly's voice brought me back to the moment.

"Brad, let me go," she said softly.

I looked at her and saw the fear in her eyes for the first time. Fear that I had put there. Immediately, I released her arm. I shut my eyes in an attempt to turn back the clock and make this whole scene a figment of my imagination. Unfortunately, I didn't have those kind of superpowers and when I opened my eyes I was greeted by the look of concern on Kelly's face and the anger still plastered on William's.

"I can't keep doing this with you Brad. I told you before that I can't just be your friend. Until you figure out what you want, please leave me alone," she practically begged.

Even through the alcohol and pills I could tell that I was hurting her and I took a step forward to reach out to her.

"I think you should go," William interrupted and in an instant the anger was back.

"You don't get to tell me what to do. This is between Kelly and me," I seethed.

"I want you to go," Kelly said, and I swiveled my head back to her in shock.

"Kelly?" My eyes were now begging her to change her mind, but she didn't.

"Please, go."

It was nothing more than a whisper. I saw her eyes begin to water and her lips trembled. She wouldn't look at me. Once again, I took a step forward and raised my hand to reach out for her, but I stopped when the first tear fell.

So much for keeping my promise to Kevin. I stepped away and ran out of that library and tried to chase away the memories.

I spent the next two months ditching classes, skipping out on practice, ignoring Lily's calls and falling further down the rabbit hole. Matt and Serena both tried to get me to talk to them, but I made it clear to them that I wasn't interested. I had even told Serena that Matt was marrying her out of pity and slammed my door in her face. I half expected Matt to come charging into my room to beat the shit out of me but that never happened.

If hitting rock bottom is an actual thing than I hit mine a few weeks before the term was to end for the summer of my second year in college. At that point I had no idea what my grades were, nor did I care. I'd managed to alienate the remaining people that cared for me and all I could see was blood against stark white tiles.

In my mind Kevin hadn't died from a gunshot wound to the temple. No, he had died on the day I discovered him lying in his blood on the bathroom floor. He had died because I had failed to save him. I clutched his letter to me in my hand as I took another long drink from the bottle I was holding. It didn't matter what was in that bottle anymore. It also didn't matter that I had tried, and failed, to break my foot in a mad attempt to get more pain medication. The nurses and doctors had looked at me suspiciously the entire time I sat in the emergency clinic. It was clearly obvious that I was drunk, but

I wasn't nearly high enough to chase away the memories. That was why I needed the pills. I had depleted my latest stash. The doctors really didn't want to prescribe me anything, but the purpling of my left ankle left them no choice. I hadn't broken anything, but I had managed to severely sprain it. Of course, in my current state I wasn't grateful that I had botched my plan. Nope. I was furious with yet another failure.

I read Kevin's words and was struck by how right he was. It didn't matter how hard we tried because it would never be good enough for anyone. We were destined to be nothing but failures, undeserving of love. I was nothing more than a burden to those around me and it would just be better for everyone if I just disappeared for good.

I released Kevin's letter and reached for the orange bottle beside me. I had already taken four of the little round pills. There were maybe ten more in there. The doctors usually gave me a full bottle, but this doctor had been crafty and gave me such a limited supply. I wasn't sure if ten would be enough, but I poured them out onto the floor beside me just the same. I was putting the second pill into my mouth when my phone rang from my desk. I groaned when I heard it because it was interrupting my task.

Ignoring the ringing, I reached for the third pill, but the phone kept on ringing. I couldn't do this with that noise distracting me, so I reached behind me and pulled the phone off the desk I was leaning against.

The intent was to turn the phone off but for some reason I found myself looking at the screen and saw a familiar name blink across it. Closing my eyes, I leaned my head against the side of my desk and let out a breath. Tears were falling down my cheeks and snot dripped from my nose. I set the bottle I was holding aside so I could unlock my phone and answer the call.

"Jenny?" I cried into the phone.

"Brad? Brad what is wrong? Where are you? Kelly called me

and said she was worried and asked me to call you. What is happening?" Jenny asked desperately while I continued to sob into the phone.

"Jenny?"

"Yes, Brad. I'm here. Talk to me," she begged.

"I don't want to die," I managed to whimper.

"Oh, Brad. We don't want that either. Tell me where you are so I can get someone there. Please, Brad, let me help you."

This time, for some reason, I listened to Jenny, and I let her help me. I told her where I was and what I was about to do.

"Listen to me Brad. Pick up every one of those pills and take them to the bathroom right now. Flush them down the toilet. Pour out all the liquor. Do this right now, okay?" She instructed.

"Okay," I sniffled and managed to pull myself up off the ground. I gathered the pills and did as she instructed. It was painful limping to the bathroom, but I ignored the voice in my head that told me one more pill wouldn't hurt. I flushed them and the rest of the liquor down the toilet.

"Now what?" I asked as I stumbled out of the bathroom.

"I want you to go sit on your bed and stay on the phone with me. Is there someone nearby that I can call to come sit with you?"

"I don't know. What day is it? Everyone might be gone already," I said because I couldn't remember if school had ended or not.

"What about your friend? Matt? Is he still there?" Jenny asked.

"He isn't talking to me anymore," I said and put my head in my hand because I was starting to get a headache.

"That's okay. Give me his number so I can call him."

I managed to look through my contact list and give Jenny the number. I heard her talking to her husband about calling the number she gave him and telling Matt to come to my room right away.

"Jenny?"

"Yes, Brad, I'm still here," she answered.

"I messed up really bad," I said.

"It's alright Brad. We will get you help," she replied, trying to soothe me.

"No. No one can help me with this."

"Yes, we can Brad. There are places that help people like you all the time. We can make sure you get the help you need to treat your addiction," she said, and I realized that she and I were talking about two separate things.

"No, Jenny. I'm not talking about the pills. I'm talking about Kelly," I clarified.

"What do you mean Brad?"

"I violated her," I confessed and began to sob uncontrollably.

"No, you didn't," she said with sympathy.

"Yes, I did. On the day of Kevin's funeral. I had sex with her in the bathroom and then I left her there like she was nothing to me, but she isn't nothing, Jenny. She is everything and I'm no good for her. I only bring darkness and pain. Kevin was right. We are just no good for anyone," I sobbed.

"Bradley Jason Klauzek you listen to me, and you listen good. You do not bring darkness and pain to anyone. You are the kindest man I have ever known, and you are loved by many, and I will not let you talk about yourself like that. You are so much more than you think you are and if you ever try to take yourself away from us again, I will kill you, do you hear me?"

Between the sobs and tears, I managed to laugh.

"If I'm already dead you can't kill me," I pointed out.

"Not true. I will bring you back to life and then I will kill you," Jenny said, and I laughed again.

She kept talking to me and about ten minutes later there was a knock on my door, followed by Matt calling out to me. I got off my bed and stumbled to the door. The booze and pills were wearing off so the pain from my ankle was coming through and I was having difficulty moving around. I nearly stumbled into Matt when I opened the door. He caught me and put his arm around me to help me back

188

to the bed.

"Matt's here," I said to Jenny on the phone.

"Okay, good. Give him the phone."

I did as she instructed me and lay back on the bed. While Matt talked to Jenny, I closed my eyes and tried to ignore the pounding in my head and throbbing in my ankle. I really needed another pill, but they were now circling down some pipe.

"I understand. I won't leave him. I'll make sure there is a car for you two at the airport," Matt said and hung up the phone. I could tell he was staring at me even though my eyes were still closed.

"I'm a dick," I said.

"Yeah, well, I already knew that. You also smell like socks that have been left in a pile of cow shit for two months and then set out in the sun," Matt said, and I chuckled.

I opened my eyes and stared at my friend. A friend that I didn't deserve.

"I'm sorry," I said, and fresh tears began to fall.

"You'll make it up to me. And Serena. But right now, we need to get you in the shower," Matt said and helped me stumble my way to the bathroom.

As Matt helped me undress, stand in the shower, and wash the body that I had been abusing for so long, I was struck by what real love looked like. I had said hurtful things to him and his fiancé. I had been pushing him away for months and yet, here he was, washing my naked ass like none of those things had happened. I definitely didn't deserve this kind of friendship.

"You shouldn't be here," I said as he wrapped a towel around me.

"What is that bullshit?" he responded.

"I've treated you and Serena like shit. You should run as fast as you can from me. I'm no good for you," I said and lowered my head, waiting for him to leave.

"Brad, I'm only saying this to you because you are my friend and

189

I love you like a brother. You are a complete jackass. *I* decide who is good for me and who isn't. *I* choose my friends, and *I* choose you, so stop trying to fucking get rid of me because I'm not going anywhere. You're stuck with me for the long haul and if you can't handle that then to fucking bad," Matt said, and he helped me stumble back to my bedroom for clothes.

I had never heard Matt cuss before, so it had an impact on me. He was always the picture of calmness and poise. If he was dropping f-bombs then this shit was serious.

"Can a man love another man without it being weird?" I asked.

"Hell yes we can," he answered and gently placed me down on my bed. He turned and started going through my drawers and closet, looking for clothing.

"When was the last time you did laundry?" he asked.

"What day is it?"

"Point taken," he said and started smelling the items he found. After he identified the least offensive items, he helped me dress and then tucked me into my bed. Yes, a grown man tucked in another grown man and there was nothing weird about it.

I waited for him to leave but he pulled my desk chair over and sat beside the bed.

"What are you doing?" I asked.

"Staying here with you," he answered as if I had asked him the dumbest question.

"What?"

"Really? Are we back to that again? Because you're my friend, jackass, and I care about you," he answered and folded his arms across his chest.

"No. I mean what happens next?"

"Well, Jenny and your sister are on their way here. Once they get here, we will figure out what to do about your classes but I imagine you haven't been going to those," he said and looked at me for confirmation. I nodded and he continued on. "Whatever the university decides about your scholarship and such depends on them, but regardless of that you will go to a rehab program." Matt finished and looked at me pointedly, making sure I knew that was not up for debate.

"I understand," I said.

"I'll call my dad in the morning and get you a spot at his facility. It's a really good place and they can help you, Brad," he said, looking at me for the first time with worry in his eyes.

"Matt?"

"Yeah?"

"You have a really great girl. Don't ever let her go," I replied.

"Not a chance in hell," he said, and I slowly drifted off to sleep.

23

Rehab

Withdrawals are a bitch. There is just no other way to describe the agony I was in. Everything hurt and all I wanted to do was find one of those orange bottles that had brought me release in the past. My hands twitched for the press of a glass bottle. I needed to escape this wrenching pain, but I was encased in a place where I had no access to the things I desired most.

I would cry out for the very people I had pushed away. During the sweats I called out for Kelly and asked her to forgive me, then cursed her in the next breath. I begged Kevin to come back and take away the pain. I even called out to a mother that had never loved me or showed me any affection. It didn't matter that I hadn't heard from her in months, I wanted my mother beside me. In hindsight, I was probably calling out for Lily when I called for my mother, but the facility workers didn't know that and they had to remind me that I couldn't make any phone calls just yet.

Lily and Jenny had shown up within hours of my breakdown. I'm not sure how she managed it, but Lily convinced the Dean to put me on academic probation and let me return to classes in the fall, after my treatment. Matt called his father, and I was whisked away to begin my rehabilitation less than twenty-four hours after my cry for help. I was lucky. It was because of those around me that I was still alive, let alone in a place that could help me.

All three of them came with me to the facility that first day.

Lily had it the hardest. I could tell she was barely holding herself together when we had to say goodbye. She was crying but she kept trying to hide it. After I had said my goodbyes to Jenny and Matt, I went to Lily, and she broke before my very eyes.

"I can't lose you too. I'm just not strong enough for that," she sobbed and wiped the tears away.

"I'm sorry I'm putting you through this," I apologized and hung my head.

"I will go through this a million times over as long as it means you are still in this life," she said and took my hands in hers.

I looked at her and she smiled at me.

"I don't des,"-

"Stop right there," Lily interrupted me. "You do deserve all of us and you need to realize that. You are important. To us, and so many others. We aren't giving up on you," Lily said and squeezed my hands.

"It is time, Brad," Dr. Stone, Matt's father, said behind me.

I nodded and let go of Lily's hands.

"I'll call as soon as they let me," she said and stepped back.

Jenny came forward and took Lily's hand in hers. I tried to reassure them with a smile, but it mostly came out as a pained groan. Between the withdrawals and my ankle, I hurt all over.

Lying in my bed, sweat dripping down, as I writhed in pain I was brought back to that day and how defeated my sister looked. She had already lost one brother and here I was following down the same path. I needed to get through this, for Lily.

The days fell into one another and I lost track of time. I eventually came out of the withdrawal stage and entered full on to anger. I barked at the staff and other patients because all I wanted was to get out of there. Some of the residents tip-toed around me when I entered the common areas because I had developed a reputation for snapping rather quickly.

It had been three weeks since I entered rehab and it was my first day of group therapy. Up until this point I had only done one-on-one sessions with one of the counselors at the center. Dr. Stone finally believed I was ready to do group because I was more in control of my outbursts than I had been previously.

Personally, I dreaded group because I had a hard enough time sharing my emotions and thoughts with a single person, let alone a whole group of people. What made me go through with it, however, was Lily. I had finally gained phone privileges, and she had encouraged me to participate in group when I had spoken to her the night before.

So, I found myself sitting in a circle with Dr. Stone and five other residents. We were called residents, not junkies or patients. Dr. Stone said we weren't ruled by our addiction and the other labels implied that we were, so our official title was resident. I didn't exactly second his belief, but I wasn't the doctor, so I kept my opinions to myself.

"Thank you all for coming," Dr. Stone said when the group session began.

I laughed internally because it wasn't exactly like we had a choice to be here.

"We have a new member this week so I would like to begin today by introducing ourselves and making Brad feel welcome," Dr. Stone continued.

I was sitting in my chair, my legs spread out before me and my arms crossed over my chest. There was no clock in here and it was annoying the hell out of me. This was supposed to last two hours and I really wanted to know what time it was now.

"Jan, will you start us off?" Dr. Stone asked the woman to his right. She nodded and moved up further in her chair.

"I'm Jan. Hello everyone," she said and waved. The group echoed a greeting.

I remained silent.

"I'm an addict and have been since I was thirteen. It started when my father's girlfriend thought it would be funny if she shot me up too. I had seen them get high before, but I really didn't know what they were doing. When Lilah put the tourniquet on me, I didn't know what was going to happen. She injected me and I remember feeling light and free. After that they made sure they shot me up every time they got high. This went on for a couple of years before a teacher of mine noticed the needle marks and called in the authorities. I was taken away from my dad but by then I was already hooked. I spent the next three years in various foster homes and seeking out any drugs I could find. I couldn't get my hands on heroin, so I settled for speed and meth.

"Settled? That sounds funny to me now. Like there is somehow a chart of what drugs are better for you than the others. I was lost, and alone for so long. I thought I deserved the hell I found myself in. Drugs were the only thing that ever loved me, and I loved them. I aged out of the system and ended up on the streets. I spent five years there, chasing my next high and doing whatever it took to score. My come to life moment happened when I was going through a dumpster, looking for some food. A family came out of the restaurant whose dumpster I was looking through and they stopped to stare at me. I was angry at first because they wouldn't just walk away like so many others before them had. The kids looked terrified of me, but their mother started to walk towards me. Her husband tried to pull her back, but she shook him off. She walked up to me like I was a feral cat. I guess I must have looked like one after five years on the streets.

"Anyway, this woman slowly walked up to me with her hands up. Then she did something that nobody had ever done before, she smiled at me. She said if I wanted, she would help me look through the dumpster for something to eat, or I could go with them and she would buy me lunch. I didn't answer her at first because I thought

195

she was playing a game or something. Then, she asked me my name and stuck her hand out. She told me her name and waited for me to respond. I told her. I hadn't told anyone my real name for years, but I told this woman, and I shook her hand. She introduced me to her family, and they took me to the same restaurant they had just left. When the manager tried to kick us out, she fought him. While I ate the family talked to me like I was a person. Even the kids started to ask me questions.

"When we left that restaurant, I thought for sure that would be the end. But I was wrong. The husband asked if I had anywhere to go and I told him I slept in the alley. He told me that wasn't good enough and asked me to go with them. I said no at first, but he insisted. They drove me here. That was two months ago and every visiting day that family has been here to see me. The kids, Kate and Devin, draw me pictures every time and Connie and James tell me they care about me. I didn't even know these people, but they have shown me more kindness then my own father ever did," Jan finished and accepted the tissue that another resident gave her to wipe away her tears.

I had sat up straighter as her story was told but I just couldn't find it in myself to believe her. People like that didn't exist and I wondered if she was a plant by Dr. Stone to get the newcomers to open up. Dr. Stone moved on to the next person and I listened to story after story. Suddenly, it was the guy's turn sitting next to me.

"Hello everyone, I'm Gary. I'm an alcoholic," he said. The group returned the greeting, and I waited.

"I was married for thirty years to the most beautiful woman I have ever met. Thirty years. We had three children. None of them will talk to me now, of course. I don't blame them. I put them and their mother through hell. You see, I didn't just enjoy the occasional drink. No, from the moment I woke up to the time I passed out I had a drink in my hand. I thought it wasn't a big deal because I provided for my family, you know? I made the money and paid the bills. They had a roof over their heads and food in their bellies. So, what if I spent most nights at the bar? So, what if I got mad sometimes and broke things? I was doing my duty, and they didn't want for anything. Thirty years. I thought Carol would be with me forever, but as soon as our youngest had left the house she told me she was leaving. She told me she only stayed because of the kids. She said she hadn't loved me for twenty years. She said I loved the drink more than her and she couldn't live this way anymore. She was going to live with her sister in Poughkeepsie. Who the hell moves to Poughkeepsie? I didn't even know where Poughkeepsie was.

"She left and I found myself alone in a house where my children had been raised but I couldn't remember a single minute of it. The day the divorce papers showed up is the day I checked myself into here. I know I can't get Carol back, but I want my kids to at least talk to me. Right now, they refuse to answer my calls, but I know I need to do this, for me and for them." Gary finished his story and looked at me.

It was now my turn.

After listening to the others, I wasn't sure what I should say. The things that had happened to them seemed so much more monumental then what had happened to me. Besides, I had never spoken to anyone about what haunted me. I wasn't sure I was ready, but all eyes were now on me and it was say something or punk out.

"I'm Brad," I started.

"Hi Brad," the group echoed.

I swallowed and looked at Dr. Stone. He smiled at me encouragingly and looked back at the group. It was now or never.

"I'm an addict," I said.

The breath that escaped me felt like I had released much more than a simple breath. It felt like so much weight had been lifted.

"I wasn't always an addict. I actually used to avoid places that brought me into contact with things that I used to equate to weakness, to my brother," I said and stopped.

197

I had never before acknowledged that I thought my brother had been weak and I was stunned by the revelation. The others waited patiently for me to begin again.

"When I was nine when I found my brother lying on the bathroom floor in his own blood. He had tried to kill himself and hadn't succeeded. He viewed this as a failure for the rest of his life and he let me know that. You see, I was the one that called 9-1-1 and saved his life. I was the one that spoiled his plans and forced him to live. He never actually told me he blamed me for that, but I knew. I knew it every time I looked at him and saw that look in his eyes. He didn't want to be here, and it was because of me he still was. My parents blamed me too. I heard them when they talked about him. They were embarrassed by him and said he should have finished the job. Like he was getting paid to kill himself or something. I was nine and I didn't understand any of that, only that I had parents that would rather see their son dead than be embarrassed by his attempted suicide. I had a brother that would rather be dead than live with me. And I had a sister that had escaped to forget about me. I was surrounded by people that wanted nothing to do with me.

"So, I made myself invisible. If they couldn't see me, they couldn't hurt me. That all changed the day I moved in next to her. Until that day I was content to go through life without people noticing me but from the moment I saw her I only wanted her to notice me. God, did I try to get her to actually see me, but she had eyes for someone else and I sat on the sidelines, waiting. She never did notice me though, not in the way I wanted her too. I was the friend, the surrogate brother, she always wanted. It didn't take long for my life to corrupt what I had with her. I hurt her over and over again and I justified it because she wouldn't look at me the way I wanted her too. I blamed her for everything. When my brother finally managed to end his life, I blamed her. I told myself I could have saved my brother if only I hadn't been distracted by her. But Kevin would have done what he did regardless of what was happening in my life. I actually never told him about Kelly. I think I kept her from him because I didn't want him to ruin things. All my life I thought everything revolved around Kevin and his moods. I thought if I desired something I was being selfish and abandoning my brother, so I hurt her over and over again. After Kevin was gone, and I read his shitty letter to me, I reached for the pills, but I had been lost long before then. I blamed her. I blamed Lily. I blamed my parents, and I blamed Kevin for choices I made, but really the only one to blame is myself.

"There are people in my life that have begged me to let them help me and I pushed them away. Even Kelly was there for me after all the hurt I put her through. Instead of accepting it and telling her how I felt I lied to her and pushed her away again. I used to say it was for the best because I was no good for them, but I was just a coward. For so long I have been afraid to let anyone in because the moment you do they have the power to hurt you. I thought I was doing the right thing but the only reason I am alive today is because the very people I tried to push away refused to give up on me. They loved me anyway and I still don't feel like I deserve that love," I finished.

The room was silent, and I started to squirm from the nerves I felt.

"Thank you, Brad, for sharing your story. Let's now shift topics and talk about our triggers," Dr. Stone took control of the group again. I was grateful for his presence, and I spent the next hour listening to the rest of the group. For some reason, it was easier to confess those things to strangers. I had been carrying them for so long that I needed to unload them. I didn't participate again during that session, but I found I was eager to talk to the group again.

24

Group

"Why won't you let your friend tell Kelly where you are?" Jan asked me during a group session.

A month had passed since my arrival, and I had gained visiting privileges. Of course, Lily was eager to visit. I had told her that, for now, I only wanted her to visit me. I just wasn't ready to see the others.

"Because, Jan, I'm ashamed," I said honestly.

I had stopped holding back during group sessions and found that I enjoyed them more than the weekly one-on-one session I still had with Dr. Stone.

"I get that," Clarence, another group member and my roommate, said as he nodded his head.

"But you have someone out there that is desperately trying to find you. Isn't that what you wanted all along? For her to notice you? Well, she's noticing but you are still keeping her in the dark," Jan said and threw her arms up in frustration.

"It's his choice to tell her," Justice, a shy middle-aged woman replied. She cowered slightly when Jan's glare turned towards her.

"Jan, it is important to remember that control won't always be a possibility," Dr. Stone reminded her.

Now that Jan was clean, she was battling with control issues. For someone who spent so long out of control she desperately wanted to ensure her environment developed a certain way.

"I know. I know. I just don't understand it. I would have given anything to have someone care about me the way this girl cares for him. I don't understand your hesitation," Jan said and sat back in her chair.

"I understand," Gary said. Aside from the first group session I attended, Gary was by far the most reluctant to contribute. So, we all turned to him when he spoke up.

"Even though my kids know I'm a drunk, and have known for years, I don't want to tell them where I'm at. My dad taught me to be 'a man' and a man doesn't admit his weakness," Gary finished.

"Is that why you won't tell her? Because you think it makes you less of a man?" Jan asked me.

"Sort of. I've already done so many hurtful things to her. I don't want to add one more thing to the long list. Maybe it's easier to have her thinking I don't want anything to do with her than it would be to have her tell me, once again, that she doesn't have the same feelings as I do. I don't know. But I do know that I'm not ready to talk to her."

"That is an excellent observation, Brad. I'm sure you have all experienced this same thing at some point. There is no magic formula in determining when one is ready to communicate with their loved ones. However, that is a part of the healing process. Brad, I encourage you to write down the things you wish you could say to Kelly. This will help you prepare for the time when the actual conversation occurs. Now, let's all take out the project I gave you from last session," Dr. Stone said, and the residents began shuffling in their chairs to remove folded up pieces of paper from their pockets.

I did the same.

"Clarence, would you mind starting us off," Dr. Stone said, and Clarence cleared his throat. He held his unfolded paper before him and read what he wrote.

"Clarence, I'm sorry I told you crack was good. I'm sorry I made you hurt your girlfriend because the drugs had you believing she was a demon sent from hell to castrate you. I'm sorry I got you in trouble at work and lost everything you had worked for. I'm sorry I got you arrested, but I'm not sorry that arrest finally got you the help you needed. I'm glad that Shanice has forgiven you," Clarence coughed and folded his paper back up.

"Very good Clarence. Can you now share your goals for the future," Dr. Stone encouraged Clarence to continue.

"Yeah, sure, Doc. I know Shanice and me are done but I want our baby girl to know her daddy loves her and will take care of her. So, I'm going to complete all the therapy sessions my firm has placed, get back to work and make my daughter the center instead of the drugs. This may be crazy, but I also want my mother to move in with me. She is getting older and needs someone there for her. I thought, maybe we could both be there for each other. Besides, I know she would love to be near her grandbaby," Clarence finished.

"Thank you for sharing with us Clarence. Brad, would you go next?" Dr. Stone turned to me.

I unfolded my paper but hesitated.

"Brad, is everything alright?" Dr. Stone asked.

I stared down at the paper I held and shook my head.

"I'm not sure. I want to read this, but I don't know if I believe it yet," I said.

"That is perfectly fine. You hold on to it and when you feel you are ready you can share it with the group. Justice, can you continue for us?" Dr. Stone turned his attention to the next resident, and I put my paper back in my pocket.

I was making progress, but there were still some things I wasn't ready for.

The days continued on. Lily kept her word and visited me every weekend. I told her she didn't have to, but she told me she did and nothing I could say would keep her away. Jenny came to visit me as well. She begged me to let her tell Kelly where I was, but I made her promise she wouldn't. Jenny told me Kelly would call her and demand answers, but Jenny kept her promise and never revealed my whereabouts. I hated asking Jenny to betray Kelly, but I just wasn't ready to face her yet.

My time at the center was drawing to a close and while I felt ready to return to college, I wasn't sure I was ready to function without the support of the connections I had made while in therapy. Dr. Stone had managed to set me up with a counselor and group closer to my college, but I worried it wouldn't be the same. He assured me that I needed to allow the process to work, and that life wasn't built on guarantees. He told me I needed to realize our realities weren't always going to go as planned and that I needed to accept things would be okay, even if I wasn't pleased with the results. I heard what he was saying but there was still a part of me that feared the moments when I lost control. I didn't want to go back to the person I was, but I still didn't know what kind of person I wanted to be.

I discovered my answer in the strangest of places. Since I had been in rehab, I wasn't able to return to work with Reyann and Jeff. Of course, I allowed Lily to tell them what was going on because I didn't want them to worry. The week before I was scheduled for release Jeff came to visit me. After our initial greeting he walked around the room I shared with Clarence. He examined the few personal items my roommate had on his nightstand before turning to me.

"You think you're ready for the outside again?" he asked and gestured towards the world visible from my window.

"I don't know," I shrugged.

"Fair enough. Reyann told me to tell you she doesn't pay you to go on vacation. I told her that was insensitive, but she said if I didn't tell you she would dock my pay. We missed you, little dude," Jeff said and sat down beside me on my bed.

"Thanks."

"Yeah, well, you aren't just an employee, you know," Jeff said.

"Okay."

Jeff looked at me skeptically before punching me in the shoulder.

"You still think you are just a number on a tax form to us? Reyann considers you the son she wished she had. She's always on my case about how much better you are at things than I am. And, well, Tom is the black sheep, and you know what she thinks of him," Jeff said and raised his eyebrows.

"She loves him," I said.

"Of course she loves him. He is her son. She loves you too. And I, well, I'm fond of you," Jeff said and shrugged. He seemed to be a bit uncomfortable, and he stood. After taking a few steps towards the door he turned and came back to stand before me.

"Why didn't you call me?" He held his hands out before him, palms up.

"I didn't know I could," I admitted.

"Bullshit! You're my brother," he said, like it was a fact. He must have noticed the confusion in my face because he sighed and sat down beside me again.

"I know we aren't blood or anything but there isn't anything I wouldn't do for you that I wouldn't do for Tom. Brothers don't have to be related. You can always call me," Jeff said.

"I don't think I could. It would be…weird," I said.

"Why?"

"Because I had a brother. I don't know if I'm ready for another one," I said flatly.

"Yeah, what happened sucked, and he was real selfish to put all this on you. Just because you had one brother doesn't mean you can't have another," Jeff said.

"He told me to forget about him," I whispered.

I hadn't shared with anyone what Kevin had written to me and I don't know why I chose that moment and Jeff to reveal the catalyst for my downward spiral.

"Well, that was dumb. He's your brother. Of course you aren't going to forget about him," Jeff said like it was the simplest thing in the word to understand.

"He tried to do it before, twice. I was the one that found him in the bathroom the first time he did it. I wish I could forget finding him like that. I've tried to forget it but no matter what I do the images keep returning," I replied and tapped my forehead with my index finger for emphasis.

Jeff nodded, letting me know he understood that I'm telling him this is why I took the pills.

"Look, I'm not going to pretend to understand what was going on in his head or why he felt he had to do what he did. I don't know anything about wanting to end your life. But I do know a little bit about being a big brother. If Tom pulled this shit, I don't know what I would do and I don't know if I could have handled it for as long as you did. It's a shit thing your brother did to you and your sister. It sounds like he was sick, and no amount of sibling love was going to change that. You did all you could. In fact, you did more than you should have done. Your brother shouldn't be the cause of your misery.

"I love Tom more than I love myself but there comes a time when you have to just accept them as they are and realize you can't make them change. Kevin twisted his feelings and thought he was doing what he did out of love but that isn't the right kind of love. What you and Lily did, now that was love at its best; unselfish and

205

self-sacrificing. They say we hurt the ones we love the most, but I think that's crap. In the end, you ended up hurting yourself the most by allowing your entire world to be about Kevin. You treated others like shit, sure, but they are alright. It's you that is sitting in this place trying to forget a brother that you loved more than your own life.

"As for that letter Kevin wrote you, you can't take any of it seriously. He wrote it during his worst moment and while it may say he was thinking of what was best for you, he wasn't. He used you and your sister as justification to do what he did and that's the mark of a sick man. His thoughts and feelings had nothing to do with you. I know you think you failed him, but he failed you, man. Maybe it's time you stop the twisted cycle. Remember him during the good times and accept that the bad times weren't his entire identity. And Brad, you need to stop seeing yourself as the villain in this. You were just a kid. You've carried this with you long enough. How much longer are you gonna punish yourself for things that were never in your control?" Jeff placed his hand on my shoulder, and I turned to look at him, tears forming.

"I'm not Kevin. I'll never try to be. But, I'm here and if you ever need me I'll come, because that is what brothers are supposed to do for each other," he said and clapped my shoulder once more before removing his hand and standing. "Now, I'm starved. What kind of food does this place have?"

I laughed, wiped my eyes and stood. We had lunch together and he left two hours later with a promise to be there on the day of my release. He hugged me goodbye and while it was a little awkward at first it quickly morphed into the parting I had so often seen between him and Tom. He even gave me the customary brother shoulder punch the two of them engage in. I found myself smiling at Jeff's departing back while I rubbed my throbbing shoulder.

For the first time, I understood what if felt like to watch a brother walk away and not feel panicked that this would be the last time you ever saw each other. I knew I would see Jeff again and I also knew that his affection came without strings. For the second time in my life, I felt a burden released and it was replaced with a sense of hope.

25

Junior

Dr. Stone and the others at the center had bid me farewell on my final day. Gary had even given me a hug and told me not to repeat his mistakes. He told me to go after the girl and treat her like she deserves. He said there was only room for one idiot in our group, and that spot was reserved for him. I was surprised by the hug and didn't get a chance to respond before he walked away. Gary still had a long way to go before he forgave himself. I still hadn't read the apology letter to myself. I suppose I wasn't quite ready to forgive myself either, but I was working on it.

Lily and Jeff were both there to take me home. I had moved in with Jeff after the fiasco with my parents at Kevin's funeral and he told me my room was still available. I was only going to stay with him for a week before I returned to school. Somehow my amazing sister had managed to secure my place at college and on the track team. I was on academic probation and had to maintain a 3.5 grade point average in order to keep my scholarship, but I was hopeful I could do it.

There was only one detail I was dreading about returning to school. I knew that it was only a matter of time before I crossed paths with Kelly. I still hadn't allowed Jenny to tell her where I had been, or what I was doing. Jenny told me that Kelly no longer asked about me when they talked. A part of me felt hurt by that but the other, more controlled, part of me wanted to believe that she was finally moving on and living the life she deserved.

Dr. Stone had told me that I had a tendency to catastrophize things to the point where I believed the only course of action was to disappear. He said it was most likely a response to the childhood I had. I was programmed to be silent, to disappear, when my parents became uncomfortable, or annoyed with me. Dr. Stone said I carried this behavior with me into adulthood and used it as a coping device. It was a piss-poor one and didn't get to the root of the underlying issues I had. I recognized the behavior for what it was now, but I still struggled with correcting my response.

Another aspect I feared that would hinder my reentry into the life I had before my downward spiral was the absence of Matt. He and Serena had graduated and would no longer be close by. Of course, I was still in contact with Matt on a regular basis and sometimes Serena would talk to me. Matt had told her what had happened, and he assured me she would not tell Kelly. Of course, Serena had spent nearly twenty minutes yelling at me for being beyond stupid. She didn't like that I was keeping this from Kelly, and she really didn't like that I was asking her to keep it from Kelly.

"She's my best friend and I don't like lying to my best friend," she scolded through the phone.

"I know. I'm sorry you have to do this," I replied, and I truly meant the apology. I knew the difficult position I was putting everyone in by asking them not tell Kelly about my addiction.

"I'm not doing this for you. I'm not even doing this for Matt. I'm doing this for Kelly. She's finally in a good place and I know her. If I tell her what happened and where you were at, she will come rushing to your side and put aside her own happiness once again. She has a weakness for you, and she deserves a life outside your needs," Serena said, the calm returning to her voice.

"You're absolutely right," I agreed.

"Of course I'm right." She declared and gave the phone back to

Matt.

"Do you think you are going to see her?" Matt asked me.

"No. Serena's right. I need to give her a chance to live her life without me."

And that is what I did. I returned to school and did not seek Kelly out. I dedicated myself to my studies and earning back my teammates trust. They had witnessed my slow decline and some had even tried to reach out but I had done what I always did and pushed them away.

"I'm glad you got your shit together," Terrence, my former roommate, said to me one day after a practice. We had finished our run and were trying to catch our breath. I took a drink of water, offered it to him and began to stretch out.

"Yeah, I was a mess. Sorry for all the crap I put you guys through," I said to the few guys that had gathered around us.

"It's all good," Derek, a guy who had joined the team late last year, said. "Your running has improved since then."

"Yeah. It probably helps he's staying in a straight line," Clark, another former roommate of mine, joked as he slapped a hand on my back.

I grinned at him, but he was accurate. A few months ago, I rarely ran with a purpose other than to forget the nightmares that haunted my waking hours. Direction had been lost to me then.

"How's Addy," I asked Clark, changing the subject from my drunken running to his girlfriend.

Clark's grin fell and Terrence sucked in his breath. I glanced around at the guys and saw the looks on their faces. I had definitely stumbled into something.

"What?" I asked.

"Addy and Clark aren't together anymore," Terrence answered.

"Oh."

Derek, the new guy, changed the subject and the guys began gathering their things and dispersed. I didn't know what had happened between Clark and Addy and I didn't ask. I had plenty of my own baggage to deal with.

The days developed into a routine. I woke, went for a run, showered, went to class, ate lunch, went to class, went to practice, showered, went to therapy, ate dinner, studied then went to bed. Rinse. Repeat. I usually heard from Lily, Jenny or Matt on a daily basis. It almost seemed like their calls had been coordinated before-hand. I wouldn't put it past my sister to have developed some sort of schedule with the others, just as we had done with Kevin. I didn't ask about it because I recognized it for what it was. Lily needed this in order to feel I was doing okay. So, I always answered their calls and talked about my day. On the weekends I would talk to Jeff and Reyann. On some weekends Jeff would drive up and visit me. He always came prepared with some new adventure Reyann had discovered for us. While neither one of us was particularly interested in the sites, we did it because we were both afraid of incurring the wrath of Reyann.

I went through the motions, time passed, and reality found me one day when the new guy on the team approached me after practice, when the others had begun to depart.

"Hey, Brad, can I talk to you for a moment," Derek asked.

I was putting my things away in my bag and was barely paying attention to him when I said, "Yeah, sure."

Thinking he was going to ask me about an upcoming meet or something related to the team, I wasn't prepared when Kelly's name spilled out of his lips.

"So, I've been seeing this girl and some of the guys let me know that she and you kind of had a thing a year ago. They made it sound like it was pretty serious, and I just figured it would be best if you heard about it from me, you know? The team has some good cohesion, and I don't want to mess with that. I thought it best that I come to you and tell you straight up about Kelly and me," he said.

Stunned, I dropped my bag. Fumbling, I picked it up and clutched my fingers around the strap as tightly as I could. Doing my best to keep the fact that his news was nearly crushing me, I gave my best attempt at a friendly smile. The guy was doing the decent thing, approaching me and telling me himself. He could have punked out and just pretended he wasn't dating a teammate's former…

Former what?

Kelly had never been my girlfriend. We had no relations between us. And she wasn't even technically my friend anymore. The only thing that connected was a past that I had yet to come to terms with. It wasn't right for me to keep holding on to her, denying her a chance at something that had the potential to be great.

Derek seemed like a nice guy. The fact he was standing in front of me proved that. Maybe this guy was the kind of guy she truly deserved.

Maybe it wasn't up to me. It was up to her, and I shouldn't get in the way.

"Yeah, we were friends. I appreciate you letting me know, but there is no issue here. It's between you and Kelly," I told him. Surprisingly, the words came out easier than I thought they would.

Derek slowly nodded and visibly relaxed after I spoke. He thought my reaction was going to be something else entirely. I wondered if that was because Clark or Terrence had told him what had happened the previous year, and how much I had been affected by my friendship with Kelly.

I didn't ask him, and he didn't stick around to tell me. He said he would see me later and left. For days I played that scene over in my head and wondered if maybe I should have responded differently. But I knew I wasn't ready to be the man Kelly deserved, the kind of man I was trying to be. I didn't know if I would ever be ready and holding her hostage in my dreams was not fair to either one of us.

I know I made the right decision.

One day, nearly a month later, I was getting a coffee from a rolling cart when I heard my name called from behind me. I won't lie. A part of me thought it was Kelly, and my heart stopped for a single moment. I wasn't prepared to see her, but I also desperately wanted to talk to her. I had managed to avoid her because Jenny had told me her schedule and where her dormitory was. I made sure I wasn't in the same part of campus she would be in. I turned to the voice with thoughts of Kelly in my head. When I saw Addy standing there, I wasn't sure if I was disappointed or relieved.

"Brad, it's Addy," she said because I hadn't reacted to her yet. She must have thought I didn't remember her.

"I know. Sorry. How've you been?" I asked her.

She smiled and stepped forward to place her order with the barista.

"I'm doing okay. I haven't seen you in a while. Where did you disappear to?" she asked, still smiling at me.

I don't know why I answered her the way I did. Maybe it was because she had always been so nice to me and had been concerned for me long before others had been paying attention. Whatever the reason, I didn't do my usual dodge.

"Rehab," I answered truthfully.

Addy paused in the middle of handing her money to the barista and stared at me. She quickly recovered, handed over her money and took her coffee. She thanked the barista and gestured to a nearby bench. I nodded and followed her. We sat down and drank some coffee in silence for a little bit.

"I'm glad you got some help. I was really worried about you," she said and put the lid back on her coffee.

"Yeah. Sorry about how awful I was to you. I wasn't exactly the greatest person back then."

She just continued to smile at me as she said I was forgiven and asked what I had been doing lately.

"Mostly just practice, studying and therapy," I said.

"I understand that. I don't really get out much either."

"Why is that?" I asked the question without intending to cause pain, but her expression changed, and she stopped smiling. She suddenly looked so sad, and I felt like a dick for making her sad.

"I'm sorry. I didn't mean anything."

"You didn't do anything. I've just had a rough time of things lately, I guess. Clark and I aren't together anymore," she said, looking down at her coffee cup. I watched her fingers fiddle with the open flap.

"I heard."

"He told you?" she asked, her head snapping up.

"No. Terrence did. I mean, Clark was there but he didn't say anything," I replied. She sighed and her shoulders released their tension.

"Sorry. I probably seem like a crazy person right now."

"You don't seem crazy. You seem sad," I said and placed my hand on hers to quiet the obvious nerves she was experiencing. She stopped fiddling with the flap and instead intertwined her fingers with mine.

"I am sad," she admitted and I saw the slow tears begin to fall.

"Me too," I told her and she looked at me with a tentative smile.

We just sat there on that bench, holding hands and drinking our coffee. Perhaps it was our pain that brought us together or the journey of healing we were on, but Addy and I began to spend more time together.

At first, we would meet for coffee and study together. Soon after we began sharing meals together and sometimes, I would go with her to social gatherings. It was only with Addy that I would go places I knew large groups would be. I didn't drink. I told Addy she could if she wanted to, but she never did. She always seemed to know just when I would reach my threshold for socializing, and she would manage to say her goodbyes with ease. I told her she could stay but she never did. She always left with me, and I would walk her back to her room. Sometimes we would hold hands when we walked but we would always part ways at her door.

One night, after returning from a gathering in which she had run into Clark and his new girlfriend, she invited me into her room. I released her hand and took a step back.

"I don't think I should," I said and put my hands in my pockets.

"Please, Brad. I don't want to be alone tonight," she said.

I saw the tears on her cheek and just nodded my agreement. She moved aside and I stepped into her room. She had a roommate, but the roommate went home on the weekends. The room was dark, and the silence was so deep that every move Addy made sounded ten times louder than it should. I stood in the middle of her room, my hands in my pockets, not sure where to go.

Addy put her purse down on a chair and turned on the lights. I blinked as my eyes adjusted and watched her disappear into the bathroom. I stayed glued to my spot while I listened to the sounds of Addy getting ready for bed in the bathroom. She exited, wearing a T-shirt and shorts, no longer crying. She had removed the makeup from her face and put her light brown hair into a ponytail. She walked past me to her bed and began pulling the covers down.

"You can sleep in Jessa's bed if you want," she said, her back to me. I turned and looked at her roommate's bed behind me.

"Okay."

"Can you sleep in mine instead?"

I turned back to Addy and saw the same deep sadness in her eyes that I had seen that day on the bench.

"Okay," I said and watched as she climbed into her bed.

I finally took my hands out of my pockets, walked to her bed, sat down and began removing my shoes. Addy held the covers while I placed my legs beneath them. Once I settled, she draped the covers over me.

We lay there in silence, the light on her desk still glowing. I stared up at the ceiling and remained stiff beside her. I wasn't sure what was happening here, so I just remained still.

"I saw them together and it just brought everything back to the surface," Addy finally spoke.

I turned my head to her and saw she was staring at the ceiling too. Despite spending time with her these last few weeks Addy had never revealed to me the particulars of her split with Clark.

"I really loved him," she sobbed.

"I know."

She wiped away some tears before speaking again.

"I was pregnant," she said softly as more tears fell.

I wanted to reach for her hand then, but she had them clasped together on her chest. I recognized the pose for what it was. She was holding on tightly so she wouldn't fall apart completely while she told me about her pain.

"He didn't take it well. He was mad at first and just kept shouting how a baby would ruin his life. He eventually calmed down, but he never really was okay with it. Things didn't exactly get better between us, but he stayed with me. I was into my third month when I lost it. Lost her," her voiced wavered and she took a calming breath before she continued on. "He freaked when he saw the blood and rushed me to the ER but it was too late. I sat in that hospital bed and watched his face when the doctor told us I had miscarried. I saw the moment when the concern left his eyes and relief replaced it. He was relieved that the baby that was ruining his life was now gone.

"Driving away from the hospital I knew there was no going back. He tried to tell me things would be alright. He told me we could just go back to the way things used to be before. He wanted to just move on and forget any of that had ever happened, like there had never been a baby in the first place. I couldn't do that, and I couldn't look at him the same anymore. When things got tough, he fell apart, and he wasn't the person I loved. We broke up. Over the summer I started having severe cramps and abnormal bleeding. The doctors discovered abnormalities with my uterus that were irreversible, and I had surgery. I can't have children anymore and every time I see him all I can think about is the one and only baby I will ever carry and how I lost her. How he never wanted her to begin with."

Addy broke apart then and her body shook from the sobs. I reached for her, and she came into my arms. She tucked her head into my shoulder and wrapped her arms around me. I kissed the top of her head and held on to her while she cried. I didn't tell her it was going to be okay because I knew it wouldn't be. This was a hurt that she would carry the rest of her life and there were no words that could make it better. I cursed Clark for his selfishness.

She eventually cried herself to sleep and I turned off the lamp. I held her in my arms that night and took comfort from the warmth of her body against mine. For so long I hadn't been in any condition to offer support to someone else. I was grateful that, for once, I was able to be there when it counted.

When I woke in the morning Addy was still lying beside me. She was awake and staring at me. She smiled at me when I opened my eyes, and I smiled back at her. Silently, she reached up and put her hand on my cheek. I must have startled a little because she released a small chuckle as she stroked my cheek. I didn't stop her as she moved closer and placed a soft kiss on my lips.

She moved back but continued to stroke my cheek. She moved her thumb over my lips; her eyes followed the path of her thumb. My mind was telling me to stop this, but my body reacted differently from her touch. It had been so long since anyone had touched me so affectionately.

"Addy, I,"- She cut me off by placing a finger on my lips to silence me.

"I'm not asking you to love me. I know neither one of us can give the other what we really want. We are both still in love with other people, but we can't have them. I'm not asking for forever, Brad. I'm only asking for a glimmer of something other than pain and regret. We may not be able to forget but we also don't have to be alone," she said and moved her hand from my cheek to my chest.

I looked down at her hand and then back to her eyes. It was me that initiated the next kiss and she leaned into me further. Her hands wrapped around the bottom of my shirt, and she lifted it up off of my body. I threw it to the floor and went back to her. We repositioned our bodies and I was lying over her, kissing her. She returned every kiss with a hunger that was both desperate and filled with pain. I reached down and caressed her side, moving my hand beneath her shirt to cup her breast. She gasped when I squeezed her nipple, and I inhaled the gasp into my mouth.

This felt different than all the times before. It wasn't love, not in the sense she had Clark, but it was something meaningful. I knew this mattered to both of us. And for the first time, I didn't think about someone else beneath me, wish for her touch. I was present with Addy and whatever misgivings I had moments earlier no longer lingered.

I leaned back so I could remove her shirt. She lifted herself slightly off the bed and threw her shirt onto the floor with mine. This time I ran both hands up her body and kissed a trail from her stomach up to her jaw and ended with her lips. She bit my lip slightly and this time I gasped. Her hands were on their own journey of discovery and they dove into my shorts. She cupped my erection as she leaned up and took my mouth with hers.

"If you keep that up, I won't last much longer," I said into her ear as she moved her hand back and forth.

She smiled at me, removed her hand and shoved my chest. We rolled and this time she was the one lying atop me, straddling me. She smiled at me as she removed my shorts. I watched her lean forward and she kissed my thighs. My dick jumped, literally jumped, from the contact. She wasn't even touching it, and she made it jump. I had slept with many women, but I had never really let them explore my body. I had never wanted them to take their time with me, and I certainly hadn't wanted to take my time with them. What Addy and I were doing was new to me.

Her tongue slicked up my length and I sucked breath in between my teeth and my dick jumped again. She took me into her mouth and the warmth of her lips enveloped me. I gripped the edges of her mattress and raised my hips up. She sucked and I held my breath.

When I reached the point just before breaking, I reached out and gently pulled her up to me. I kissed her and brushed some lose strands of hair away from her face. I was naked before her, but she still had on her own pair of shorts. I glanced down at the clothes she still wore and groaned slightly.

"I really want to continue but I don't have any protection," I said regrettably.

"There's no need," she said softly, and I mentally kicked myself for reminding her that she could no longer have children.

Quickly, I reached for her and spun us around, so her back was now on the mattress. Without another word I removed her shorts, spread her legs and brought my mouth between her legs. I didn't give her a chance to say anything or think any more about her sorrows. I gave to her what she had just given me. I felt her fingers moving in my hair and when she felt pleasure she would grip onto my hair while her legs tensed around me.

"Brad," she whimpered, and I knew she was telling me she was ready. I moved up her body and used one hand to open her legs further. With a kiss on her lips, I pushed inside her.

She cried out and crushed my lips to hers again. I took her leg and wrapped it around me as I continued to plunge inside her. She wrapped her arms around my neck as I developed a rhythm.

This was the closest I had ever come to actually making love to a woman and I couldn't look her in the eyes. I wanted to, wanted to give myself completely to her, but there was still something inside that held back.

With my eyes closed I listened to Addy as she climaxed, and a name escaped her lips. The name wasn't mine, but I ignored it. When she said his name, I understood she hadn't uttered it because she wanted him. She was saying goodbye, releasing the hold he had on her.

Afterward, I lay on top of Addy and told my chest to stop thumping. Once my breathing evened out, I pulled out of her and rolled to the other side of the bed. I didn't know what to say to her. Now that we were finished the doubts seeped in. She must have read the concern on my face because she reached out and intertwined her fingers with mine.

"It's okay, Brad. Sometimes people just need to feel again. Let's promise each other that the moment this becomes something other than comforting we end it. We don't have to be anything more to each other than a friendly ear and a sympathetic touch," she said and smiled at me.

It was her smile that made the dark thoughts disappear. She had the most welcoming smile that was also vulnerable at the same time. I squeezed her hand and agreed to the promise.

When I left, I kissed her goodbye at the door. Something else I had never done before.

That was how I went from addiction to avoidance. With Addy there it was easy to forget that I still had a lot left to atone for. She became my distraction. We would often fall into each other's arms if the thoughts overwhelmed us. We connected in those intimate moments, and there came a point when we were both fully present. It wasn't long before we spent nearly every night together. Sometimes we would just hold one another while we slept.

I would later come to understand that it was Addy who broke through my walls and taught me the difference between the good and bad touches. I don't mean acts of violence against another, but how a touch could be hollow and meaningless, as opposed to the kind that held true feeling in them. Sex to me had just been an act of release before. I never understood how it could connect two people in more ways than just with bodies. But with Addy, I was connected, and I didn't fear it.

Our arrangement did have another unintended positive aspect. I had never before spent an entire night with another person in my bed. Therefore, no one had ever witnessed my night terrors. The first night it happened with Addy there I was embarrassed. I had woken up in a sweat with a scream on my lips. I bolted up right and was already reaching for my running shoes when I felt Addy's hand take hold of mine. I looked at our hands and then at her. She was concerned but she didn't say anything. She got out of bed, picked up my shoes, knelt before me and put my shoes on for me. I watched her get dressed and put on her own shoes. I was confused as she held her hand out to me.

"No more running alone," she said and waited for me.

Slowly, I placed my hand in hers and let her guide me out into the night. I hadn't expected her to keep pace with me, but she did.

We ran for two miles.

In the past I would have run further than that. I would have run until I had nothing left in me but for some reason, with Addy by my side, I hadn't felt the driving force to keep going. When we got back to my dormitory I told her about the nightmares.

"You've had them for that long?" she asked as we slowly walked around campus.

"Yes. Ever since I found him in the bathroom."

"Did you ever tell him about them?"

"Tell Kevin?" I asked, horrified.

"Yes. Did you ever tell him how that had affected you?"

"Of course not."

"Why not?"

"Because he didn't need to know that. He had enough to deal with," I explained.

"Hmm," she said and kicked a pebble with her toe.

"What?" I asked. It was obvious she had more to say.

"Well, it just seems to me that you used his condition as an excuse to avoid your own. You're doing it again, you know."

"How so?" I asked, curious. Kevin was dead. How could I be avoiding it again?

"With Kelly. You've been back now for months but you still haven't gone to her or let anyone else tell her the truth about where you were," Addy said.

"She's dating Derek now. He came up to me at practice and asked me about her. He wanted to make sure I would be okay with them dating. I told him I was. He's a good guy and she deserves to be happy," I said, and I believed every word. Kelly didn't need me coming around and screwing with her life again.

"And what do you deserve, Brad?" she asked me point blank.

I stopped walking and stared at her back as she kept moving. Once she noticed I had stopped, she turned to look back at me.

"I don't know," I answered, and I saw the compassion in her

eyes as she walked back to me. She took my hands in hers.

"You deserve to be happy too. And if you think finding your happiness has anything to do with Kelly then you need to risk it and go to her. It's time to stop avoiding the things that are unavoidable. You will always have regret in your life until you stop running. No more running," she said and reached up to gently touch my cheek.

She smiled at me, and I smiled back.

"I'm sorry," I said to her and placed my hand over hers.

"For what?" she asked and tilted her head in confusion.

"You are simply amazing, and I think in another time, maybe another life, I would have loved you," I said, and she still smiled at me, even as I was rejecting her in a way.

"We weren't meant to love each other, not like that. But I do think we were meant to find one another during our broken parts. You've given me so much, Brad. I had lost myself for so long but, somehow, during this time with you the pieces have been coming back together. Because of you, I know that there is life after loss, and I'm ready to step back into that life," she said.

We continued our walk, still holding hands. While we didn't say another word on that walk, we both knew that our time together was drawing to a close. There was nothing more we could give the other.

It was time we found out how to stand on our own.

26

The End of Avoidance

In group, with Dr. Stone, Jan had described the day she had been brought to the facility as her come to life moment. She had equated her lowest point and her rescue in the same context and believed the two moments were linked. Listening to her story I became convinced that my come to life moment had been crying on the floor, whiskey bottle in one hand and pills in the other, reaching out for a phone that I hadn't wanted to hear. I thought Jen's call that night had been my rescue during what I believed had been my lowest point.

Turned out, I was wrong.

Despite my conversation with Addy and our acceptance of needing to stand on our own, we continued to exist in the insular universe we had created for each other. She still held on to the pain of her loss and broke every time she saw Clark around campus, not because she missed him, but because she longed for the child that would never be. I still continued to avoid the places I knew Kelly would be. She was still dating Derek and while I interacted with him during team events, we never again discussed Kelly. He seemed content, just as I was, to pretend there wasn't this tension between us in the form of a blonde pixie whom I used to call short-cake and tease regularly.

I would often overhear Derek talking to other teammates about Kelly. It usually involved things they would be doing that weekend,

224

or the parties they would be attending together. One day, Kendrick, another teammate was giving Derek shit about how he had flaked out on them because he was in love and had time only for his girlfriend. I doubt they knew I was nearby because these conversations would typically end once I came into earshot. This time, though, they continued talking.

"So, what if I love her? She is definitely better to look at then your ugly mug," Derek responded, and Kendrick laughed.

"Yeah. She is a fine specimen of a woman. How did you land her again? Because your just as ugly as I am so I don't understand what she sees in you. It's your dick, isn't it? She's fallen for 'The Major'?" Kendrick joked.

"'The Major'? What the hell is that?" Derek asked, standing up from his stretch.

"It's your junk, man. What? That's what I call mine. What do you call yours?" Kendrick asked as he pulled an arm across his body.

"Nothing because I'm a grown man and not a juvenile that finds vindication in the size of his penis, or naming it," Derek ribbed.

"I bet Kelly has a name for it."

"Okay. I'm done discussing my penis with you. Can we run now?" Derek asked and they took off running, Kendrick's laugh echoing behind them.

I stood there staring after their disappearing forms.

Hearing Derek say he loved Kelly snapped me out of the fog I had existed in with Addy since I returned from rehab. It was easy to avoid the feelings I still had for Kelly as long as I didn't see her, hear her name or admit that she was in a healthy relationship with a great guy. But hearing Derek so openly admit his feelings for Kelly had snapped the curtain I had been using to cover what had been so obvious to Dr. Stone, Jen, and even Addy. I couldn't truly heal if I continued to avoid Kelly and the feelings I still had.

My past, and my present, was still so very much wrapped up in her. As I began to follow the same path Derek and Kendrick had just run down it occurred to me that I was falling into an old familiar pattern. When I had been drinking, I would often see or hear about Kelly with some other guy and I would use that as an excuse to go to her and it always ended in disaster. I believed that it had ended so badly in the past because I had been drunk, or high, when I went to her in my altered state. They weren't my finest moments, but I honestly believed this time would be different. This time I wouldn't be drunk. This time I would go to her with a clear head, and I wouldn't react with anger or spew out accusations. This time I would tell her the truth. This time I would stop avoiding my feelings.

That is how I found myself going to a diner a few days later. A diner that I knew Kelly would be at because Derek had told Kendrick he was meeting Kelly there after our meet. I suggested to the rest of the team that we go there too and get some food to refuel. No one thought anything of me making the suggestion because I had never discussed Kelly in front of them. They didn't know that the real reason I wanted to go there was because I wanted to see Derek's girlfriend. They honestly believed I was hungry.

Addy knew better though. She had come to the meet to cheer us on, and she pulled me aside after the others started to disperse to their vehicles. She waited until we were alone before she questioned me.

"What do you think you're doing? This isn't your best idea," she said, dropping my hand.

"I know. It's time. I need to talk to her, to tell her how I feel," I said and nervously ran my fingers through my hair. I was beginning to doubt my plan. Well, this wasn't exactly a plan but rather a spur of the moment impulse.

"And you can't wait to do it when you won't be blindsiding her and Derek?" Addy pointed out the absurdity of my plan.

"I just don't think I can put this off any longer," I shrugged.

"I admire your gusto, Brad, but your timing sucks. Okay. Well, if

226

this is something you need to do tonight then let's do this. Put your game face on," she said, slapped my ass and walked over to my truck.

I chuckled as I watched her put her seatbelt on and grin at me. She really was a special girl. Whoever she ended up falling in love with again would be a lucky man. I was grateful to her for being my friend these last few months and saddened by the realization that if things went as I hoped with Kelly, I wouldn't be able to continue my friendship with Addy. What I had with Addy would only interfere with what I wanted with Kelly. While I knew Addy had already accepted this, I couldn't help but feel responsible for the hurt I would be causing her by my withdrawal from her life.

I got into my truck, buckled my belt, started the engine and paused after putting the truck in drive. I remained still for a moment and Addy turned to look at me, confusion clear in her eyes.

"You aren't getting cold feet already, are you?" she joked.

I put the truck back in park and turned to face her.

"You're probably one of the greatest people I've ever met," I said.

She smiled and patted my hand.

"I like you too," she said.

I must have grimaced because she stopped smiling and her expression became serious.

"We promised to end things if this stopped being comforting. I can see the torture in your eyes, Brad. There is absolutely no choice when it comes between me and Kelly. You have always longed for her, and I knew that from day one. You have no reason to feel beholden to me and I'm sorry that this is hurting you. I'm actually happy for you. I've known for a long time now how important it is for you to tell Kelly the truth. I'm glad you finally realized it and are willing to go to her. I'll be fine, Brad. Don't worry about me," she said and took hold of my hand. She gave it a comforting squeeze and smiled at me again.

"You've helped me so much. I just wish I could help you," I said.

"You have. I don't know when I'll be able to look back on this time with fondness instead of sorrow, but I do know that that day will come. You are so much stronger than you think you are, Brad. Now, let's go get your girl," she said and slapped my thigh.

I laughed and we drove to the diner, to Kelly.

When Derek's eyes met mine upon our arrival, I began to seriously doubt my actions. Here I was, once again showing up at a time when Kelly was happy, uninvited. When Kelly saw me and her smile dropped, I must have taken a step back because I felt Addy slip her hand in mine and give it a squeeze. She leaned into me and whispered in my ear.

"Now or never. Time to stop running," she said.

I nodded and we walked past Derek, Kelly and her friend William. They were sitting in a booth close to the entrance and the rest of the team went to an area towards the back of the diner. I purposely sat in a position that allowed me to keep a visual on Kelly's booth. Derek had sat back down next to her, and they were soon laughing and talking with William, her ex-boyfriend. I wasn't sure how the three of them could hang out together, but I also knew how difficult it was to walk away from Kelly. I assumed William had similar difficulties after him and Kelly stopped dating. He appeared to be good terms with Derek, and I watched the three of them talk and laugh together.

Thirty minutes later I saw Kelly leave the booth and go towards the bathroom area. I motioned towards the area and Addy smiled at me, giving me silent encouragement. I abandoned our group and took the back way to the bathroom so I wouldn't have to walk by Derek and William. I made sure no one was near before I walked by the women's bathroom. Kelly had been on her way out as I came near. When she saw me she immediately withdrew back into the ladies bathroom.

I hesitated. Glanced, to both of my sides and repeated what Addy had said to me. *Now or never. Time to stop running.*

I put my hands up and pushed open the door. She met my eyes with shock as I stepped inside. I saw the moment panic set in, and raised my hands, trying to let her know that I wasn't there to fight and that I meant no harm. It didn't occur to me that I was invading a private space for her, a space she had retreated to get away from me.

"Get out!"

"Don't shout," I said softly.

I didn't want the others to hear and interrupt us. I just needed a few minutes alone with her to explain everything.

"What do you think you are doing?" she asked and shoved my chest. I took a step back to put some distance between us. The last thing I wanted was to make her angry and if I had learned anything from my previous ambushes it was that I needed to give her space and not crowd her.

"I just needed to talk to you, and I didn't want an audience. When I saw you get up, I followed you," I explained.

"Well, I don't want to talk to you," she said and tried to step around me towards the exit. I took another step back and leaned up against the door, blocking her exit. So much for not crowding her. I knew it was the wrong move to make the instant I did it.

"Please just give me a minute," I pleaded.

"What? What could you possibly have to say to me?" she demanded as she crossed her arms across her chest and planted her feet. I was seriously starting to doubt my strategy and my nervous habit took over as my fingers ran through my hair.

"I was so messed up Kelly and I am so sorry that I hurt you. I never wanted to be that guy to you. You were so important to me, and I just fucked that all up that day." I saw her impatience grow and I nervously continued on, stumbling over my words.

"Losing Kevin like that just broke me and I-I didn't know how to act after that. I know I began pushing you away before that and that

229

had nothing to do with you either. There were things going on that I just wasn't ready to tell anyone about and I didn't want you to be disappointed in me. I made some bad choices, and I was ashamed. I thought if I could just keep you at a distance, you wouldn't find out and then Kevin died and I just lost it," I rushed to get it all out before she tried to leave again. I didn't know how much time I had left so I quickly continued talking.

"And I don't know what I was thinking, coming after you like I did in the library. I never should have grabbed you like that. You will never know how much I regret that. I know the things I've said and done are unforgivable, but I am sorry. I miss you, Kelly. I miss you," I said and tried to reach out for her. She took a step back and I instantly stopped reaching out. I pulled my hand back, and drew it behind me, letting her know I wouldn't try touch her again.

It was then that a knock sounded on the door behind me.

"Kelly, are you alright in there?" Derek called out.

I had so much more to say, and I didn't want to miss this chance, so I made a request that probably only convinced Kelly that she needed to get away from me.

"Tell him you are alright, so he'll go away," I whispered, and she narrowed her eyes at me.

Shaking her head at me she responded to Derek's question.

"I'm not alright," she called out and defeat washed over me. I closed my eyes and tilted my head in surrender.

"I'm coming in," Derek said and pushed against the door.

Of course, I was still standing in front of it so it hit my back and only opened a few inches. I heard Derek curse, and he put his full weight against the door and pushed it open the rest of the way. I stepped off to the side and Derek went to Kelly.

"What the hell, man?" he said to me.

"I just wanted to talk to her," I explained.

"In the fucking bathroom!" Derek shouted as he put his arm around Kelly. Another part of me split when I saw her lean into

Derek, just how she used to lean into me on our nightly porch visits.

"I saw an opening," I shrugged. It was a pitiful excuse for what I had done.

"Oh, well, as long as you saw an opening I guess it's okay that you accosted my girlfriend in the bathroom," Derek responded in a way that clearly said it was not okay with him.

"I didn't accost her. I just spoke to her," I said and held my hands up in a feeble attempt to show that I meant Kelly no harm.

"Stay the fuck away from her," Derek ordered.

I wasn't angered by the order. Actually, I understood completely where he was coming from. What sparked my anger was the way he started to steer Kelly towards the door, like he was in charge of her or something. That didn't sit well with me, and I responded with an equally snide remark.

"She can speak for herself," I pointed out.

She did not hesitate, and her responding words cut like a knife.

"I don't have anything more to say to you," Kelly said, effectively making my comment irrelevant. She walked out of the bathroom with Derek. I let them go and intended to let them leave the diner without further incident but then I caught my reflection in the mirror, and I flashed to another bathroom in which I had been in with Kelly.

I had refused to stare at my reflection in Lily's bathroom on the day I had had sex with Kelly against a sink on one of the worst days of my life. Now, staring back at my reflection after watching Kelly walk out, I realized that my lowest point hadn't been the day I was going to kill myself. No. My lowest moment had been the day of Kevin's funeral. Kelly had reached out to me, and I had rejected her in the worst possible way. That was my lowest point and this moment right now, standing in another bathroom was my come to life moment. I couldn't walk out on her again.

Turning, I rushed out of the bathroom and after the girl I loved.

27

Amends

Derek and Kelly were at the booth with William, gathering their belongings to leave. I rushed over to them and stopped short behind William.

"Kelly, please," I said and came face to face with William. He looked at me and then back at Kelly before turning his attention back on me.

"Are you fucking serious right now?" Derek shouted. "She told you to back off. So back the fuck off!"

I saw the grip on his duffle bag tighten and recognized a man being pushed to the brink. I didn't respond because the last thing I wanted was to make this worse than it already was.

"Hey, let's all simmer down okay. Brad, why don't you let Kelly and Derek pass and you and I can talk?" William said, trying to diffuse the tension. I felt his hand rest on my shoulder, and he gestured for Derek and Kelly to leave. I took a step towards them and watched as Derek pulled Kelly behind him.

"Don't you fucking dare," Derek warned, and I held my hands up, letting him know I wasn't going to touch either one of them.

"Just let them go Brad," William said and put a little bit of pressure on the shoulder he was holding. I knew he was giving me a silent warning and I heeded it. I stepped aside and watched as Derek led Kelly out of the diner.

When they got to the exit, I called out to her.

"I'm not going anywhere Kelly," I said and noticed the slight way her shoulders tensed as she heard me, but she did not reply, and she did not turn back. She left.

"Damn. That was close. You nearly got your head taken off," William said as he released my shoulders. I was still looking at the door Kelly had just walked out of and fighting the voice in my head that was shouting at me to run after her.

As I stood there, I felt a presence come up behind me and a hand slipped into mine. Turning, I saw Addy standing next to me. She smiled at me sweetly and I smiled back at her. William stood there, staring at the two of us.

"Color me confused. Weren't you just trying to convince another girl to stay here with you while your girlfriend was sitting over there the whole time?" William scratched his head in a dramatic exaggeration of his confusion.

"I'm not his girlfriend," Addy stated.

"Now I'm really confused," William said and sat back down in his booth.

"I take it things didn't go so well?" Addy asked me.

I shook my head, and her expression shifted to sympathy.

"Why don't you two sit down and fill me in on what the hell is happening?" William said to us.

We turned to him, and he must have seen that I really didn't want to talk to him because he sighed heavily and gestured towards the other side of the bench.

"Look, if you want to talk to Kelly then you are just going to have to talk to me first. You aren't going to get anywhere near her without my help. So, sit down," he gestured to the booth again.

Addy was the first to sit and I reluctantly sat beside her. In typical Addy fashion she made herself comfortable and began eating some fries from a plate of food that had been abandoned by either Derek or Kelly. William chuckled at her before turning his attention back to me.

"So, it seems you still have designs for Kelly," he said.

I crinkled my forehead at him because who the hell said things like that anymore.

"He does," Addy confirmed, and I turned my scowl towards her. She laughed and waved me off.

"Okay. So, what gives? Why have you been the world's biggest dick head to her?"

"It's complicated," I replied.

"Okay. Then simplify it," William instructed.

I glanced at Addy for support, and she just shrugged. She wasn't going to be any help with this. I was on my own. We had agreed it was time, and she was sticking to that.

"How much has Kelly told you about me?" I asked William.

He leaned back in the booth.

"You two were like super close growing up. Like share your darkest secrets close. You basically hovered on the side lines her whole life when it came to her romantic relationships, and I gather that was because you weren't particularly happy about them. She said you started becoming distant and then shit went sour with your brother. You two had sex and you rejected her. She thinks it's because you don't love her, but I think it's because you do love her and are scared shitless about it. How am I doing so far?" William asked.

"Spot on," Addy answered, and I scowled at her again.

"What? The man nailed it."

"Now, what I don't understand is this," William said and gestured between Addy and me.

"Well, the two of us were both on our own journey of healing after some massive emotional breakdown shit and we sort of just fell into each other. Strictly of the support variety, nothing romantic," Addy explained.

That wasn't entirely true, but I wasn't about divulge her private details without her permission, so I kept silent.

"Okay. None of this explains why you basically have been persona non grata since last year." William once again addressed me.

"I wasn't around," I supplied.

"No shit. I know that, but what I don't know is where the hell you went. Kelly told me you just disappeared, and no one would tell her where you went. It's like there's this big conspiracy and Kelly is the one left in the dark. Why the silent treatment?"

"I had a problem with drinking and drugs," I answered.

"Oh, yeah. I totally knew that," William said and waved away my answer like it simply wasn't good enough. I looked at him in surprise because I hadn't exactly been forthcoming with the information and wasn't sure how he could have known.

"Your behavior completely shifted, and you were toasted in the library that day. I have family into drugs. I recognized the signs right away and that was why I didn't want you near her. You were unpredictable."

"Have you told Kelly?" I asked, a bit panicked. I had worked hard to keep this from her, and I didn't want her to find out by someone else.

"No. I'm not an idiot. She would have gone running to rescue you or some shit and she didn't need your hot mess fucking with her head any more than it already was. So, I take it your disappearance had to do with getting clean?" William guessed.

"Yes. I was in rehab and asked everyone to not let Kelly know. I didn't want her to know that side of me," I said.

"Yeah, I get that, but you went about it really shitty. The fact that others knew what was going on and that you had deliberately kept it from her hurt her bad. Probably worse than the other things you have done."

"Yeah. I just can't seem to get anything right when it comes to her. I need to talk to her, William. I need to tell her the truth and if she tells me that she wants nothing to do with me then I will walk away, for good this time."

"And what if she can't walk away? You're her weakness, Brad, and I don't know if she is capable of ever letting you go, whether you are good for her or not. Derek is a really good guy, and he adores Kelly. She deserves to be happy."

"You're right. She does. I'll walk away then and leave the decision up to her. I won't pursue her," I said and glanced at Addy. She smiled her sweet, sympathetic smile at me. She knew how hard this was going to be for me.

"Hmm. I wish you luck with that," William said, like he knew how difficult it would be.

"How did you do it? How are able to watch her be with someone else after you dated her?" I asked him.

William blinked back at me several times before he smirked, then laughed.

"Are you joking?" he asked.

"No. How do you do it? Doesn't it hurt?"

William looked between me and Addy, amused at my question. I didn't find it amusing and I was about to leave the booth when William revealed why he thought I as so amusing.

"I'm gay. I never dated Kelly. We are truly just friends. She wasn't kidding about you. You are clueless. I understand now why you kept fucking things up. You had no idea she loved you," he said.

Stunned, I practically leaned over the booth when I said, "What? No, she didn't."

"Still clueless. I mean it, Brad, best of luck," William said and vacated the booth, leaving Addy and I alone.

I took Addy back to her room. The drive back was spent in

236

silence because we both knew this would be the last time the two of us would rely on the other. There was no returning to the way things had been after all that transpired.

In the past, I would have come up to her room and we would spend the night in each other's arms, trying to drown out our pain with our bodies. This time, I parked the truck and didn't get out. She smiled her sweet smile at me one last time, looking me over with a longing that I knew wasn't for me, but for whoever the guy in her future would be that captured her heart. Silently, she got out of the truck.

We didn't talk to each other again after that day. Sometimes we would cross paths on campus, but we never talked. If our eyes met, we would silently acknowledge the other but walk away without a word spoken. We had said everything we needed to say to each other in my truck before going to the diner. Our goodbye had already occurred, and we were finally trying to stand on our own.

Days passed and I waited, waited for Kelly to come, but she never did. She was still with Derek, and I kept my promise to William. I didn't seek her out and my only interaction with Derek was during practice. If you could call letting him glare at me and saying nothing in return an interaction.

Surprisingly, William would sometimes appear and spark up conversations with me. We never talked about Kelly, and I was strangely okay with it. The guy began to grow on me, and I even found myself looking forward to our conversations. He had this uncanny ability to brighten my mood, and I found myself opening up to him without even realizing it. I mentioned it to him one day and he told me it was because he was an emotional ninja that snuck up on people. I understood why Kelly had been drawn to his friendship.

The days turned into weeks, and I found myself, for the first time in a long time, in a place where I wasn't being chased by demons. I even replaced the guitar I had destroyed and began playing music again. I no longer felt guilty when I reached for the strings. Music became what it used to be for me, a release. My current therapist had encouraged me to return to music and I was glad I had listened.

There were still nights in which I woke from visions that lingered. With Addy, I would reach out for her and we would chase away the visions with our touch. I realized that what we were doing was just another form of avoidance. With my music I didn't avoid the feelings. I channeled them and turned them into something that I could understand. The visions no longer frightened me. I simply accepted them for what they were and did what I needed to do to ensure they did not overpower me again.

One evening, I was putting the latest nightmare down on sheet music when a knock came on my door. Not thinking anything of it, I answered the door and found Kelly standing there. Surprised, my eyes widened and all I could manage to say was her name. It escaped my lips like a one-word prayer.

"May I come in?" she asked.

Still in shock, I nodded and stepped aside to let her in. After closing the door, I continued to stare at her in disbelief. Eventually I snapped out of it and grabbed the chair from my desk for her to sit in.

"Thank you," she said as she sat down.

I ran my fingers through my hair and saw her smile at me. Her smile broke me free of my trance and I spoke to her for the first time in a month.

"Why are you here? Wait, let me start over. I'm glad you're here. Why are you here?" I asked and sat down on the edge of my bed.

"You were right. We need to talk. I think this is better than a ladies bathroom," she stated. The nervous joke fell flat, and I chuckled at her obvious unease.

Not sure how to diffuse the situation I began to rub the back of my neck.

"Yeah. Sorry about that. Derek wanted to pound me and he would have been justified," I laughed, just as nervous as she was.

238

A part of me scolded me for being so nervous. This was Kelly, after all. She had seen me snort soda out of my nose on more than one occasion. I had no reason to be nervous with her.

"Yes, he did," she said softly, and I saw her wring her fingers together in her lap.

"I just saw you and I couldn't let you go without trying," I explained the reasoning for my behavior that day in the diner.

"Why did you disconnect your phone? Why didn't you want me to know where you were? Why didn't you come and find me right away? Why did you avoid me?" She fired the questions off without pausing in between them and I sighed.

"I'm not sure I can answer all those right now," I said because the answers to those questions weren't as easy as she thought.

She nodded at me and started to stand. Realizing she thought I was refusing to answer them and was getting up to leave I immediately jumped to my feet.

"No, wait! Sit down," I said and held my hands up to stop her.

She looked at my hands and I made a slow downward motion to show her I wanted her to sit back down. She did and I breathed a sigh of relief.

"I just meant that it's hard to tell you everything by just answering questions. Can you just stay and listen?" I asked her.

I was terrified she was going to leave, and I would never again have this chance. I had stayed away from her because I wanted her to choose and here she was, before me, finally. I didn't want to mess this up again.

"Yes," she agreed.

I sat back down on the bed and ran my fingers through my hair, trying to decide where to begin.

"Okay. Thank you. Well, you already know how shitty my parents are." I began at the beginning.

"Yeah, well, they've been like that my whole life. Lily is right, I don't know why they ever had kids, but they had three of us. Lily was Kevin's and my whole world. She took care of us, loved us and made us feel wanted. After she left, Kevin and I just fell apart. Looking back I realize that Kevin had always been kind of broken and Lily was just the band-aid. I tried so hard to make him happy, but I just couldn't. The first time he tried to kill himself he was sixteen and I was nine. I found him in the bathroom and there was so much blood," I said and paused because the visions were flashing before me again. Kelly had gasped and was leaning forward to reach out to me, but I knew if she touched me I wouldn't be able to continue on so I leaned back and threw up my hand to stop her.

"No, I need to get all this out," I explained, and she stopped moving towards me.

"I called the ambulance, and they took him away. I remember my father saying something like if Kevin was going to embarrass them, he might as well have finished the job, like Kevin's whole intention was to piss off our parents. That was the moment I began to hate them. My mom didn't stick up for Kevin; instead, she comforted my father, like he was the one that was bleeding. From that point on I became Kevin's shadow. I was so terrified he would do it again and leave me alone with them. He never once acted like I was a nuisance to him and he became my world, just like Lily used to be. Except, Lily used to be the one that took care of me, this time I was taking care of Kevin.

"When he graduated high school and announced he was going away to college I panicked. Who would be there to watch him? To stop him from trying again? He insisted he wouldn't do it again and I made him promise me that he wouldn't. I told him I would never forgive him if he ever left me like Lily had. He promised he was better and so he left. It wasn't long after that that I moved in next door to you. I still remember that first day I met you. You were pressed up against that moving truck, terrified out of your mind," I said and smiled at her. She had been so breathtaking even then.

"I wasn't very good with new people back then," she replied

shyly.

"No, I suppose you weren't. But you were still just as beautiful."

Her mouth dropped open in surprise and I laughed at her shocked expression. Surely, she had known how beautiful I thought she was.

"You've always been gorgeous. You just never noticed it yourself. I think that was one of the reasons why I fell in love with you. Everyone around you was so captivated by your beauty and you just never accepted it. You were always so humble and so kind to everyone," I said and paused for a brief moment, shifting to memories from before.

"Jen used to tease me all the time because I had feelings for you and would never tell you. She called me a coward a few times and she was right. I was so afraid that you wouldn't share my feelings, and I had grown accustomed to having you in my life. I didn't want to lose that, so I kept quiet and just continued to play the part of your friend. Then Mark came along, and I just wanted to rip him apart. You always thought my distance was because I hated Mark, and I guess you were right, but I hated him because he had you. I hated him because he got to touch you, kiss you and listen to your secrets. You used to tell me your secrets but then he came along, and you only had eyes for him. I couldn't tell you how I felt then because you wouldn't have believed me. So, I waited.

"I never expected you and Mark to last as long as you did. Jen told me what his parents had done to her when they dated, and I knew it was only a matter of time before you realized how awful they were. But you never did, and you kept on dating him even after he refused to go to college with you." I took a break to swallow down the old hurt.

"His mother let me know just how awful they really were. After losing my mother, and then you, I was afraid to lose Mark too. So, I pushed away the warning signs and just kept holding on," she said.

"I'm sorry about that. I shouldn't have pulled away like I did. I just thought once Mark was gone things would somehow work out between us. My timing was never right, though. Just when I thought I could let you know how I felt it seemed like something with my family would always get in the way. Kevin would relapse, my parents would lay on a guilt trip, or I just got cold feet. Then you met Justin, and it was like you turned into a different person. I didn't handle that very well either. I couldn't stand seeing you two together because it should have been me doing those things with you. I tried to tell you, but it always came out wrong. I thought, after the night you met Justin and slept in my bed, that you had felt what I was feeling. I thought our chance had finally arrived but then you asked for Justin's phone number, and I just got so mad at you. I didn't understand how you could just ignore what was happening between us and the only explanation I could come up with was you didn't feel the same as I did. So, once again I pulled away.

"Then things went to shit. Kevin wasn't taking his meds, and he fell into a deep depression. He would call me at odd hours just crying and saying he wanted it all to end. I was back in that terrifying place I used to live in, and I couldn't do anything about it. I just couldn't focus on anything other than keeping my brother alive. I pushed so many people away because I honestly believed I didn't have enough in me to be there for anyone but Kevin. It was just easier to tell myself the best thing for everyone was if I just distanced myself and focused on Kevin. Lily and I started to communicate more frequently, but we only ever talked about Kevin. Between the two of us we had a pretty good system going."

"But I saw you with other girls," Kelly broke in.

"Yeah, but I never actually dated any of them. I'm not proud of this Kelly but I used those girls. I couldn't be with you and there were times I just needed to forget about all the craziness so I would find some girl and use her until she started getting too close, then I would ditch her. I was a complete ass, and I justified it by telling myself they all knew what they were getting into. I'm not a good person, Kelly," I said, and she shook her head at me, dismissing my statement.

"I'm not finished. You might not feel the same after I tell you everything. I thought things with Kevin were finally getting better and that I'd be able to take a step back and get back to my life but by then I thought you were dating that William guy and once again I had lost my chance. And in typical fashion I reacted in anger and lashed out at you. I think- no, I know- I began to blame Kevin for all the missed opportunities with you. I was so damn mad Kelly, but I couldn't take it out on Kevin because that might send him over the edge. So, instead, I took it out on the next available target – you. I started to think you knew how I felt, and you were just toying with me like it was all just a game to you. I know now how crazy that was but I couldn't see past my rage and so I went after you again."

"William and I were never dating," she provided, and I just nodded because I already knew that.

"That day at your house for Christmas I decided I was done waiting on the sidelines. I decided I was going to fight for you and then Lily called, and Kevin was just gone. At first, I blamed myself because I hadn't done enough to keep him alive. Then I blamed Lily because she was closer, and she should have seen how bad it was. Then I blamed my parents because they were shitty parents. Then I blamed you because you had distracted me. Then, God help me, I blamed Kevin. I blamed him for everything. My life was in chaos because he had to be a selfish bastard and kill himself. He knew how much it would hurt Lily and me, but he just didn't give a damn and did it anyway. I didn't want you to come with me because I was just so angry, and I didn't want you to see it.

"When Lily and I went to clean out his apartment and she gave me his suicide note something just snapped in me. I wanted to shout at everyone. I wanted to punch everything. And I wanted Kevin to be alive so I could finally tell him how he had fucked up everything. But Kevin wasn't alive and all I had left of him was this stupid fucking note and all his prescription medications. I told Lily I got rid of them, but I didn't. I kept them all. He had so many painkillers and anti-depressants. One doctor had even prescribed him an anti-psychotic thinking he was schizophrenic. He wasn't, but he just kept going to so many different doctors that he had a collection of drugs. I don't know what made me keep them, but I did.

"Then my parents showed up at the funeral and since I couldn't release my rage on Kevin, I let it loose on them. I don't think I've ever loved them. How can you love someone that has never shown you any affection? I learned how to love from Lily and to this day I still don't know how she ever learned it herself. Our parents are the coldest people I have ever known; except for me that is."

"You aren't cold, Brad," she said and tried to reach out for me again. And again, I brushed her off. I wasn't ready for her to comfort me. Like before she stopped advancing and sat back in her chair.

"But I am Kelly. I knew what I was doing in that bathroom. I took advantage of your kindness, and I used you just like I had used all those other girls. But you weren't those other girls, Kelly. You were so much more, and I just tarnished you. I took what I wanted and didn't care how it would hurt you. Nothing about that had to do with love. The only thing I felt in that bathroom was hatred. I hated my parents, I hated Kevin, I hated myself and at one point I even hated you. After, I just couldn't look you in the eye. I violated you and I had to get as far away from you as I could so I wouldn't hurt you again.

"I just kind of wandered for a few days before showing up at your room and I only made things worse. It never occurred to me that you had fallen in love with me and when you tried to tell me I didn't believe it. I was so consumed by grief and anger that I convinced myself you could never love me. The only way I could see salvaging any friendship with you was to tell you we had made a mistake and beg you to start over, but you couldn't do that. It was foolish of me to think you could ever just forget what I had done and go back to the way things used to be. I hurt you and I can never make that up to you. I left your room, and I realized that I didn't deserve your forgiveness. I went back to my room and took out Kevin's suicide note. I don't know how long I sat there reading it but eventually my brain started to tell me there was a way to numb the pain and I took out Kevin's pills. That was the night I started taking pain killers so I could forget you."

She gasped and brought her hand to her mouth to hide the shock. I ignored her reaction and forged on.

"I told myself I didn't deserve to be happy because all I ever did was fail those around me. My parents thought I was a failure. I had failed to save my brother, and I failed at loving you. I began drinking more heavily and mixing the alcohol with the pills. When I ran out of Kevin's stash, I faked injuries to get my own. I even tried to break my own foot once so I could get more pills. Thankfully, I had been so drunk at the time that all I managed to do was trip and bruise my ankle. Matt tried to convince me to stop. He begged me to get help, but I ignored him.

"For six months I just spiraled downward. I'm pretty sure the day I assaulted you in the library I was drunk. I don't really remember much of it. I avoided Lily's calls and told myself she didn't need me anymore since Kevin was gone and all we really had in common was him. I stopped going to classes. I just stopped living and one day I decided Kevin had the right idea all along. This whole life thing was just too painful, and I couldn't do it anymore. As soon as I had that thought my phone rang and it was Jen. I don't know why I answered it, but I did. She told me you had called her again and asked her to check up on me. I think it was just hearing your name that broke me. I came clean to Jen, and she got Matt to my room to stay with me. She called Lily and they both flew out the next day. They checked me in to a clinic and I began rehab."

My mouth suddenly felt dry, and I quickly got up to get some water from my fridge. When I came back to sit down, I handed Kelly a bottle of water before opening my own and gulping some down.

She took the water from me but didn't open it.

"Withdrawals were more painful than anything I had ever experienced. I must have cried out for everyone at some point. I think I might have even begged for my mother, which is silly since she wouldn't have cared. Maybe I really meant Lily when I said mother. Who knows? Your mind is in such a fog during withdrawal. The only thing I could focus on was wanting the next high, and you. I thought about you a lot. Once I was coherent enough to participate, I began group therapy. I resisted at first, but I opened up eventually and it helped. Just talking about all the anger I still had somehow made me feel better.

"Eventually, I realized it was okay to be angry at Kevin. I just never believed I could be angry at my dead brother before. I thought by being angry at him I was somehow dishonoring his memory or something. I was using painkillers and alcohol in an attempt to rid myself of the anger but they only intensified it, so I took more thinking that was the answer. While I was in rehab my phone was disconnected because we weren't allowed to have them. I made Jen swear she wouldn't tell you where I was. I didn't want you to know. I was so ashamed of what I had allowed myself to become. I couldn't let my darkness touch you again." I finished and hung my head, waiting for her to get up and leave. To my surprise, she didn't.

"Why didn't you come to me and explain all this sooner? Why did you wait so long?" she asked.

I lifted my head and looked at her painfully.

"I'm damaged, Kelly. There will always be a part of me that lives in darkness and you are so pure. How could I place this on you?" I asked.

"Then why approach me at the diner? Why corner me in the bathroom?" She needed answers and I wasn't entirely sure I had the answers to those questions.

"Derek came to me when he started dating you. He wanted to let me know so I wouldn't be blindsided. I told him were had just been friends, but I knew when I said that we were never just friends. I told him we were and that whatever happened was between you and him, but then I saw you there, with him, and old habits die hard I guess," I said and half smiled at her.

"Weren't you there with your girlfriend?" she asked me, confused.

"Yeah, Addy. I had told her about you and, even though she was hurt, she walked away. She knew about the drugs too," I said.

I wasn't sure I could explain what Addy and I had been to each other in a way that Kelly would understand, so I provided an explanation that she would understand. Besides, Addy had been my girlfriend in a way, even if we both knew that there was an expiration date between us.

"I don't understand. All I've ever wanted was to be there for you and you pushed me away on purpose," she said, and I noticed her eyes begin to water and tears started falling.

My body twitched, a natural response that wanted to move to her and comfort her, but I remained where I was.

"I can't explain it. My mind was all messed up and I had convinced myself that I didn't deserve you in any form. You deserved so much better than me. You deserved someone like Derek. Someone who wouldn't cause you pain or bring so much ugliness to your life. Since the day we met, all I ever brought into your life was pain. I couldn't do that to you anymore," I explained and clasped my hands together to prevent them from reaching out for her.

"That is total bullshit Brad, and you know it! Most of my happy moments in my life are because of you," she cried and stood, knocking her chair down from the force. I stood with her and this time I did reach out for her.

"Don't cry. I can't stand to think I'm hurting you again," I said and wrapped her in my arms. "Please don't cry because of me," I whispered into the hair on the top of her head.

"You just left, and I never knew why. I thought it was because of something I had done. I thought I wasn't good enough for you," she sobbed as I held her.

"I am so goddamn sorry I put you through that," I said and held on to her just a little bit tighter. It was me that wasn't good enough for her.

"What am I supposed to do now?" she asked me.

I didn't know what to say to her. I knew what I wanted but I couldn't do that to her. This choice had to be hers, so, I shrugged and said the only thing I could say.

"Nothing. Whatever you want. I don't deserve, nor do I expect, your forgiveness. I've never stopped loving you Kelly and all I want is for you to be happy. I've seen you with Derek. You're happy and he loves you. Be with him, if you want, just be happy," I said, kissed the top of her head, stepped out of the embrace, and away from her.

"How can I after everything you just told me?" she asked desperately, wiping away tears.

I smiled sadly at her and wiped away a single tear she had missed.

"You just do it. You live, Kelly," I said and smiled at her when she nodded her head at me. I walked forward and gave her the briefest of hugs because I knew if I lingered any longer, I wouldn't be able to let her go.

"Be happy, Kelly," I said and went to my door. I opened it and she looked at me quizzically. She didn't say another word to me as she quietly walked out of my room. I watched her leave for the briefest of moments, silently begging her to turn around.

She didn't and I closed the door.

28

Confrontation

For the first time in my life, I felt like I was actually doing the right thing, the unselfish thing, by letting Kelly go. I wanted her to be able to have a life filled with happy moments that weren't marred by a history that elicited hurtful memories. I figured she could have this with Derek, a man that loved her and had never betrayed her or hurt her like I had. The time marched on and I returned to avoiding the areas I knew she or Derek would be.

The track season ended, and I no longer had to attend the mandatory team practices. I still ran, but only with Kendrick or Terrence. While I was friendly with them, we weren't exactly friends, so the conversation of Derek and Kelly never came up. I assumed after I had finally told Kelly everything she would have gone back to Derek and continued on without me. William would try to talk to me about her, but I would cut him off and tell him I was no longer a part of her life. He yelled at me one day and said I was being more foolish than Kelly was. I didn't ask for an explanation. I should have though, because it would have provided me with information that would have prevented an encounter I later had with Derek.

I had become very good at avoiding the places he would be, but I came upon him by chance one weekend while out for a run. It was early morning, and the air was thick with cold from the last night's snow. My lungs were burning from the ice in the air, and I could feel the frost through my clothing. I ended up cutting my run short because the cold was so biting. I came off the path and didn't see Derek until we were both standing at the same cross path. Our breath lingered in the air surrounding us and our pants echoed in the silence.

After a few minutes of silent staring, I started to continue on my path but his answering scoff made me pull up short. I squinted my eyes at him and he laughed at my expression.

"I'm standing here, hating you, and you are so fucking clueless it's laughable," he said.

"I'm sorry," I replied even though I was not entirely sure what I was apologizing for. Why would he hate me? I did what I said I would do – I walked away and stayed away.

"Why didn't you just tell me the truth? I came to you. I gave you an out and you lied to me. You said you had only been friends. You said you wouldn't be a problem. Well, guess what fucker, you weren't just a problem. You were the only problem!" Derek shouted and before I could react, he lunged for me.

The impact of his body knocked mine down and we both fell into a mound of snow. He managed to land a few ineffective punches to my side before I recovered from the initial shock and pushed him off me. His gloved hands and my sweatshirt had cushioned his punches, and I was able to roll to my side and get up without any pain. He grunted, slammed his fist into the snow and stood, getting into a fighting stance.

"I don't want to fight you, Derek," I said and put my hand up in front of me.

"Well, to fucking bad because I want to fight you," he said and lunged for me again. I was able to sidestep out of the way.

"This is crazy. Stop for a second," I said and had to jump out of the way again as he tried to charge.

"Stop fucking jumping around like a damn rabbit," he said

250

angrily.

"Derek, you don't want to do this. Think about Kelly. She wouldn't want this," I said in an attempt to bring him back to his senses. If Derek showed up with a black eye and he told her I had hit him it would unravel everything I had done.

He stopped advancing when I said Kelly's name and instead started to laugh.

"You're so fucking clueless. Kelly broke up with me, you jackass."

I stared at him in disbelief. This couldn't be right. She was supposed to go back to him and live out her life. She was supposed to be happy with him. Why would she break up with him? I was so lost in my thoughts that I didn't notice Derek had removed his gloves until the impact of his fist on my face told me. The punch had enough force behind it that it knocked me to the ground. As I lay there in the snow, my face began to sting from the punch and the cold, Derek stood above me, cursed and shook out his hand.

"God. I can't even manage to punch you without hurting myself," he said and reached out with his other hand.

I stared up at the offered hand, not sure what to do. He shook it slightly at me with impatience and I wearily reached out to take hold of his hand. He hauled me onto my feet and put his gloves back on. I rubbed my cheek and winced from the pain of my touch.

"I don't understand." I said.

Derek guessed correctly that I was confused about Kelly breaking up with him, and not about him punching me. That I completely understood entirely.

"After the two of you had your little chat, she came back and told me she couldn't be with me anymore. She said a part of her would always belong to you and she couldn't continue to hurt me. You ruined everything," he said and bent to pick up the hat he had been wearing that had fallen off during our scuffle.

"She wasn't supposed to do that," I said and just stood there,

251

staring at the broken man before me.

"Yeah, well, maybe you should tell her that. Actually, you know what, don't. Stay away from her. You've got her head so jumbled up she can't figure out what she wants," he started to walk back down the path he had come from.

"I did stay away," I called after him.

He stopped, turned, and came back to stand before me.

"I don't get it. I don't get you," he said and shook his head.

"What do you mean?"

"She's fucking amazing. You are supposed to be madly in love with her or something but every time you have an opportunity you fucking blow it. All I know is that if the roles were reversed, I wouldn't stay away from her. If she loved me even half as much as she loves you, I would never walk away. You're an idiot," Derek said and stared to walk away from me again.

"Derek?" I called after him.

"What?" he shouted back, still walking away.

"I'm sorry!"

"Whatever. Just stop fucking things up," he responded and then sprinted away, the snow kicking up with heels.

The next few days passed in a haze and the semester ended. I packed up my things and made the drive back home, my confrontation with Derek playing over in my head. I was spending the holiday season with Jeff, Reyann and Lily, but my mind wandered over to the family across town. The family I used to spend the holidays with, laughing and feeling loved. Kelly wasn't the only one I missed desperately. I missed her entire family, especially her father. Paul had always been there for me, and I hadn't seen or spoken to him since the day of my brother's death. This would be our first Christmas without Kevin and to say I wasn't feeling the loss would be a lie. I knew Lily was feeling it to. I was originally supposed to go to Philly and be with her, but she decided she needed a change of scenery, and she came to Wisconsin instead.

Jeff and Reyann welcomed her, and they all quickly hit it off. Jeff didn't skip a beat and started calling her little sister. It didn't matter that she was older than him by about six years; he kept giving her noogies and putting her in head locks.

"God, if this is what it's like to have an older brother than I am glad mine were both younger," she joked as Jeff had her in a head lock again, but her laughter quickly faded as she realized what she had said.

Reyann was in the middle of putting a platter of mashed potatoes down on the table for our dinner and she noticed Lily freeze. Jeff, ever oblivious, continued to pull Lilly around the room in the head lock. I glanced at Reyann and she smiled at me.

"Jeff, let the young lady go. It's time for dinner," Reyann said, and she sat down at the head of the table.

"But Mom," Jeff whined. He was a grown man in his thirties, but he still acted like a teenager around his mother. She gave him her sternest look and he immediately released Lily.

"I apologize for my Neanderthal son, Lily. My other son, Tom, isn't as brutish as this one," Reyann said as she gestured to Jeff, who was pouting as he sat down at the table.

"I'm sure Tom is lovely," Lily replied as she sat down next to me.

"He'll be arriving tomorrow with his new girlfriend," Reyann provided.

"I wonder how long this one will last," Jeff said as he spooned some beans on his plate.

"At least he tries," Reyann barked back at Jeff.

"Don't worry about me, Mother. I have plenty of options

available to me," Jeff bragged.

"Don't be crass at the dinner table. We have guests."

"Family doesn't count as guests," Jeff announced and promptly threw a roll at me. It bounced off of my shoulder and rolled onto the table. Lily looked at the roll and then at Jeff.

"What?" he asked and bit into a drumstick.

"Jeff, put your food down. We haven't said our thanks yet," Reyann instructed her son, and he dutifully put his chicken down and folded his hands together in a prayer stance.

Lily glanced at me in a panic. This was all new to her. I smiled and gestured for her to mimic Jeff and me. She did and we waited for Reyann to begin the prayer.

"Lord, we thank you for the food on our table and the many blessings you have bestowed upon us. We are forever grateful for the love you have provided in our lives and for sending Brad and Lily to us. Please send our love to Kevin and let him know that he has not been forgotten. Bring him, and those still mourning his loss, peace during this holiday season. Oh, and please forgive my eldest for his language and sinful ways. He really does have a good heart. Amen," she finished and picked up her fork.

Lily froze in her seat and stared at Reyann with tears in her eyes. Reyann noticed Lily's tears and she reached out to take hold of Lily's hand. She gave it a reassuring squeeze.

"Aww, shucks, Mom. I knew you still loved me," Jeff said and effectively lightened the mood. Lily laughed and wiped away her tears.

"A mother's love is eternal. Even if her son continues to live his life in debauchery and refuses to give me grandkids to spoil," Reyann said affectionately.

"Tom will have to cover that area for you. I'm strictly bachelor bound for now," Jeff stated and picked his chicken back up.

The conversation continued and thoughts of sad times were quickly replaced with laughter and happy stories. Lily became engrossed in the magic that is Reyann and Jeff's bond. My sister was finally witnessing how a mother was supposed to love their child and she was thrilled by it.

When Tom and his girlfriend arrived the next day Lily bore witness to another time-honored family tradition – a holiday family fight. Turned out, Tom's new girlfriend was Jeff's high school ex. There was shouting, a bit of pushing, some name calling followed by a stern warning from Reyann and ended with two brothers crying and awkwardly hugging each other.

"I love these people," Lily said to me as we watched on.

I smiled knowingly because I loved those people too. Finally, I had a family that was all my own. I had always felt accepted by Kelly's family but had never actually felt a part of it. I knew my presence was dictated solely by my friendship with Kelly, so I never actually thought of her family as mine. But Reyann, Jeff and Tom chose me without any strings attached and I would be forever grateful to them.

On Christmas day, Lily and I took a moment to ourselves to remember our lost brother. We took a private walk among the trees that still remained at Reyann's landscaping business. The scent that had brought me comfort for many years was now bringing back a flood of memories as we walked amongst the rows.

"Have you forgiven him yet?" Lily asked me. I was taken aback by the question because it was so abrupt.

"I don't know," I said honestly.

"I hadn't, until I came here. Until I saw this family. I think Kevin did the best he could given what we had to start life with. I was so mad at him for leaving so soon but I think he gave us more years than he had in him. I'm thankful for that extra time, you know?" she looked at me.

"I never thought of it like that," I admitted.

"Yeah, me neither. Brad, why are you here?" she asked, stunning me with another abrupt question.

"I'm spending time with you," I answered.

"No, I mean, why aren't you across town? I know you miss her."

She was talking about Kelly. I told Lily everything that had transpired since I had returned to school six months ago and she had tried to convince me to go to Kelly. No matter how many times I explained it to her she simply didn't accept that I was doing the right thing.

"It's not about what I want any more," I repeated for the hundredth time.

"The two of you are just too stubborn for your own good. Let's head back. I don't want to miss Jeff pummeling Tom again," Lily said, and she put her arm through mine as we started walking back to Reyann's home.

29

A Wedding & A Promise

Lily returned to Philly, and I began getting ready for Matt and Serena's wedding. They were tying the knot right before I was set to return to finish out the second half of my junior year. This would be the first time I had seen them since I left rehab, and it would also be the first time I would see Kelly since I had told her the truth about everything. Surprisingly, I wasn't dreading any part of this wedding. I was happy for my friend, and I wanted to see Kelly. I wanted to be sure she was happy with her life, just as I had asked her to be.

I was unable to attend the rehearsal because I had a meeting I had to go to. I felt terrible about it, but Matt told me they understood. He knew how important it was to my sobriety that I attended the meetings regularly. I told him I could go to another one, but he told me he needed me to be solid on his big day and encouraged me to attend the meeting. That meant I would arrive on the morning of the wedding. When I arrived, I was taken aback by the massive embrace Matt gave me, but his greeting explained things to me.

"She's freaking out. You know how she hates surprises, and she got it in her head that since you didn't come last night you would forget what time to be here this morning. I'm so glad you are here," he explained the bride's to be current state of being. He quickly took me in to the area the groom's party was getting ready in.

"Sorry I couldn't make it yesterday," I said and greeted Matt's father, Dr. Stone.

"We are just thankful you are here today. How have you been?" Dr. Stone asked me as he shook my hand.

"I've been good, sir. Really good," I say, the pleasure seeping into my voice.

"I am happy to hear that. Now, between you and me, I think my son is more nervous than the bride," Dr. Stone said. He laughed when Matt sent him a scathing look.

"I don't know why. Serena is a catch, and she can clearly do much better than this frog," I joked, joining in on the good-natured ribbing Matt's father had started.

"Don't," Matt warned.

"What?" I asked innocently, sharing a conspiratorial look with Dr. Stone.

"Do not remind my soon to be wife that she is crazy for marrying me. Wait until after I clinch it to tell her she can do better. Now help me figure this cursed thing out," he said and tossed the bow tie at me.

I catch it but look over to Dr. Stone in desperation. He chuckles and takes the fabric from me to assist his son. I had never in my life ever wore a bow tie and had only a handful of occasions when I wore a regular tie. There was no way I was going to be able to tie that thing.

The rest of the morning passed with Matt jumping back and forth between elation and panic that Serena would come to her senses to run off with someone who wasn't so interested in numbers, someone not boring he said. We did our best to convince him, but it wasn't until he saw her walking down the aisle to him that he relaxed.

Later, I stood beside Matt as the wedding march played and the procession began coming down the aisle. After the ring bearer and flower girl passed, Matt's sister came down the aisle and Kelly followed behind her. She was absolutely stunning in the light purple bridesmaid dress she was wearing. All I could think about when I

258

saw her was springtime. She had a crown of flowers in her hair and curled wisps of her blonde locks swayed freely on her shoulders as she walked towards me. It isn't until she turned to take her place on the bride's side that I remembered she wasn't walking towards me and I shook my head to clear my thoughts.

Serena appeared at the altar, escorted by her grandmother, and she placed her hand in Matt's as he helped her up the few steps. I could hear the minister begin the ceremony, but my focus was on Kelly. She was watching Serena and Matt, but I couldn't keep my eyes off of her. I tried to decipher any sense of her state of happiness but was unable to meet her gaze. The few times she noticed me staring she quickly averted her gaze.

When Matt and Serena exchanged their vows Kelly's gaze once again landed on mine and I stared back, trying to see if she was happy, but all I saw was sadness and it washed over me, crushing the hope I had been holding on to that I had done the right thing by walking away. I break our eye connection because I can't face the hurt, I see in her expression. I did that. I put that there.

Once the ceremony was over, Matt and Serena walked back down the aisle together, followed by the bridesmaids and I pulled up the rear. The reception was in the same building and the guests all filed into the hall. The wedding party is shown to their seats after the customary photo session.

Matt and Serena's entrance is announced, and everyone cheers for them as they take their seats. I am seated next to Matt and Kelly is seated next to Serena. We are separated by our friends and neither of us attempts to bridge the gap. Within moments, a voice rang out over the speakers and asked for the guests to welcome Matt and Serena to the dance floor for their first dance as a married couple. The music played and my friend took his new bride into his arms and they both laughed as they gazed into each other's eyes.

My gaze is fixed on the dancing couple, and I did not realize Kelly had left her seat until my chair was bumped by a guest walking behind me and I turned to see her gone.

I quickly scanned the crowd but was unable to find her. I stood and started heading toward the entrance doors when a movement from the patio caught my attention. I saw a brief glimpse of purple fabric through the glass doors. Turning on my heels I went back to my chair and grabbed my jacket. It was winter and the weather had not been kind that year. She was wearing a strapless dress that provided very little warmth.

Opening the patio doors, I felt the instant bite of the cold and searched for her. She was standing towards the edge, staring into the night sky. She looked breathtaking in the moonlight. I was so entranced with her that it took her shiver for me to break free.

"They really do seem happy," I said to her as I walked up behind her and placed my jacket on her shoulders. She tilted her head slightly and pulled the jacket across her body for warmth.

"They really do," she responded.

"What about you Kelly? Are you happy?" I whispered. I stood behind her and all I wanted to do was wrap her in my arms, but I knew I needed to give her space.

"I'm trying to be," she replied.

"What would make you happy?" I asked and took a step closer to her.

"You," she said softly.

I started to take another step towards her, but I hesitated. She moved slightly and it was then I saw the tears shining in her eyes. Without another second thought I rushed to her and pulled her into my arms.

"Don't cry because of me," I begged.

"I can't help it. Missing you hurts," she admitted, and I felt her arms constrict around my waist.

"I just can't seem to stop hurting you," I whispered into her hair. She really did fit perfectly into my frame.

"You could," she said and pulled back out of the embrace. She looked up at me, tears glistening in the moonlight. "Stop avoiding me."

I smiled down at her and laughed slightly. All this time I thought I was being noble by staying away and she had thought I was avoiding her again. Lily had been right. We really were too stubborn for our own good.

"I'm no good for you," I said and caressed her cheek. She leaned into my hand and let out a soft sigh.

"You're wrong. Nobody else will ever be good for me as long as I love you", she said and that time I'm the one who sighed. The dam just broke and I leaned my forehead against hers and took hold of her hand. I placed our joined hands between our bodies.

"If you let me, I'll spend the rest of my life making sure that is true," I said. Despite all I had revealed to her in my dorm room, this was the most vulnerable I had been before her. Asking her to give me a chance, knowing full well her answer could be no.

She nodded.

I leaned in and stared into her eyes briefly before I kissed her. That kiss was exactly what our first kiss should have been like, innocent and filled with nothing but love. Our lips were feathers that brushed against each other, caressing tenderly, making up for all the hurt. Our hands were still joined between us when I spoke against her lips.

"I will always love you short-cake," I said.

"Promise," she replied and released my hand, crossed her fingers and placed them over her heart. I smile at her as she performed our childhood ritual.

"Promise," I vowed and completed the ritual by mimicking her gesture.

The next time I kissed her I put everything I had into it, letting her know I meant everything I said. She placed her hands on my hips and gripped onto me. Mine were her face, tilting her up to me. Her lips answered my every call, and we lost ourselves in the moonlight.

We broke apart only when we needed air and even then I kept my body pressed against hers and my face as close to hers as possible. She smiled at me, and I smiled back.

"What now?" she asked.

"What do you want to happen?" I asked, giving her all the power. For so long I had been the one making all the decisions in our twisted dance.

She pursed her lips as she thought about what she wanted.

"I want to live. I want to be happy. Will you be happy with me?" she asked, and I grinned down at her.

"That's the only time I've ever been happy," I answered and kissed her again. A few more minutes passed and again it was her shiver that broke me from my trance.

"You're cold. Let's go back inside," I said and started to move towards the door. I was holding her hand and when she didn't move with me, I was pulled back. I glanced at her questioningly and she nervously looked around before her eyes settled on mine again.

"I'm afraid if I move out of this moment it will end," she admitted.

Not sure I was going to say the right thing I took a moment to think about my response.

"Well, all moments have to end eventually. But that's okay because we will have many more moments together," I reassured her and this time she moved with me.

Back inside, the festivities continued on around us. We were walking back to our table when I heard Serena call out to us. She ran up to us, Matt trailed behind her. She stopped abruptly when she saw our joined hands and squealed. Matt looked at her with concern and she turned to him to slap a hand on his chest.

"I don't believe it," she said.

"What?" Matt asked.

"They're together," Serena gestured to us and Matt looked around her to us.

"How do you know?"

"I just do. It's about freaking time you two. I was about ready to have you both kidnapped and locked in a room until you figured it out," she laughed.

"Figure what out?" I asked her.

"That you belong together. Duh. Now come dance with me," she said to Kelly and grabbed her free hand to pull her to the dance floor. I watched them run to the dance floor, laughing the whole time.

"How about that?" Matt said and patted me on the shoulder.

"What?"

"My crazy, beautiful wife just put you in your place and stole your girl all at the same time," Matt chuckled, and he awkwardly danced his way towards Serena and Kelly. I laughed and Kelly looked at me, beckoning me with her hands.

Without a second thought I went to her and danced the night away.

30

Back To You

"We don't have to do this," I said to Kelly as we stood outside my hotel room door.

She glanced nervously down the hallway and hugged my jacket closer to her body. I had tried to walk her to her room and say goodnight, but she refused. She said we had spent enough time apart and she didn't want to miss out on any more moments.

"I want to do this," she said and put her hand over mine.

She turned my hand and took my room key from me. Turning, she put the card into the reader and opened the door when the green light flashed. I followed her into the room and watched as she wandered over to the windows and looked out at the skyline.

"Have I told you how stunning you look tonight?" I asked her and she looked at me over her shoulder with a smile.

"Only a thousand times," she said.

"Well, that isn't nearly enough times," I said and walked over to her and wrapped my arms around her waist. She leaned back against me and closed her eyes. I kissed her cheek.

"So, this is what it feels like," she said.

"What?"

"Being happy," she replied, opened her eyes and turned in my arms. I smiled down at her and caressed her face with the back of my hand. She continued to stare at me as she removed my jacket and dropped it to the floor. She then took the loosened tie from around my neck and slowly slid it off. The movement was subtle, but seductive. With her hands free she reached between us and started to unbutton my shirt.

"Kelly." I began but she shook her head at me.

"No, Brad. I forbid you to feel guilty in this moment. Tonight, we stop looking back and only move forward," she said and looked me square in the eyes. I nodded and she continued to unbutton my shirt.

Once the buttons had been opened, she used both of her hands to push it off my shoulders. It fluttered to the floor and her hands were now moving over my arms, across my chest and landed at the hem of the tank I had worn as an undershirt. Her hands snaked under the shirt, and she moved them slowly up my body and around until she was gripping the muscles in my back. I inhaled sharply and felt my muscles tense from her touch. When we came together before our movements had been hurried by grief but this time we were deliberately moving like molasses.

I had my arms at my sides and was looking down at her. Her hands came back down to the hem of my shirt and she started to lift it higher. She went as far as her height would allow her to go and I raised my arms to remove the shirt the rest of the way. She stared at my body, swallowed once, twice before she leaned forward and began to trail kisses along every part she could reach. My hands were desperate to hold her, but I commanded them to stay still. This moment belonged to her, and I was determined to do nothing more but watch the beauty that was her.

After she had touched and kissed every portion of my upper body her hands drifted down to my waist. She plunged one hand beneath the material of my slacks and boxers. Before my eyes closed, I saw her smile at the sharp intake of my breath. Her fingers inched closer to my erection and just when I thought she was going

265

to reach it her fingers pulled back and she removed her hand. I opened my eyes, and my brows furrowed in confusion.

"I want you to see every moment, to be here with me," she said in explanation, and she opened the snap on my slacks.

Those amazing hands circled around my waist, and she pushed my pants down, moving with them. She helped me step out of them and removed my shoes. I'd never had a woman undress me the way she was doing and the act was so sensual. She took her time with every movement, and it took all my strength to not reach for her and rush it along.

She stood up on her toes and kissed my jaw. I turned into her and our lips met. I started to deepen the kiss, and she pulled out of it. I was about to protest when she dipped back down and took hold of my boxers. Keeping my eyes on her the whole time she bent down, looked up at me and slowly began to remove my boxers. Our eyes stayed connected the entire time the cotton material left my body. She helped me step out of those too. I was standing before her, naked and she was still fully clothed. I went to reach for her, but she put her hand up to stop me. I groaned but complied.

Turning, she presented her back to me as she swiped her hair over one shoulder.

"Unzip me please," she instructed, looking over her shoulder at me. I swallowed and did as she requested. Just as we did when she removed my boxers our eyes stayed locked as I unzipped her dress.

She moved away from me when I was finished and took a few steps forward before turning to face me. Staring at me, she dropped the dress to the floor and stepped out of it. My breath caught when I saw the only clothing she had on now was a pair of purple lace panties. Before I reached for her, I asked for permission.

"Can I touch you?" I was standing in the spot she left me, a good five paces away. All I wanted to do was feel her body pressed against mine but I waited.

"Please," she said, and I went to her.

I reached out and her face leaned into my hand. I put my other hand on her hip and pulled her into me. She was startled a bit by the movement and let out a small noise of surprise. I had no doubt she could feel my hardness pushing against her purple lace panties.

"I need to feel you against me," I explained, and she nodded as if she understood my desire.

Now that my initial need had been satisfied, I took a step back bent down before her. I repeated the process she took with me and slipped my fingers beneath the lace. Keeping my eyes fastened on hers I slowly removed the material and helped her step out of them. With our gazes locked I caressed up her body. I was still on my knees before her and I pulled her towards me, buried my face in her stomach. I kissed her and felt her fingers running through my hair. On my knees, before the woman I loved, I looked up at her and started to cry.

"Don't cry," she said and wiped away a tear.

"I can't help it. I'm just so damn happy," I said and to my surprise she dropped to her knees and cupped my face with her palms.

"Make love to me," she said.

I nodded and she leaned forward to join our lips. Still joined, I reached around her and lifted her. She put her arms around my neck and I stood from my knees and placed her gently on the bed. We continued to kiss, caress and explore each other. There wasn't a single part of our bodies that we did not cover and when the time came, I entered her and stared into her eyes the whole time.

"I love you," she said as my hilt reached her pelvis. We were one in that moment.

"I love you," I told her and kissed her gently before I began to create a rhythm that suits us both. She clung to me and gasped every time I pushed back into her. Nothing else mattered in that moment, except her. All the wasted moments were shattered in that single space in time, and I finally knew that I had begun living as life was meant to be. She cried into my shoulder and I soon followed her into the bliss.

Something stirred me from my slumber and I woke with a start. I had felt the beginnings of a nightmare but something had disturbed it and I quickly reached out for Kelly but the other side of the bed was empty. Panicked, I looked around the room and saw her clothing was still on the floor where we had left it. Her shoes were still by the door where she took them off. I heard running water suddenly and realized she was in the bathroom. Throwing the covers off of me I walked over to the open bathroom and saw her washing her hands. She was still very naked, and her curves called to me as she leaned over the sink rinsing the soap from her hands. She noticed me watching and smiled at me.

"Did I wake you?" she asked. I shook my head and laughed as her eyes widened because I suddenly became hard just by looking at her.

"He likes you, and so do I," I said and she laughed.

"I like him too. And I like you. Maybe you both should come in here and say hello to me," she turned off the sink and reached for the hand towel. I followed her movements but did not enter the bathroom.

"Come out here," I said and take a step away from the bathroom. She narrowed her eyes at me, and I saw when she realized why I wouldn't enter the bathroom.

"Brad, come in here," she cajoled and threw the towel down on the sink.

"I don't want to," I replied. She knew I was refusing because the last place I wanted to touch her was in a bathroom. The guilt was still very strong in me and I never wanted to be reminded of that terrible act ever again.

"Well, I'm not coming out, so you have to ask yourself what is more important to you in this moment. The guilt you feel or me?" She asked and sat down on the edge of the tub.

I furrowed my brow at her and she raised her eyebrows at me, challenging me. With a quick frustrated glance at the ceiling, I took a step into the bathroom. I splayed my hands at her as if I had said, *well, I'm here*, but she remained seated on the tub and tilted her head, saying wordlessly, *not good enough*. I grunted again and took two more steps toward her. She didn't move until I was standing right in front of her. Smiling, she stood and took my hand.

She stood on her toes and kissed me. As the kiss deepened and she moaned against my mouth I grabbed her ass and lifted her off the ground. She threw her legs around my waist, and I started to back us out of the bathroom. When we reached the doorway she threw her arms out wide and grabbed hold of the wall and frame, stopping us.

"No. Here," she commanded and gestured with her head back towards the bathroom.

"Kelly. No," I refused and begged her not to make me do this.

"Yes, Brad. Right here," she said and put her arms back around my neck so she could put her feet on the ground. I groaned when she pulled away from me and backed up against the sink. I watched as she hopped up on the counter and scooted back until her back was almost against the mirror.

"I want you to take me right here. Just like this," she said and bent one leg, placed her foot on the counter she used one hand to push her leg open, displaying herself before me.

"Kelly," I groaned and ran my hands through my hair. I glanced over to the perfectly good bed and then back to her.

"Make a decision buster," she said and I smirked at her.

"Buster?"

She shrugged. "I took a chance. Now it's your turn," she said and trailed one finger down between her breasts and moved it to her mound. I watched as that finger disappeared between her folds and just like that, she pulled me in.

I forgot about my guilt and rushed back into that bathroom and took hold of her face and kissed her like I hadn't kiss her before. She laughed against my lips and nibbled on the bottom one. I groaned and pulled her closer to the edge of the counter. She opened her legs for me and wrapped them around my waist. I plunged into her and we both gasped from the impact of our bodies coming together.

The laughter was gone, and the heat took over. I thrust into her, and she cried out. It was then that I saw my reflection in the mirror and everything in me froze. She noticed and called to me.

"Hey, come back to me," she said, and I looked away from the mirror and into her eyes.

"I'll always come back to you," I promised and with a kiss I thrust back into her.

Her head fell back, and her nails clawed into my shoulders as I rode her on a bathroom counter for the second time. There was no guilt remaining after that. There was only the pleasure and the love I felt for her. She cried out my name and I crushed my mouth to hers, spilling into her.

"Welcome home," she said and all I would say was…

"Finally."

Epilogue

A Letter to My Brother

For so long I blamed you for all the bad things surrounding me. I'm sorry for using you as a scapegoat for my own issues. It took me a long time to accept that the sun didn't rise and set around what was happening to you. You see, Kevin, neither one of us came out of that house unscathed. Your demons came in the form of sadness and feelings of constant failure. My demons centered around the fear of losing those I loved. When I lost Lily, I placed all those demons on your shoulders, and that was unfair of me. You couldn't even defeat your own demons, and I gave you mine to carry as well. I used to think that it was me saving you but now I realize you were the one that was trying to save me. You did it in the complete wrong way, of course. Then again, it seems we were both wrong about so many things. You thought you were saving me by leaving and I thought I was saving you by making you stay.

I've learned a lot over the years and from continuous therapy. Dr. Stone says that healthy people are in a constant state of learning. It is when we reject the process that we are truly in danger. I guess that is what happened with you. You stopped learning. Me, I discover new things about myself every day. I used to think I was strong, until I realized how weak I really was. It took me a while, but I finally found true strength. I'm sorry it took me so long and I'm sorry it was after you left. I'm still trying to forgive myself for that

271

one. Lily says we did all we could, and she has accepted your choice. I'm still trying to learn how to do that, but I'm trying.

There are moments I find myself wanting to talk to you, to tell you about my life. Reyann says all I have to do is say the words and you will hear me. She means well but I'm not sure I share the same belief she does that once we die, we can still consciously be aware of what is happening with the living. It comforts her though, so I just nod and tell her I'll try.

I'm happy. I'm not sure if that brings you any joy, but it's true. After all the pain and hurtful things I did to those I loved, I am finally in a happy place. I'm sorry I never told you about Kelly. I should have. That's what brothers do. They tell each other things. That is what Jeff tells me. He's constantly telling me things, even if I don't want to hear them. He calls it brotherly bonding, but I think he does it to amuse himself. Most of the time I don't mind. It's actually quite nice to be able to sit down with a brother and be honest with him. I regret not being honest with you. I used to think I couldn't share things with you because you had enough burdens plaguing your mind. I know I shouldn't but sometimes I think maybe if I had opened up to you then you would still be here. Dr. Stone says that is an uncertainty and it will only cloud my judgment. He's right. When I find myself having those thoughts, I usually call Tasha, Kelly's mom, my mother-in-law. She knows a thing or two about having those thoughts. Her first husband did what you did and took himself away from her. Besides Lily she is the closest thing I have to someone who understands my thoughts sometimes. She's really good at conceptualizing things for me.

Oh, I got married a few months ago. We set a place for you at the reception. Some of the guests thought it was morbid, but I didn't give a damn. I wanted you there, so we made you a place. I don't know how you would have felt about your picture being there next to the place setting, but it ended up being fine. Until Jeff decided it would be a good idea to start talking to you. That definitely freaked some of the guests out. You should probably know he's still mad at you for calling his date a moose. And he's still mad at me for agreeing with you. Don't worry though; he never stays mad for long.

I should probably tell you why I'm writing you after all this time. It seems even in the happy moments; darkness can seep through when you least expect it. I lost somebody I loved this week. Her death was a gut punch and not expected at all. I'm not even sure if I've completely accepted it yet. I know she's gone but my heart doesn't want to believe it. Even when I stood before her casket and watched it get lowered to the ground, I didn't want to believe it. Her husband held on to their little girls like if he let go, he would drown in sorrow. I never told you about Jen either. I should have. I should have shared her story with you. Maybe if I had you would have realized that if she could find a way to heal than you could too. There I go again, dealing with the uncertainties Sorry Dr. Stone.

I guess what's tearing me up about Jen's death is that she didn't want it. She fought really hard to stay alive, but it just wasn't enough. Maybe it is twisted but I find comfort in knowing that you actually wanted your death. You wanted it so much you tried to get it three times, but others kept messing it up for you. I did it the first time and the second time some fellow traveler on the road called for help too quickly and you once again watched your death float away. Jen had everything to live for and I know she would have kept on going if she could have. In my grief I reverted to old habits and suddenly I became angry with you. I'm still learning how to stop using you as an outlet for my rage.

Let me explain. As I stood there watching a broken man say his final goodbye to the woman he loved beyond this world, the mother of his children, I was struck with the thought that you had simply thrown away your chance. You could have been some guy loving your wife the way this guy did, but you just pissed all over the possibility and in that moment I hated you again. Here I was, at my friend's funeral, hating you. I carried that hate with me up until later that night. Until the moment my wife broke down before me and confessed, she was pregnant.

I'm not exactly proud of this next moment. Instead of comforting her I froze. What the hell was I supposed to say? I couldn't lift her into my arms and twirl her around with joy after coming back from her best friend's funeral. I couldn't ignore her because that would make me a dick and I promised her a long time ago I would stop being a dick to her. I was stuck trying to figure out what to do that it just slipped out.

"Damnit, Kevin," I said, and Kelly stopped crying to look at me like I was crazy. Who knows, maybe in that moment I was. She asked me what was wrong. Here she was, practically falling apart before my eyes because she just lost her friend and found out she was pregnant at the same time and all I could do was curse you. I know it doesn't make any sense now but in that moment, I thought about how once again you were missing out on something and Jenny was missing out on everything now. So, naturally, it must have been your fault. It's absolutely bat shit but that was where my mind took me.

My wife set aside her hurt and set about comforting me. About halfway into it I realized how completely ridiculous and selfish I was being and immediately apologized to her. I did what I should have done in the first place. I took her hands and told her how incredibly happy I was she was carrying my child. It was then she confessed that she was happy too and felt guilty about it because Jen had died, and she didn't feel right being happy when she was supposed to be sad. She put a crack in my heart then and I wrapped her in my arms and told her that death didn't take away how happy Jen would have been for us.

And that right there was the moment I realized what Reyann had been trying to tell me all along. Death wasn't the end. There is no such thing as a final goodbye. We are forever surrounded by those we love. They are in the happy moments filled with laughter and the sorrowful ones marked by tears. You and Jen may no longer be alive, but you surround me every day. I am reminded of both of you on a daily basis and it's time I stop being angry about it and be thankful for it. It seems, along with continuously learning, I constantly keep having 'come to life' moments. I've had so many over the years that I've lost track. I'm sorry you never found your come to life moment, but I'm no longer saddened by it because that is one uncertainty I have come to accept.

So, in closing brother, I would like to share with you something I wrote in rehab. I was never able to share it with anyone back then because I don't think I had forgiven myself yet for the choices I had made. It took losing someone that was an integral part in saving my life to realize the greatest power any of us has is the power to forgive. I forgive you brother for leaving, and I forgive myself for loving you the wrong way. I hope this reaches you.

In this life all we have are the moments that mark our soul
Many of my moments have been marked by you
I offered my love, and you ran from it
You ran so far that I couldn't see you anymore
I tried to catch you but all I did was fall behind
I blamed you for the scars on my heart
I cursed your name, and I reached for fleeting pleasures to fill the void
In this life all we have are the moments that define us
Many of my moments have been cast in shadow because of you
For so long you were the monster behind my fears
Your loss crushed me and once again I fell
The spiral consumed me, and I lost myself in the bottom of a bottle
It wasn't until I reached the end that I broke free
In this life all we have are the moments that pass us by

You floated away and I broke
You broke me
I broke me
This life broke us both
But I don't want to be broken anymore
Please forgive me for not forgetting you
Forgive me…In this life and the next

Always, your brother

About the Author

Angeline Larson is a product of imagination and life. She is not perfect, but she tries. She is a human who loves dogs, likes watching chickens go about their daily tasks, reading, and even creating her own books. She is a mess, but she is a mess carefully crafted and that makes her unique in her own way.

More to Read by Angeline Larson

<u>Contemporary Romance</u>

Finding You – Kelly's story
Finding Hope – Jenny and Evan's story
Lost in You – Addy and Derek's story
Finding Me – Stacey and Josh's story